"Set in the deep, dark waters of Australia, where danger lurks under and above the surface, *The Offing* is terrifyingly brilliant. As the boat rocks and sways, so do the suspicions swirling around everyone on board. My heart hammered, nails digging into my skin, as I breathlessly turned the pages, gasping at each stunning reveal. Roz Nay has written a chilling, gripping tale of deceit, revenge, and justice, proving once again that she's an undeniable force in the thriller genre." —SAMANTHA M. BAILEY, *USA TODAY* and #1 national bestselling author of *A Friend in the Dark*

"Roz Nay remains one of my favorite thriller writers with *The Offing*, her latest page-turner about two young women on vacation—and secretly on the run from danger back home. A locked room mystery on a boat in Australia, a police investigation unfolding in a split time-frame, and a nail-biting first person narration had me on the edge of my seat from start to finish. Another must read from a masterful storyteller!" —WENDY WALKER, bestselling author of *What Remains*

"Roz Nay takes us Down Under for a creepy cat and mouse chase in Australia's tropical waters. . . . Atmospheric, immersive and incredibly addictive, with all Roz's trademarks: a strong sense of place, complex characters with secrets, and hot but dubious men. I'm a huge fan of Roz's writing and this is her best yet!" —ALLIE REYNOLDS, author of *Shiver* and *The Swell*

THE OFFING

ALSO BY ROZ NAY

The Hunted
Hurry Home
Our Little Secret

THE
OFFING

ROZ NAY

VIKING

VIKING
an imprint of Penguin Canada, a division of
Penguin Random House Canada Limited

Canada • USA • UK • Ireland • Australia • New Zealand •
India • South Africa • China

First published 2024

www.penguinrandomhouse.ca

*Publisher's note: This book is a work of fiction. Names, characters, places and incidents
either are the product of the author's imagination or are used fictitiously, and any
resemblance to actual persons living or dead, events, or locales is entirely coincidental.*

LIBRARY AND ARCHIVES CANADA CATALOGUING IN PUBLICATION
Title: The offing : a novel / Roz Nay.
Names: Nay, Roz, author.
Identifiers: Canadiana (print) 20230556981 | Canadiana (ebook) 2023055699X
| ISBN 9780735248250 (softcover) | ISBN 9780735248267 (EPUB)
Subjects: LCGFT: Novels.
Classification: LCC PS8627.A98 O34 2024 | DDC C813/.6—dc23

Book design by Emma Dolan
Typeset by Erin Cooper
Cover design by Emma Dolan
Cover image: (moored sailboat) © mjr5house / RooM / Getty Images

Printed in Canada

10 9 8 7 6 5 4 3 2 1

Penguin
Random House
VIKING CANADA

For my son, Cash

For the sky and the sea, and the sea and the sky
Lay like a load on my weary eye,
And the dead were at my feet.

SAMUEL TAYLOR COLERIDGE,
"The Rime of the Ancient Mariner"

Severed arm found on beach in Far North Queensland

By Taj Weyman

Queensland Police are continuing to investigate the discovery of a human arm on the shore of Flint Beach, NQ, early this morning. In a statement released by the Far Northern Region, it was confirmed that the limb showed signs of "a traumatic injury" at the elbow joint. Since the investigation is ongoing, no further details can be made public until the forensic analysis of the arm is complete. Anyone with information relating to the incident is asked to contact their local police department immediately.

Posted Jan 7 2020 / Updated 6h ago

1

I STEP OUT OF THE Airlie Beach hostel this morning as if into the aftermath of a flood. Remnants of last night's celebration are strewn all over the sidewalk, city workers cleaning up the garbage and beer cans while backpackers sleep off their hangovers inside, Regan among them. The town went big for New Year's Eve—fireworks at the lagoon, dancing in the streets, DJs at every bar—and most people seemed to be having the best night ever. All around me there was revelry, and it felt a bit like those Times Square celebrations I used to watch on TV once I was thirteen and allowed to stay up. I'd sit cross-legged in a quiet room, witnessing other people's fun through a screen.

The cab driver honks his horn, reminding me the meter's running. From under the shade of the paperbark tree, I give him a thumbs-up. *All good, buddy. Not much longer. She'll be right out.* Ten minutes ago, I shook Regan gently awake in our dorm, the air in there sour with sweated-out alcohol.

"Hey, come on," I'd whispered. "Our interview at the marina is at noon. The crew jobs—remember? The cab's already outside."

She'd winced as if my face was a garish beam of light, a question in her eyes even though she'd been right there yesterday when we made the plan. We'd both spotted the handmade ad for two crewmates and a cook on a little yacht, *Alone at Last* painted in cursive along the stern in the overexposed photo. How calm it had looked; how perfect. The boat was heading north to Darwin—exactly where we needed to go—and we'd get paid, do tons of sailing, and avoid spending money on flights. We'd agreed that as long as the guy wasn't asking for super-experienced help, it was totally worth checking out. I'd torn the tab from the fringe at the bottom of the sheet.

But this morning Regan just groaned, truffling into her pillow. "Stop, Ivy. Sleeeeep. Let's blow the crew thing off."

I stood there for a minute, realizing I could just go on my own. I'd report back. To me the interview felt fated. It hinted at a whole different way of traveling, one I might be better at. "You stay. I'll go check it out myself," I said, and her eyes snapped open. Perhaps she was remembering last night. We'd meant to celebrate New Year's together, mark the symbolism of turning a corner, of finally putting my shitty year in the rearview mirror. We'd bought miniature bottles of champagne, and were going to link forearms at midnight and swig at the same time, as a toast. But Regan hooked up with some guy from Switzerland around eleven, forcing me to make small talk with his buddy—which was okay until he inched closer and closer, then lunged for me at the first strike of twelve.

"Jesus," I'd said, pushing his whole face away with a flat palm. "What? It's for luck. *Happy new year?!*" He fixed his hair, shaking his head and expelling air through his nostrils, as if I wasn't playing by the rules.

I downed all my champagne, left the bottle on the grass, and walked home on my own feeling raw. And this morning, I can't get rid of the sense that he was right, that I need to get better at this game. We've been here ten days, and it's not that I don't like Australia, or that I regret flying out here with Regan. On the contrary, I love the comically loud birds, the bright cobalt skies, all the spiky red bottlebrush shrubs. Everything's bold in this country, nothing's half-measured— hard sun, hard rain, hardy people—and I still get excited to see the water swirling counterclockwise in the sink, or when the crescent moon slivers horizontally, like smiles in the night sky. All these southern hemisphere details feel like a fresh page, and I need that, a chance to get away and mend. It's just the backpacker *scene* I can't handle. Plus I'd been looking forward to spending more time one-on-one with Regan. I've missed her since she dropped out in the middle of our sophomore year.

"We're twenty-one," she'd said, suggesting the trip having already booked us the flights. "We're young and we're free." It was mid-December, a couple days after the end of semester, although Christmas break was going to be permanent for me. "I say we get out of here for a month. Forget about Thatcher Kane. Forget *all* the weak-ass guys. Let's have an adventure, just you and me."

"But I can't— I don't have—"

"I put the tickets on my credit card," she said, shrugging, as if it was the bank's fault for enabling her. "Into Brisbane, out of Darwin. And there's tons of room left on the card. So, you know. Happy holidays."

Regan was the richer of the two of us, undeniably—she'd had a lucrative year in the city while I was holed up reading literary tomes in the NYU library—but the idea of just flying away was outrageous. Wasn't it? A vacation in tropical Queensland at the height of their summer, with nobody there we know. It didn't take long for it to go from an outrageous to a genius plan. So, with conditions in place that I'd use the remainder of my scholarship money and pay her back the rest later, I took the lifeline she was offering me.

The cab driver lowers the passenger window and leans toward me. "We right, darl? Good to go?"

"Two minutes," I say, glancing back at the main reception, just as my cell phone dings in my back pocket with the noise that can only mean Thatcher. He's texted again. He changed his number recently, although I don't know why, since his messages are always so clearly him. I've assigned him a doom-ridden, horror-movie footstep of a tone because these days, anything he sends me is ominous. Shudder-inducing. There's no way I'm reading the text.

"That them with an update?" The cab driver is eyeing me, and I shake my head, leave the phone buried in my pocket. January 1st is a fresh page. A day to at least make *new* mistakes, not jump straight back into the old one. Talking to Thatcher will never happen again, nor will the intimacy I had with him, the very image of which makes me want to throw up in my mouth. What the hell was I thinking, sleeping with a college professor? With *my* college professor? It's so cringingly awful, and that's *before* I found out what he was really like.

"Ives! Hey, ready, I'm here!"

I turn to see Regan hurrying from the hostel, pulling her dark curls back into a claw clip. She stops beside me, long-limbed, flat-stomached, tanned.

"Sorry," she says. "I had to get water. Want some? How was your night?" She passes me the ice-cold bottle as we move toward the cab. "Sorry about that guy in the dorm. We were just fooling around."

"I know, it's—whatever." I sip, one eye closed in the sun. "Can we make a new rule, though? No more bunk-bed boning? At least not while I'm below you."

She snorts as she takes the bottle back, and there's nothing more that needs to be said. The entire backpacker lifestyle hinges on hookups, conveyor-belt romances, easy-come, easy-go fun. Regan fits in, but then she always does. This morning she looks clammy, like she barely slept, but the world will still bend for her. It's never been any different.

"So, where is this boat thing at?" She reaches for the rear door handle, just as a guy with a surfy blond man bun emerges from reception. He's high cheekboned, wearing harem pants and a scoop-neck T-shirt that shows his collarbone and the circular top edge of a tattoo.

"Regan!" He says it like *Ray-Gun*. She doesn't bother to correct him, just turns to me fast. *What is his name?* she mouths.

I roll my eyes at her. He's the Swiss guy, but I know she won't have listened to a word he said between fireworks. "Hi, *Milo*. We were just heading out."

"For the crew jobs? But it's not safe," he says, incredulous. "You don't know these people. What if they're secretly smugglers? Traffickers? Or you run into pirates who take you, use you, throw you into the sea?"

I bite the skin near my thumbnail. Is he right—are we being stupid? But the very essence of travel is a dice roll from what I can tell. Since we got here, I've been sleeping in rooms full of strangers, going on waterfall hikes in flip-flops, signing waivers like they're checks to be cashed. And anyway, what's riskier than being pursued by Thatcher Kane?

Beside me, Regan blusters. "We're not reckless girls, you know. The yacht's family-owned. They're hardly a crime syndicate."

She's right: the boat in the picture looked folksy and cute, and the wording spoke of a dad and daughter, plus pet. There were ten other posters pinned up around it, most of them out of date, but they proved that job offers like these weren't unusual. Airlie Beach is a crewing town. Milo probably just wants Regan to stay.

"And there aren't any pirates in the Whitsundays," I add. "They're in, like, Somalia or somewhere. Gulf of Aden." I wait while he considers this shaky fact I gleaned from a Tom Hanks movie. The thing is, as hesitant as that wave of doubt just made me, there's also something that seems so destined about this opportunity. I can feel the prospect of it tingling under my skin. Finally, Regan and I would get some solitude, a chance to properly catch up, on a journey we'll remember forever. I've been imagining the sunsets we'll get to see, the brightness of stars when there's no land in sight. Plus, the whole ad had a comfy, mom-and-pop feeling—or at least pop-and-daughter feeling. What's not to like?

"We'll be fine," Regan says, batting her hand at him. "See you later. You'll be in the bar?"

He shrugs as if he really might not be, but who is he kidding? Regan's magnetic. Even hungover, she doesn't have to try. We climb into the cab, its back seat covered in heavy clear plastic that feels greasy under my thighs.

"We'll be fine," Regan murmurs again as we take off through the deserted streets. She nudges me, and I feel a rush of certainty, just like I always do when she and I are a united front. Things are going to get better now, and it's almost as if we got our champagne toast after all. Here's to a totally fresh start. College roomies back together. *Alone at Last.*

2

WE GET OUT IN A windswept forecourt, where old boats sit in scaffolding, damaged or riddled with mollusks. The place looks sad to me, somehow. Like a hospice. The sick and the dying.

"New Year's is a weird day to hold interviews," Regan says, as the cab pulls away in a crunch of gravel. "Look, the office isn't even open." She points at the crooked sign in the dusty window. *Back Jan 2.*

"Good," I say. "Weed out the competition."

She laughs, shakes her head. "You really want this, don't you? Why—you just want to get away from the crowds?"

"Sure," I say. "And do things that are . . . unique, I guess." *Unique, quiet. Off the grid.*

Her dark eyes search my face, wondering if there's something I'm not telling her. And there is. But now's not the time.

To our right is a wire gate, equipped with a sensor, that opens onto a walkway to the boats. Regan rattles it, but it's locked. "Should we call the number you got off the poster?

You'd think the dad would be up here to meet people."

She waits while I unzip my shorts pocket and find the paper scrap, but then we hear footsteps. Two men are walking up the wharf. The one in front is younger—late twenties— wearing board shorts and a pale-yellow T-shirt. He's dark haired, fit-looking, confident in his stride, and he's holding some sort of file folder. Is he going for the cook job, or is he our direct competition? He seems worryingly self-assured. Behind him is definitely the guy from the ad, about forty, in a polo shirt buttoned all the way to the throat. He has sporty sunglasses on top of his head, sandy-gray hair, and there's a faded stripe of zinc across the bridge of his nose and cheek-bones. They stop at the top of the walkway and shake hands.

"Thanks again, Mr. Edwards," the younger guy says in a faintly British accent, dimples evident as he smiles and brushes a sweep of curly hair from his brow. "It was great to meet you."

"Thanks, Desh. Likewise. Looks like we've found our chef!" He opens the gate from the inside. My shoulders relax an inch.

The boat owner—Mr. Edwards—spots Regan and me, and catches the door before it closes. "Are you two here about the *Alone at Last*?"

"Yes, sir," Regan says, stepping forward. "The crew jobs."

"Fantastic. How exciting. Come on in."

"Good luck," the younger guy says, teeth white and straight when he grins. I notice the lean cut of his chest as warm air buffets his T-shirt, the beachy necklace around his smooth neck, the sun-worn woven bracelet on his right wrist.

Regan moves past him, but her head turns as he walks away. I can tell she already likes him. Mr. Edwards wedges the gate open with a brick, and the three of us stand in a little circle at the top of the wharf.

"How are you going? I'm Christopher." He extends his hand for us to shake. His fingers don't press, aren't alpha-male dominant. Mostly he just seems sun-smart, practical-looking, eager. Like a dad at a swim meet.

"I'm Regan Kemp," she says, adding her winning smile.

"And I'm Ivy McGill."

"What great names. How striking." When he rubs his hands together, the sleeves of his polo shirt reveal a line of tan at his sinewy biceps. "You're both keen sailors?"

Right, I think. *Here we go.* Now I'm nervous. How should we answer that one? As much as I want this adventure, we can't outright lie. Sailing's no joke, and this is a family vacation. Imagine if we sank the boat. I stare down at Christopher's sneakers, hoping Regan will handle the negotiations. She's the one with the gift of the gab.

"Ivy's dad is into sailing," she says. "Right, Ives?"

"I've been out quite a bit," I nod. "But just small boats, dinghies, nothing major."

There's a long pause while Christopher scrutinizes us both. He has a kind face, although he looks tired around the eyes.

"Neither of us have crewed before," Regan says. "If it's dangerous work, or you need really experienced helpers, we might not be your best bet."

"But we're fast learners. Hard workers," I add quickly, then hold my breath, fingers laced so tightly behind my back that I'm certain they're white at the knuckle.

"I appreciate your honesty," he says quietly. "I take it you're both backpackers. What lives have you left in the dust?"

It's a strange way to phrase things, and we both hesitate.

"I work in fashion in New York City," Regan says, and Christopher's eyebrows shoot up. I wonder if he gets she's a model. She was scouted two years ago buying a Coke at a deli, handed a business card, signed by a top agency, and that's what I mean: life rolls open for her like a lavish carpet. But she's not bigheaded. Regan's likeable. Her casualness unlocks everything.

"And I'm an English lit major in my senior year at NYU."

There's no way I'll graduate, I manage not to add.

"How good is that? My daughter, Lila, is eleven and an avid reader. It's such a dying passion in youngsters, but I've tried all along to nurture it. We couldn't pack her enough books."

"I have hundreds," I say quickly. "On my Kobo. Including a whole range of classics she might like. *Jane Eyre, The Secret Garden, The Outsiders.*"

He shakes his head in wonder like I've just told him I wrote them all.

"And we're a good team, Mr. Edwards. I mean, Christopher." Regan puts her arm around me. "We lived together freshman year. We're tight."

"That's true," I say, flushing, but I notice Christopher isn't looking at us anymore. His gaze is out at the water, dreamy and faraway. After a few seconds, he turns back to us with a sigh.

"Can I tell you a secret, girls? I reckon it's my turn to be completely transparent."

"Okay," I mumble, frowning. I feel Regan reach for my hand.

"The truth is, I don't really *want* crew. No, I don't mean that rudely. It's just that I'm on a trip with my daughter, and it's very bonding, very . . . special. We should have done this a long time ago, to be honest. We're both finding it extremely therapeutic." He dips his head, as if bashful at his own fatherly devotion. "But the next leg is up over the top into the Gulf of Carpentaria, and that's a major shipping channel. I need to make sure we don't stray into the path of bigger vessels. And for that, I need a rota system. Through the night. So, when I say 'crew,' I really mean glorified boat watch. Looking for lights out at sea."

"You just need bodies awake?" Regan grins. "Night watchmen?"

"Exactly. Shift work. Nothing technical or navigational. I do all that. I'm taking on a chef—the guy you saw—to rotate faster, make the watches shorter. And get better grub! But your job would be lights in the night. That's it."

"And what if we see one?" I ask.

Christopher laughs, stares at me like he wants to give me a hug. "You wake me up!"

"Oh," I say, turning to Regan. "We can *totally* do that."

"It's not a long passage," he goes on. "Once we get up there, it's two days through the gulf, if we motor. I really only need crew for a limited time—a week or two at the most. I'll pay you sixty bucks a day each. Cash. And all your food would be covered. Then you'd jump off in Darwin, and Lila and I would carry on with our trip on our own."

"Right on," Regan says, her expression hard to read. "Where's your final destination?"

"I'm not sure," Christopher says. "We're winging it. It's a moving target."

"Well, we could stay out of your way for the crewing portion," I say. "Let you have all the time you need with your daughter. We can keep to ourselves."

"I appreciate that. It's not that we're unsociable . . ." He smiles, and the zinc on his face creases. "It's just that Lila can be painfully shy. And recently she's . . . Well, there were kids at her school who weren't the kindest. So, she's on the mend. She'll be quiet. Don't take it personally."

"Poor kid," I say, and Regan murmurs agreement. I remember being eleven—fifth and sixth grade—when bullies were everywhere, cloning themselves, and nobody dared reveal a quirk or an idiosyncrasy. I wouldn't go back there for anything.

"I should show you the boat and introduce you to Lila," Christopher says. "That is, if you're still interested."

"Sure," we say in unison, and we follow him down the wharf, past empty-looking, padlocked catamarans and a few battered old fishing vessels. The closer we get to the *Alone at Last*, the cozier it looks. It's mostly white with patches of faded summer-blue, and while it's not super big—and a bit vintage—the top deck is tidily organized. All the chrome is polished, the ropes tightly coiled. There's a mop in a bucket by a wide wooden steering wheel. And beneath the boom is a wicker cat basket with a big hairy dent in the cushion. No cat.

I grab Regan's elbow, pull her into my side. *Look at this sweet little home*, I'm saying. It's adorable. Like a cottage that bobs.

"She's ramshackle." Christopher waits at the edge of the dock, thumbs hooked near the cell phone clipped to his belt. "I don't know if you're used to heaps of comfort and luxury, but I have to tell you, this isn't that."

"Don't worry," Regan says. "We have deceptively low standards."

"I love everything about this," I say. "Including that you brought your cat on vacation."

"She's Lila's cat. They're best mates." He climbs aboard, then reaches over the railing to help each of us up.

"Where is Lila's mom, Christopher, if you don't mind me asking?" says Regan.

"At home. Down south." He moves toward a sliding door to our left. "She couldn't get away. It was a last-minute thing. Lila and I set off from the very bottom of the country just over a week ago."

"Wow, so you've sailed a long way north already." I follow Christopher as he ducks into a cabin that smells of hot sun on old fabric. There are cushioned bench seats along each wall lined in a sweet daisy print, and dusty little shelves at knee height with barbecue fuel, tongs, a lighter. But it's tight in here, and behind me, I hear Regan's lukewarm "huh." She must be thinking exactly the same thing.

We squeeze ourselves down skinny steps into a tiny kitchen with a couple of cupboards, a netting-fronted shelf, and a two-person Formica table.

"The cabin—" Christopher begins, just as my cell phone starts ringing. Quickly I decline the call before Regan can see the screen. She doesn't know much about Thatcher. I downplayed it, told her I'd only seen him a couple of times. I'm not sure I'd have said anything at all, but after we broke up in early December, my roommates texted her when I wouldn't get out of bed. Even when she heard the diluted version, disgust and anger had mottled her face like a bruise.

Thatcher as in Kane, the English prof? Are you for real? No, Ivy, no! What the fuck were you doing with him?

"Sorry, ignore that," I say, jamming my phone back in my pocket. "You were saying—about the cabin?" I hear a thump like a depth charge detonating. Thatcher's left me a voice-mail. It's obvious I don't want to talk to him, and he's only getting pushier. How far will he go? For a second, I get that heady feeling, the sway that signals I'm on the edge, at a precipice. And Thatcher is approaching steadily from behind.

3

CHRISTOPHER WANTS REGAN and me to meet Lila, so I push
all thoughts of Thatcher away, and we follow him into a hot
shadowy corridor, an inch of space at each elbow. He taps a
closed door at the end with a forefinger, turning back to us.

Very shy, he mouths. We smile supportively.

"Yes?" says a little voice, and Christopher steps into what
must be the main bedroom, a six-foot-wide space filled
entirely with two twin beds, a muslin curtain between
them—hooked back right now—the hatch like a skylight
above. Sitting on the bed to the right with a copy of *The
Night Circus* in her hands is a young girl, big-eyed and freck-
led, auburn hair sticking out from under a colorful baseball
cap. By her thigh is a gray and white cat, facing away from
us, its haunches padded and ample. It doesn't turn or seem
interested in us at all.

"Hi, Lila," Christopher says softly, sitting down at the
edge of her bed like a visitor to a children's ward. "Aren't you

boiling hot down here? You should come up on deck, pumpkin. Hang out in the shade."

"I'm fine," Lila says timidly. Her voice is raspy, like she barely uses it at all.

"Regan and Ivy wanted to say hi. They've come to see about crewing on the next leg of our trip. They'd join Desh, who you just met, but you can speak up more this time."

"Really?" She shuts her book, crossing her legs so the knee bones jut. "Are you letting all these people come with us?" Her dad's smile seems to falter. "We can't sail this bit on our own. We're worn out, aren't we? And beyond Airlie, there won't be big towns to get decent help."

"Oh, right." Lila bends forward, nuzzling her face into the fur of the cat. By her hip on the white comforter is a scattering of little shells that she's been organizing into a line, starting with the tiniest.

"Those are pretty," I say. "Are they shells you've collected?"

She nods, running her forefinger over a smooth dappled cowrie that's so shiny she must have polished it.

"When I was little, my mom gave me a shell to keep in my pocket at school." I pause, glancing at Christopher to make sure I'm not overstepping. But his face is calm, impassive. "I didn't like school very much. I think the shell used to make me feel braver."

She looks up at me like a mouse peeping out from a burrow. "How did it do that?"

"Well, they store secrets. That's what my mom told me." My voice wavers, but Regan nudges my side. *Keep going,* she's saying. *You're doing great.* "So, when I was sad, I'd hold the shell to my ear, and it was like I could hear messages she'd left." I laugh, slightly embarrassed. "I had that thing in my pocket the whole of first grade."

There's a long silence. Lila moves the cowrie shell to the top of the line, but doesn't say anything. Regan and I look at each other, then at Christopher, who seems a little watery-eyed. Should I not have told his daughter that story? The last thing I want to do is talk about school if she's still feeling upset.

"What's your cat's name?" Regan breaks the awkwardness. "She's very elegant."

"Pearl."

"Is it okay if I pet her?"

The little girl gives us some room, the freckles on her nose crinkling as Regan runs her hand over the bridge of Pearl's arched back. I join in, the fur like spun silk under my fingertips.

"She likes you," Lila says, surprised. "Mum gave her to me. She's heaps moody and doesn't normally like anyone. Pearl, I mean. Not my mama." She frowns for a second, then seems to retreat inward again. "Mum couldn't come on this trip. We had to leave her behind at home."

"I told them that already!" Christopher claps his hands, making us all jump. "Do you have any other questions, girls? About the boat?" We shake our heads, caught off guard. "All the safety features on board are to code. I keep a flare gun in the tender for emergencies. And I don't use GPS, but my maps are new and updated."

"It's a really good boat," Lila whispers. "We put up lanterns. At night, it's beautiful."

Christopher smiles, reaching forward to toggle the brim of her cap. "It's true. They're lovely. You girls should join us and see."

"You're offering us the jobs? You've already decided?" I feel a rush of triumph. Isn't he going to interview anyone else?

"Thanks, Christopher. Ivy and I will have a chat and let you know." Regan's smile seems a little fixed.

"Sure, of course," he says. "The only thing is, Lila and I spoke earlier and we'd like to leave at around eight p.m. tonight. We don't want to waste any vacation."

"Tonight?" Regan's voice is high. "In, like, six hours? Why didn't you say so before?"

"That is quite short notice," I concede. Though what do we really have to do before we leave? Get back to the hostel and pack a bag? I'm not sure it has to be a deal-breaker.

"Could we let you know within the hour?"

Regan gives me the side-eye. *The answer's no*, she's saying. *We can tell him right now.*

"That'll work." Christopher clears his throat. "Well, let's be good hosts, Lila, and walk these two out."

The little girl crawls off the bed and tries to pick up Pearl to bring with her, but the cat seems to hunch to get heavier, its ears flat, until Lila gives up. Christopher guides us out of the bedroom, through the galley, and up into the stifling heat of the afternoon. At the railing, he and Lila stop and watch us jump back down to the dock.

"I hope you decide to come along," Christopher says. "I know it's short notice, but I think you'd both be a great fit. And it'll be the trip of a lifetime, so much more than most backpackers get to see."

Lila nods, looking pleased. She pulls her hat lower in the sun, leans into her father's ribs, her knees knobby below the line of her pink paisley shorts.

"Thanks for meeting with us," Regan says blandly, as if that's that.

"The boat's awesome! We'll be in touch," I add, throwing in a little wave. "Bye, Lila."

We turn, heading back up the wharf. Regan doesn't say anything, but her body language, the pace she's setting as we approach the gate all tell me it's over. We're not taking the jobs. I'm about to say something—at least make it a debate—when I hear the clack of little flip-flops behind me and turn. Lila is running toward us. She stops a few steps from me, holds out her hand, passes me the polished cowrie shell.

"It's for you," she pants, pivoting one of her feet. "I put a message in it."

"Wow! Thank you." I crouch a little, trying to look at her face. "I'll treasure it. Honestly."

"'Kay, bye." She trips away again, back to the boat, gangly and angular, all elbows and legs.

I turn to Regan, show her the shell in my palm.

"Somebody's won somebody over," she says with a small smile.

"Right? How sweet is that?" I grin, flattered. The shell is her favorite. *I'm* her favorite. I hadn't realized how much I'd missed that feeling.

We walk through the gate, kicking the brick aside so it clicks shut behind us, and while Regan calls a cab, I step away to listen to Thatcher's voicemail, my phone feeling radioactively charged in my pocket. I take a breath, one fingertip pressed to my ear as the wind blows.

"Ivy, it's me. You haven't answered my texts, but I'm hoping you listen to this today." His voice makes my skin crawl. He's talking too fast. And in the background is birdsong, louder and more tropical than it should be. "I'm in Sydney." *Sydney!* My eyes widen. *What the actual fuck?* "There's a conference, I'm a keynote . . . whatever, it doesn't matter. But I have some free time, so I'm flying up to Airlie Beach right now. Stay there so we can talk, okay? I know where you are. We need to clear things up; I want to apologize, and hope we can be friends again. I miss your brilliant mind."

What the hell is happening, and how does he know where I am? I turn back toward Regan, my brain rattling, one hand hooked at the back of my neck.

"What?" Regan says. "What is it?"

Oh, God, I think, *what should I say? Does he really miss me?* Thoughts tumble dry like rags in my head. What if he's come to his senses, had some fit of conscience, and realized that he's swept through my life like a human tsunami? I squeeze my eyes tight. *Except, no.* Do not get sucked in. He hasn't come here to be friends.

So, I could face Thatcher, end it once and for all. Deal with the real reason he's still calling me, the one I haven't told Regan about. Or I could sidestep him, announce I'm flying home as soon as I can get up to Darwin, say I'm homesick. But she'd never believe that. And besides, isn't there a perfect way to avoid him altogether?

"Please, Reags," I say. "I'll explain everything later. But I *have* to get on that boat."

4

"YOU'VE BEEN IN TOUCH with Thatcher this whole time?" In the cab back to the hostel, Regan's mouth gapes like she's just found out I'm covered in slime. "And now he's here?! Block him!"

"I know, I will. Obviously." I look down at my knees, humiliated, fully aware that I've been naïve and pathetic. But in my defense, I'd allowed him to contact me purely to watch his next move. And Regan only knows the *outside* of the story. Or its ending. She wasn't in it, wasn't there when it began.

I first met Thatcher in February of my sophomore year, a month after Regan had dropped out. I'd signed up for his Medieval and Early Modern Lit course, winter semester. When I walked into his office for a tutorial, I'd been expecting other students to be there, but it was just him sitting alone behind his desk in a gray cashmere sweater, snowy-white trees behind him through the bay window.

"Ivy McGill." His dark hair seemed to make his eyes bluer,

and as he laced his fingers in front of him, I noticed he had clean, trimmed nails. "I've heard great things."

"About me?" It was warm in his office, and I tugged at my scarf. "Or, you know, life generally?"

He smiled, and I felt my heartbeat judder. "Mostly about you."

Everyone on campus knew of Thatcher Kane, the thirty-five-year-old English prof who'd published that article, taken on the literary forefathers, caused all that fuss. He was already tenured, but more than that, he was cool, antiestablishment, anti-entitled-old-white-man. Since he'd joined the NYU faculty, its stock had definitely gone up.

"Okay. Thank you. I mean, that's nice." I took out my copy of Milton's *Paradise Lost*, diligently dog-eared and sticky-note tabbed. Set down my pen.

"So, tell me what you make of the fall of man." He pointed at the poem, and I took a breath. *Please be impressive, please be impressive.*

"I think that even though we'd describe our society as more godless than it was in the seventeenth century, Milton's themes are more relevant than ever. Technology has become the new religion, and humans believe they're controlling it. We "like" things and post things, so proud of our voyeurism, our appetites. But everything's predetermined by algorithm. We're still just savages being offered an apple."

He leaned back in his chair, his ocean-blue eyes intense. "That's interesting. Wait, I might have something for you." He stood and moved to the bookshelf while the whole cavity of my head filled with golden light. Did he really just like my idea? When he turned, he handed me a floppy white textbook:

Classic Literature and Pop Culture. "Have a read. Let's meet in a couple of weeks. You can tell me what you think."

I'd walked home feeling pulled from the shadows. Regan had moved out of our second-year house share in January, having texted me over Christmas break. She'd been offered an apartment in the Village with other models. For how apologetic she was, she sure packed up quickly, and I didn't know my other roommates that well. They were a couple who hugged while they waited for their toast, sat crammed together on the couch. And everywhere I went on campus, I felt solo and adrift, as if I'd lost my compass, my north star. But now Thatcher Kane had noticed me. He had turned the beam of his focus my way—

"Ivy? What the hell is going on?"

"I didn't know NYU was going to fly him to goddamn Australia! I haven't replied to his texts, or even been on Insta. Have you tagged me at all?"

She covers her eyes with her palms for a second, then drags the skin until her whole face is ghoulish. "Were you *dating* him, Ivy? Jesus H. Christ. You are not getting back with him. I'll break both of your legs."

"I don't want to," I say quietly. *That isn't what this is about.*

We call Christopher right there from the back seat, tell him we've discussed it and we're in, even negotiating an earlier departure time of five p.m. He sounds delighted, his tinny enthusiasm so loud that Regan has to hold the phone away from her head.

"Done." She hangs up, really meaning, *Happy? Look how I'm bending over backward for you.* "But once we're on the boat, you're telling me everything."

"Okay. Yes. Deal." Inside my pocket, I feel the smooth little cowrie shell Lila gave me, run my finger over top of it. *It's a really good boat. At night, it's beautiful.*

We get back to the backpacker dorm, and Regan starts packing her bag, shoving in T-shirts, suntan lotion, damp towels.

"Does he know which *hostel* we're in?" She hurries out of the bathroom, wet bottles of shampoo and conditioner gripped to her chest. "What time does he land?"

"I don't know! Any of that!" I clip the last buckle shut on my backpack, pinching the skin of my thumb just as the door of the hostel dorm flies open and someone jogs in. Regan and I jump, nerves jangling, then wait for the guy to leave.

"I'll tell you the whole story," I say. "I swear to God, Reags. But seriously, can we just get out of here now?"

She nods, jaw muscle tight, and together we head back through the hostel, scanning left and right with each step. Is Thatcher here in the bar, watching me, laughing? He's so quick, I think, shuddering as I feel the skitter of him under my skin. In my hurry, I knock into a picnic table, shatter a game of Jenga, can't hang around to properly apologize. Regan jumps into the waiting cab, while I do one last scan of the street. Checking. Checking.

"Shut off your phone." She lowers her own as I get in, and the taxi starts moving. "Do it now."

"What—really?"

She takes a breath and puts her hand over mine, as if my name's on some kind of hit list and she's been tasked with letting me know. "I just googled literary conferences in Sydney. Keynote speakers. Any kind of bookish event."

"And? Which one is he at?"

She puffs out her cheeks. "None of them. There aren't any. No literary events running at all."

A high note starts to sound in my head, like a single violin string being continuously played. "Why would he make that up?"

But I know the answer already. Because he's so good at disguise. He's making the trip seem fluky. *Oh, hey, look at that, we're in the same spot! Let's be friends now!* He doesn't want to trigger an alarm, but he's flown out here on his own dime, just to track me down.

"Regan, I'm scared. I don't think Thatcher will stop until he finds me."

She eyes the back of the driver's head, lowers her voice. "Let's chat on the boat. Once we set sail, we're free and clear. None of this will matter." She puts her arm around me, my true good friend, but still, my throat feels dry when I swallow.

5

THE WHARF GATE IS tied open, and we head straight down the ramp. I half expect Thatcher to be a step ahead of us, springing from behind a rain barrel, tackling me off the dock. But the whole place appears as deserted as it was earlier, and at the end of the walkway, we see Christopher and Lila standing on board against the late afternoon sky. They're waving, Lila even jumping up and down a little in her worn-out Vans. The sun won't set for a couple hours yet, but already the horizon is more expansive and pastel than anything we'd see in New York. Both Regan and I pause for a second. She pulls out her phone, takes a photo.

"Just to keep," she says. "Not to post."

"We're so glad you chose to come." Christopher helps us aboard with our packs. "Aren't we, Lila?"

Lila has her flat-brimmed baseball cap on, the tops of her ears tucked into it. "We made you some Welcome Aboard food."

"You did?" Behind her, she's arranged cushions in a circle under the boom, a selection of dips and veggies spread out in the middle. And as sweet as that is—including the tea candles she's lit, all of them sputtering—I can't stomach the thought of food. "It's so pretty." I try for a smile. "Reags, you should take a pic."

But Christopher steps in front of the spread. "We're not really a *phonesy* boat. Nothing against technology, but I'd just prefer that Lila didn't grow up so reliant on screens. I'd rather you didn't involve us in any way, or hashtag the boat at all."

Regan says, "I wasn't—"

"The photo you took from the wharf, for example. Just, you know, be mindful." He looks from me to Regan, his eyebrows earnest. "That's all we ask. Isn't it, Lila?"

Lila stares at her shoes. "Yes, Dad."

"That suits us fine," I say, as Regan and I lower ourselves onto cushions. "Are we leaving soon?"

"We're just waiting on Desh." Christopher kneels, and there's a lull while he portions olives onto Lila's plate. She watches him quietly. "He wasn't expecting the earlier launch time. He'll be here any minute."

Is Desh the only one hurrying across town? I peer back up the walkway like a character in a movie willing the elevator doors to close in time.

"Do you have heaps of followers on your socials?" Lila asks Regan suddenly, raising then immediately lowering her eyes deferentially. "You're beautiful. Dad said so."

"Oh." Regan presses her lips together. "Really?"

Christopher coughs on a carrot stick. "Lila! I wasn't talking about Regan specifically. I was simply saying that true beauty's on the inside. It's not about likes or followers."

Maybe, I think, but he must have noticed Regan's looks by now.

She shifts on her cushion. "I don't care about followers—the photo wasn't about that. I just thought the sky looked cool," she says. "Amazing colors. It would make a great painting. Were you into art at school, Lila?"

"No." The girl stiffens. "I wasn't."

"Pumpkin, could you run down below and get us a knife for the hummus?" Christopher rotates his thumbs in his lap, waiting until his daughter has slipped inside the cabin. "Maybe let's keep talk of school to a minimum. I didn't tell you, but Lila's mother was head of the art department there. It threw a difficult spotlight on Lila."

Regan reaches for pita bread. I can tell by the set of her face that she's starting to dislike him. She's already been told off twice in ten minutes. "Okay, but can I ask you a personal question before we set off, Christopher? Just so we're all clear?"

Oh, my God, I think. *Here we go.*

"When did you and Lila's mother break up?"

I gawp at her. Where the hell is she getting that from? Christopher smiles sadly. "You're right. Helen and I chose to separate very recently. I was hoping it wouldn't be quite so obvious. Lila knows everything—we've been completely open with her—and it's an amicable split. I mean, we're all still adjus—"

"You don't have to go into details," I cut in, uncomfortable.

Regan looks at me, then back at him. "But we don't have to *worry* about Helen?"

His head tilts. "In what way?"

"I mean, she's okay with the trip and the addition of female crew? She won't drop bombs on us from a floatplane?" She shoots me a look that says *Dude, just ruling out a frying-pan-into-the-fire situation.*

"No, absolutely not." His chuckle sounds bleak, and I feel sorry for him. "This was a family decision."

"Hey!" shouts a voice behind us on the wharf, and we turn to see Desh standing on the other side of the railing with a backpack. "Permission to come aboard, Skipper?"

"Granted!" Christopher clambers up, helps Desh settle his things.

"Hello, everyone." Desh's green eyes are startling, and I try not to blush as we introduce ourselves. Lila pads back from the galley then, her brow furrowing. I track her gaze, thinking she's transfixed by the sight of Desh in an unbuttoned surf shirt, his ab muscles, those shoulders, that smile. But there, leaning against the railing is a speargun, tall and bright yellow, the sharp end of it spattered with old blood.

Desh steadies the weapon, realizing everyone's staring at it. "Is it okay to bring this on board? Fresh fish is pretty much the cornerstone for any chef on a boat."

"Of course," Christopher says, scratching the back of his neck. "Let's stow it safely, though. We can't have it going off, or anyone tripping over it. Come with me. I'll find a locked cupboard."

The two of them head below deck, Lila trailing behind, leaving Regan and me alone under the boom.

6

"SO, QUICK RECAP," Regan turns to me. "Bloodied death
weapons are okay, but art class is out. And—whatever you
do—do not take any photos of olives."

I smile. "He's probably just jittery. First night with new
people. We'll all settle in. Do you think we'll get going soon?"

"Yeah, I think he's as keen as we are." She stands, goes to
the railing, looks out over the water. Perhaps she's wondering
if she can last on this boat—or where the first stop is—but then
Desh walks back up on deck, and she turns, seems to brighten.

"I've taken the biggest bedroom," he says, his eyes mis-
chievous. "I hope that's okay. Regan, you're in the engine
room next to the generator."

"No, you can't—" I begin.

"I'm kidding. I'm in the engine room. Regan's actually
going to have to sleep in the john."

"Perfect," she says, her mouth curving up on one side.
"Wouldn't be the first time."

Desh laughs, and I want him to throw his playfulness my way, poke fun at me.

"Glass of wine, anyone?" Christopher emerges from the cabin with a bottle of red. "It's a Chilean Malbec. Beautiful little drop."

Oh, my God, I think, *can we please just cast off?* We're all here, and there's no time to be playing the gracious host. In my mind, I see Thatcher going from hostel to hostel. Calling cab companies, figuring out where they've taken their fares.

"We'll probably have a glass or two later," Regan says, reading my stress. "Once we're underway."

"Righto, perfect." Christopher smiles. "Then without further ado, girls, can I escort you below deck? Bring your packs. We'll get you moved in, and I'll give you the basic rundown before we leave."

Regan and I grab our stuff and follow Christopher, who sets down his wine on the galley table, then leads us along the back corridor of the boat.

"Here's the head, and the engine room—or Desh's berth," he says. "And here's where you girls will be." He steps into a boxy white cabin, even smaller than the master, also with a bed on each side under a long thin window. There's an open hatch above, just like in the front cabin, although the air smells more diesely in here, probably because of the motor next door.

"This was Lila's room before?" I ask him, as Regan and I rest our bags against the beds.

"Actually Lila has always slept in the berth at the bow, but I'll bunk in there with her now for the short time we have you on board. I've rigged her up a curtain for privacy."

There's an awkward silence, and I wonder if, like me, Regan's wondering which mattress Christopher slept on. Has he washed the sheets?

"What is that?" Regan points suddenly at our door. I follow the angle of her arm to see with a jolt that there's a sliding rod on the panel near the handle.

"Bolts," he says, as if we've never ventured into a hardware store before.

"Yes, but what the hell are they doing there? On the *outside* of the doors?" Regan crosses her arms so tightly I can see a pale bracelet of fingerprints in the skin of her upper arm.

"They came with the boat," he says, frowning.

"But you left them there? Take them off! Are you hoping we'll move into an animal hutch, Christopher? An enclosure? A *cage?*"

Wow, I think, *this escalated fast*. During the year I lived with Regan, I saw her lose her temper a few times. At tiny personal injustices, mostly: someone stealing her idea for a media presentation, borrowing her pass card for the gym without asking, or taking something she'd said out of context, simply to kick up drama. *I hate liars*, she'd always say. *Liars and frauds*. This, though; this is new. I put my hand on her forearm, a little embarrassed. She's literally vibrating. Her skin feels damp.

"Reags, I don't think Christopher's trying to contain us." I stare pointedly at him. *Fix this*, I'm saying. Because I am afraid she'll veto the whole trip right here, and I don't want to get off this boat.

"*Contain* you? Gosh, no!" Christopher bends at the knees, releasing tension in a nasal wheeze, and for a second he looks like one of those wooden toy men held up by a taut wire, collapsing at the press of a button. "I only kept the locks because Lila has night terrors. She sleepwalks all the time. And at sea that can be a real safety issue."

"There's one on every cabin? Have you been using them?" My voice sounds wary, because does he *shut her in* at night? Surely that can't be happening.

"I'm talking more about the stairwell up from the galley. If she gets through that one and up on deck, she could fall overboard and—you know. *Drown.*" He whispers the last word as if it's a campfire horror story. "We can't have that, can we?"

Regan picks up her backpack. In the second she hefts it onto her shoulder, this whole solution—and the adventure of it—starts to slip away. And where will we go? *Thatcher is in town.* Perhaps she's not as concerned about that as she seemed.

"Christopher, can you please move the rod and plate to the *inside* of our door?" I say hurriedly. "Still safe for Lila. And I don't think it's too much to ask."

My request is stalled by the arrival of Desh, ambling toward us along the corridor, trailed by Lila, who has Pearl in her arms. She looks like she's carrying a beanbag chair.

"Skipper, you want me to pull up anchor?" Desh takes in each of our faces, hesitating at the obvious friction.

"Not yet," Regan says.

"What do you think about this bolt, Desh? On the outside, right here?" I ask.

He glances at it, then shrugs. "Yeah, there's one on my door too. They're just a storm feature. I've worked on loads of boats before where we've had to batten everything down in bad weather. It's not unusual."

There's a charged silence. Christopher looks vindicated, and I can feel Regan wavering, but I know she needs more. "Let's go and look in my toolbox, Regan," Christopher suggests. "We're smart people. Every problem has a solution." He heads out of the cabin, followed by Regan and Desh.

I pivot, unsure whether I should go, too, while behind me, Lila deposits Pearl, then sits down with a sigh on Regan's bed. "My dad's a bit of a worrier," she says. "He fusses about me. And Mum. And everything. You'll get used to it."

"Right," I say. "I guess that's a good thing, though, in the long run. You kind of want that in a captain."

She tickles Pearl's forehead, quiet for so long that I'm not sure if she's even heard what I said. When she speaks again, her voice is a tiny rasp. "I don't sleepwalk."

"What's that?"

"I don't get night terrors. I heard Dad tell you that, but I haven't for years."

A cold frisson of doubt creeps up the skin of my neck, made worse by the low rumbling growl of the boat engine starting up. We're on our way.

CHRISTOPHER EDWARD FARRIS
RECORDED INTERVIEW
Date: January 8, 2020
Location: Cairns, Northern QLD
Conducted by Officers from the Queensland Police,
Far Northern Region

POLICE:	This interview is being recorded. I'm Chief Superintendent Bill Abbott, and I'm joined by Inspector Maeve Knightly. Could you please state your name for the record?
CF:	Christopher Edward Farris.
POLICE:	Farris. Not Edwards.
CF:	Edward is my middle name.
POLICE:	And your date of birth, please?
CF:	June 2nd, 1975.
POLICE:	Thank you. Mr. Farris, why did you feel the need to ch—
CF:	Where's my daughter? Where is Lila?
POLICE:	We'll get to that, sir. The first thing we need to do is establish why you've been traveling under an assumed last name.
CF:	She went into the water. Is she okay?
POLICE:	Is that the last thing you remember?
CF:	[Silence.]
POLICE:	Mr. Farris, I think it's important to—
CF:	No, I'm not answering anything until I know my daughter is safe. You can't withhold that. You can't use it like a bargaining chip. That's . . . that's inhumane.

POLICE: She's fine. Recovering. Shaken up, after all she's been through. But I think you know that.

CF: [Silence.]

POLICE: So, talk us through the name change.

CF: It's . . . it was nothing. Inconsequential. I just wanted to try it out, reinvent myself. A fresh page, a new adventure. Everyone feels that way sometimes. It wasn't hurting anyone.

POLICE: [Pause.] Perhaps we can go back to the very beginning. To what made you feel you needed a fresh page.

CF: Fine. Go ahead. I'm cooperating.

POLICE: Let's start by setting up a timeline. You've had a busy few weeks. You left Hobart, Tasmania, just before Christmas. Why didn't you spend it at home as a family?

CF: Helen and I are separated. We're taking a break.

POLICE: You purchased the *Alone at Last* on December 22nd, according to the previous owner. And set sail the very same day.

CF: Yes, yes. If you say so, yes.

POLICE: You don't remember? Was there a lot going on? Is that also why you didn't bother to register the boat?

CF: [Silence.]

POLICE: Why didn't you register it, sir? It's a legal requirement.

CF: [Long pause.] Like you say. It must have
            slipped my mind. There was a lot going on.
POLICE: Can you be more specific?
CF: Do you have kids, either of you? A daughter?
            No, well, that explains everything.
POLICE: In what way, sir?
CF: If you had a little girl, you'd know. [Long
            pause.] You'd know that sometimes you just
            have to do everything. Anything. Whatever
            it takes.
POLICE: And what is it that you felt you had to do,
            Mr. Farris?
CF: Protect her. No matter what. From those
            who would do her harm.

7

WHEN LILA AND I GET back up on deck, Christopher is standing with Regan and Desh. "I'm not much of a carpenter, especially after a few of these!" He holds up his wineglass, jovial. "But I've removed that bolt and I promise to get a new one in Bowen. I'll fix it. Top priority."

"And how far is that?" I ask, trying to recover. Surely Lila is denying any sleepwalking because she's embarrassed about it?

"Two days' sail at the most." His face looks sincere, and Regan seems to have calmed down. Add that to Desh's nonchalance over the whole issue, and it feels okay to let the lock debate go until then.

We motor on autopilot for a few hours, while the evening turns golden and the water around us glows mercury-soft. It's a million miles away from anything I've ever done or seen before, and I can't get over how vast the ocean looks, how ocher and wide the sky. I'm so grateful to be away from land, and the night is tranquil, perfectly warm, as Desh leans with me at the right-hand—starboard—rail, teaching me old nautical terms.

"See the furthest part of the ocean out there at the horizon?" he asks, pointing while his shirt wafts against me. He smells amazing. "That's the offing." I nod, feeling dreamy in the honeyed light, cocooned in this world that's nowhere near Thatcher.

"Where are you from?" I ask him, as Regan joins us, standing on the other side of Desh. "You sound like you're British but not."

"I'm American. My accent's a little messed up."

We pause, waiting. Apparently that's it for details.

"Really? Which part? I'm from Michigan. Clare, Michigan, middle of the Mitten State." I falter, pointing at the center of my palm as if I'm actually wearing a glove. "And Regan's from San Francisco." Along the railing from me, Regan chuckles. God, I know. Could I be any more uncool?

"I was born in Southern California," Desh says, "but my mom's Fijian. My parents moved back there when I was four. We lived on a boat. I went to the International School in Suva. A lot of my teachers were Brits."

"Did you like growing up overseas?" Regan asks, and I realize what she's noticed—his tone's not that happy. It's as if he's reciting a prepared fact sheet.

"Ups and downs." He smiles with his mouth closed.

Before we can ask him anything else, Christopher arrives to drop anchor in a cove for the night, and we all have to pitch in. Then, once he's overseen Lila's awkwardly enforced goodnight hugs, he heads off to read her a story.

"Early start tomorrow, guys," he says, turning by the

sliding door. "We'll aim to set off at first light. Desh, can we have a quick chat in the galley about tomorrow's food?"

"Sure, I'll be right down. Hey, did we forget to check out of the Airlie marina?"

Christopher stares at him. "I took care of all that already."

"Online? Okay. Right on." Desh watches them disappear below deck, then exhales with his mouth bunched up. "He's nice but kind of tight, hey?"

"Just getting used to us," I say. "Don't you think?"

"Yeah, probably. He'll lighten up." Desh bumps his shoulder against mine. "We'll win him over."

I feel a rush of heat at my throat. *We*, he said. *You and me.*

But as soon as he's gone, Regan turns to me, bursting my bubble. "Can we have a quick chat too?" Her eyebrows are raised, as in *Remember? Your psycho love life?*

"Okay, listen." I lower myself down, my back against the bottom rail, and Regan follows suit. "Yes, I dated Thatcher. For close to two years."

"*Two years?* How did you hide that from me?"

"I was . . . I knew you'd think it was gross. And you're away a lot. But I didn't know he was a creep! I mean, apart from that he was a prof and I was . . ." I squirm, sick of how adolescent I sound. "Anyway, I was scared you'd sniff me out. That's why every time you asked me whose class I was in, I always said someone else."

She shakes her head, still in disbelief. Back in December, after my roommates summoned her, she'd met me in a diner in the Village, bought me a sandwich, told me to eat. *Spill,* she'd said after my first bite. But all I'd managed was Thatcher's name, and the fact that I'd lost my academic

scholarship—the one that had gotten me to NYU—and that
I couldn't stay on without it.

She'd thought then that it was all about money. I'd goofed
off without her around, the handful of dates with Thatcher
just a symptom of that, the pressure of not blowing my scholarship too much, just like she'd always thought it would be.
She knew I'd been applying for grad school, too, that there'd
also be stress around that. *I'll pay your next fees and whatever,*
she said, the sandwich forgotten on a plate between us. *Fuck
it. I'll be your benefactor for as long as you need.* But even if my
problems had been purely financial, I couldn't have taken her
cash. It would have made me her charity case, jettisoned me
back into her shadow. I'd been working so hard to get out.

"It's been going on for so long." Right now, she looks
ready to throw up.

"It started in February, sophomore year. You'd moved out.
Two weeks after my first tutorial, he invited me over to his loft."

"And you went? What the fuck?"

"I get it, Regan! I'm an idiot, thanks for pointing it out."
I pause, kick my heel against the wood of the deck. "Look,
do you want the details or not?"

"Sorry. Yes. I'm just protective. Go on."

I take a deep breath and think back. Sure, I'd read
Thatcher's classic lit and pop culture book avidly, but the
invitation to go to his home to discuss it was totally unexpected. Was it sort of a date? *Hope, hope,* I thought, riding the
L in my Forever 21 dress, the midnight-blue one that clings.
His apartment was in the Meatpacking District, and when I
got there, it was clear that he must have family money. That
loft definitely cost more than his professor's salary could have

covered. All the way up in the elevator, I toyed with my coat zipper, completely out of my league.

"You made it. Come in." He answered the door in loose jeans and a faded Yankees T-shirt, with a stubbled jawline, tousled dark hair. *Oh, God, it's not a date.* I felt like a child playing dress-up as I followed him into an open-plan living room/kitchen, leather couch, soft music on the Sonos, sheepskin rug on the cement floor. His place was all high ceilings, good lighting, nice plants. "Can I fix you an old-fashioned? The bourbon is local, from Brooklyn."

I was used to drinking cheap beer straight from the bottle and suspected he'd guessed that, by the half smile on his face. What did he want from me? Why was I here? Did all his students come over? Were they all in his lending library? From the speakers overhead, the woman singing sounded throaty and sensual. I took the drink he'd made, my fingers shaking.

"Have a seat. Take your jacket off. Stay awhile."

Slowly I undid my puffer and perched on the couch while he moved behind the kitchen island, draped a dish towel over one shoulder. "I'm cooking us dinner. We can eat and talk about how your Milton thesis is developing. Do you like Korean food?"

"I don't know. Do you mean noodles?" At home, we ate pork chops and mash. My dad home-brewed beer to save money, his vats belching in the carpeted living room while they fermented.

Thatcher wiped his hands on the towel, laughing. "See, this is what I find so refreshing about you, Ivy. Your ability to ask excellent questions." There was a beat. I wondered if I should at least try to sound more sophisticated. "So, *who is* Ivy McGill? What's your favorite movie? How do you spend your weekends? Who was your first kiss, and how would you describe the experience?"

"First *kiss*?" I repeated, unnerved. I definitely didn't want to talk about Eric Oleksow, captain of my high school debate team, whom I'd dated until he came to visit me in New York. Once I introduced him to Regan, I realized what an asshat he was.

Thatcher leaned forward on the counter, one palm covering his mouth. "Ivy, I'm so sorry. Wow. That was completely inappropriate. Jesus Christ, I can't think straight."

"You—what? Really?" My body reacted as if he'd just told me he was madly in love with me. I was a live wire, every part of me zapping.

He moved five steps back from the kitchen to the couch, sat down at the other end, ran his hand through his ruffled hair. "I need to admit something. It's . . . unprofessional."

"Okay." I held my breath, heart thudding.

"I'm a little thrown by you, to be honest. You're . . . well, and I thought some book chat might keep us on track, but I can see I'm . . ." He trailed off while I blinked at him, unsure. "I'm going to have to talk to the dean. God knows what I'm going to say to her." He shook his head, studying me, as a new thought seemed to strike him. "Will you help me run through it? You be her, I'll be me."

"What?"

"Janet, have you got a minute?" He was role-playing—Janet Blau was head of NYU—and I hurried to catch up. "There's a student in my class, and I can't stop thinking about her. It's been going on for a couple of weeks now."

"Oh. Dear." My voice wobbled with trepidation, excitement. "That's . . . not good."

"No. Believe me, I want it to stop." He shifted closer. I could smell his delicious cologne, feel his heat. "But I don't think I can control it."

"Wow, that's . . . very unprofessional." Was this a dream? For days, I'd thought of little else but him, and here I was on his couch. Getting closer and closer by the second. "Has this happened to you before, Professor Kane?"

"Never." He was so close now. My fingers twitched. "The thing is, this girl is smarter than me. I don't know how to teach her, and that's new. But she sees the world in ways that I . . . can't. And she's pretty. Too pretty. I think you'd better move her out of my tutoring group."

"What if she doesn't think of you in that way?" I was trying not to smile. "Maybe she has a boyfriend. Or she thinks you're old and not hot."

His mouth opened then, faux-shocked, his blue eyes twinkling. "You make a very good point, Janet. Do you believe that's the case? It would really be so much simpler if it was."

"It's not," I said, and in one swift motion, he closed the rest of the gap on the couch, pressed against me, his lips against mine. His tongue was cool in my mouth, tasted faintly of whiskey, and I sighed into him, moving fast now, my fingers at the button of his jeans—

"Stop! I can't . . . I hate this." Regan has plugged a forefinger into each ear. "I hate *him*. He needs castrating. I'll do it myself with a machete."

"Sorry." I shake my head, trying to shake away the memory of the best sex I've ever experienced, jumping to after, when Thatcher collapsed beside me, breathing into my neck.

"Holy shit," he'd said, "that is not how it'll go with the dean."

We laughed, but when he leaned up, his face was solemn. "Ivy, if you want this, like I do . . . it *has* to be a secret. I could lose everything. I shouldn't be anywhere near you."

God, did I ever want this. I'd slept with a total of three guys, none of whom had ever made my body respond like that. I kissed Thatcher, crossed my heart. "I won't tell a soul."

Regan's voice sounds tight. "So, he manipulated the shit out of you and kept doing it for almost two whole years."

"But I let him." Every time he found excuses to keep me longer than the others after class, I'd feel my pelvis tweak and flutter, feathery with anticipation. We had sex in his office, so thrilling and dangerous, his hand over my mouth as he pressed me against the hard oak of the door. I felt so chosen when he took me for expensive dinners in hidey-hole restaurants, or weekends away in Montauk, where his beachfront cottage had vintage wallpaper and his mother's handwriting was on the calendar next to the fridge. At Thanksgiving, when I went home to Michigan for a short break, all my high school friends seemed suddenly ten years younger than me. None of those boys were men.

"Why did it end?" Regan demands, some anger still in her voice.

"Because he's a pig. I just took a long time to figure it out."

"Okay, but what he's doing still doesn't make sense. Why the hell would he follow you all the way to Australia?" When I don't answer, she takes a deep breath. "Is there something else you're not telling me?"

And this is it, the moment I choose to outright lie to my best friend. Lie rather than let her see just how mortified I am, and why. "No." I pick at my thumbnail miserably. "Thatcher likes to control women. Everything's a power game, and he can't stand that I'm no longer in his grip. But I'm not, Reags. He doesn't have me."

That part is true, and she exhales a little shakily. "Good. Okay, so relax now. No more Thatcher Kane. Thank God we got on this boat."

I cringe in the darkness, glad that she can't see my face. I know exactly why Thatcher is here. But I never in a million years thought he'd take it this far.

He hasn't come here to be friends. He's come because of what I found out about him.

And because of what I stole in a white flash of fury when he kicked me out of his loft.

8

THE ENGINE WAKES ME at six a.m. The smell of gas and hot dust permeates our stuffy cabin, catching at the back of my throat. The motor is so loud it could be inside my head, and I wonder if Desh managed to sleep a wink in his cabin. I roll over in bed, my hair pasted to my cheek. Regan's stirring, the white sheet stark against her skin.

"I slept like the dead," she says. "Must have been that wine, although I didn't think we drank that much."

We'd raided Christopher's liquor cupboard and found another open bottle of red, swigging it to the silt as we got over the difficult Thatcher chat. Desh didn't reappear; he must have just gone to bed. Above us, we hear footsteps as someone walks along the ledge of deck beside the portside window. I can see brown socks and hairy legs.

"We should get up," I say. "Christopher might have jobs for us to do."

"I need a shower." Regan drags herself up from her sheets.

"There's probably a limit on fresh water. Not to be rules-y. There probably just is."

"A swim. Something." Regan digs under her pillow. "Where's my phone? I put it here last night, I swear. What the hell?" She stands, looking under the bed, down the side of the mattress.

"Did you leave it up on deck?"

She pulls on shorts and a T-shirt. "I swear I brought it down."

"Wait. I'll come check too."

Fresh air wafts around us as we emerge from the main cabin. We're already a long way from last night's cove, the morning turning to blue, birds swooping at the prospect of a new day. It's like a different planet out here, almost a watercolor painting, two broad swathes of ocean and sky. And so *quiet*. On the front deck, Christopher has tied down long yellow cushions and set out fresh fruit, pastries, and coffee. He's leaning by the smaller racing sail that he called a spinnaker. Nobody's manning the helm, so we must be back on autopilot.

"Morning, Ivy. Hi, Regan," Lila says, sitting cross-legged in a sundress, sunglasses big on her face. Ten feet away, Pearl is curled up on her own cushion, a sheen of fur all over the fabric.

"Hey, Lila. Morning, Christopher. We're off! It's beautiful out." I look at the far-distant coastline, Thatcher way back there somewhere, the water turquoise and pristine as it spreads a vast moat of safety around us.

"You slept well." Christopher says it as more of a statement than a question. "Almost as well as Desh! Here I am on the boat with a paid chef, yet I'm doing all of the meal prep." He smiles like people do when they're irritated.

"We need alarm clocks." Regan pauses uncertainly. "Speaking of which, has anyone seen my cell phone? It's not in our room or the kitchen. Or the back deck."

"The galley," Christopher corrects her. "The aft. The stern."

"Whatever," she says.

"You didn't leave it out overnight, did you?" His expression shifts to troubled. "Things tend to slip overboard as soon as the boat's on the move."

Regan says nothing. Sits down, lifting pillows, checking under sun cushions. I help out, but the phone's nowhere to be found. Regan shakes her head at the offer of a croissant.

"I'm sure it'll turn up." Christopher pushes Pearl's cushion out of his path with one foot so she slides sideways like luggage in an airport tray. "In the meantime, I'd like to run through knots and basic sailing terminology at some point today, if that's okay. I want to get boat watch going as quickly as possible, so you need to be shipshape enough that you can sit up for a couple of hours on your own."

As he kneels, Regan's jaw muscle clenches, unclenches. "That's fine, but can you please check under *your* cushion for my cell?"

"Mine? Certainly. Of course." He leans to the side, lifts one edge of the yellow padding. Does the same at the opposite edge. Shrugs mournfully.

"It's probably under yesterday's clothes, Reags," I say. "We came up here in a hurry."

"Yeah. That's probably it." She visors one hand in the sunshine, keeping an eye on Christopher. "I'll find it. Or replace it. One or the other."

He nods once, closing the subject. "Shall we eat and get breakfast cleaned up, then? Ready to seize the day?"

"Born ready," Regan says. But her jaw muscle hasn't relaxed in the least.

—

Desh misses breakfast entirely. By the time he emerges at nine, I'm doing the dishes in the sink. Christopher has a word with him about his job requirements, and Desh says sorry, catching my eye like a naughty kid who'll likely be just as tardy tomorrow. As funny as that is, it's hot in the galley and my stomach has started to churn. Something about the continual whir of the boat's motor is making me nauseous, and there's a lurch, an unpredictable pitch now and then, a judder of waves against the hull that's making my tongue feel like paste.

"Have you sailed a lot before?" Desh asks me, taking the dishcloth from my hand.

"Just on lakes. Small boats. With my dad."

"You're green to the gills. Go up on deck. Down here is the worst place to be if you're feeling sick."

I stagger up the stairs and out to the bow, lie down in the shade of the racing sail. The cushion fabric smells of briny rotten seaweed, and by noon there's a slick sweat over the whole surface of my body. It's all I can do to take steady breaths in and out, and whenever I risk briefly opening my eyes, I see Regan with Desh, avoiding Christopher's knot lesson, hooting with laughter ten feet from me while Desh teaches her some card game.

Lila joins me in the afternoon, sits beside me reading a book, patting me now and again. Pearl settles on the other side of my hip. At around four, Christopher shoos Lila away. "She's not feeling well, pumpkin. Let's give her some space. Leave her be." I can't lift my head to tell him I don't mind her company, and the little girl withdraws. Pearl stays.

Sometime later I open my eyes when Desh crouches beside me, putting down a mug of soup. The stars are out, everything's swaying, and it's almost worse in the oil-blackness. There's no horizon, no dimension to steady me.

"Try it," Desh says softly. "It's a ginger broth. I made it specially for you."

"Thanks," I murmur. "Can you move it a bit further away?"

He smiles, or I think he does. "Your seasickness won't last. Your body's adjusting. You'll be fine by the morning."

I nod, registering that he's been thinking about me. The adjustments of my body.

After he's gone, I slowly sit up, force myself to try a tiny mouthful of his soup. It's warm, wholesome, perfectly seasoned. And to my surprise, it stays down. I venture a little more. After that, I lie back with my head on the damp cushion and drift in and out of sleep. When I wake again, the motor has stopped running and the anchor seems to have been dropped. There's no sound at all except the mournful creak of the hull as it rocks, the slap of dark waves against it. It's as if everyone's abandoned ship and not told me.

I stagger to my feet and along the thin strip of decking, sweaty palm on the railing, trying not to tumble overboard. What if I did? Would anyone even know? There's not a single light out at sea or below deck, only the distant stars and a pale moon. My legs feel rubbery, my mouth rancid and sour. Inside the sunroom, the little gate has been closed down to the galley kitchen. The whole boat is silent, everyone sound asleep in their beds, including Regan. Did she even check on me? I collapse onto the daisy-print cushioning, moving an empty chip bowl aside, my hand sinking into a wispy cobweb to my right. Gasping, I realize it's just Pearl, spread out on the bench by the board games shelf. I move closer to her, try to cuddle in, but she kicks out one leg with a jerk-jerk-jerk certainty. Giving up, I curl up on the bench seat in a fetal position. The boat moans, the ropes on the mast plink and rattle. I hug into myself, try hard to go back to sleep.

9

AS I LIE THERE in the darkness, I realize my day pack is on a low shelf to my left. My cell phone is in it. Maybe if I switched it on, there'd be a signal and I could call my dad or someone. Feel some kind of connection, a little human exchange after a horrible day. But then my heart pinches with dread again. Thatcher will have texted me, probably multiple times. If he made it to Airlie Beach like he said, he'll have wandered around town looking for me; there's no way he hasn't turned nasty. I have something on him, after all. Something he'll go to crazy lengths to get back.

I'm completely out of my depth. I was for the entire time we were together. I can see that now. Would I ever have found out what he was really like if I hadn't happened to pass by that girl on the faculty stairs late November, as I headed up to Thatcher's office? She was small, blond, and attractive, but she'd been crying so hard it looked like both eyes had been pulled out, stamped on, and put back into her face.

"Hey," I said, wanting to ask if she was alright, but she pushed on by. I climbed the last few stairs and opened Thatcher's door. He was sitting at his desk, one hand across his brow, writing something with his favorite Montblanc pen. "What was that about?" I pointed back toward the stairwell. He looked up. "Paisley? She's a freshman student. Having a hard time with the program." I lingered in the doorway. *Are you involved with her? Why the hell would she be sobbing like that?* Thatcher sighed. "She's also homesick and a sports scholarship kid. Rower, I think. I'm trying to help her balance her timetable. Sometimes the academic load can be too much."

I said nothing more. But a few days later, he told me she'd keyed his car in the parking lot. He was considering reporting her to the campus authorities.

"Why on earth would it be Paisley? I thought you were helping her." We were at his place, about to watch a movie, my head in his lap.

"I am, but I can't just fabricate good grades for her, even if I'd like to. So it makes me an easy person to blame."

I twisted, staring up at him. "She's flunking out?"

He exhaled, looked sad. "I don't know the whole picture, but I think it's likely, yes. And maybe there's pressure from home. You know what that's like—having to be the one to carry all the expectation, advance the family's good name."

"I do," I said slowly, because I *did* understand that, but even if my marks dipped and I lost my funding, there was still no way I'd vandalize a prof's car. Something was off. All evening, I kept returning to it, couldn't follow the movie's plot. The next day, I found out when the rowers had the campus gym booked out, asked one of the girls in there about Paisley, and figured out exactly who she was.

Payton (not Paisley) Nielsen was eighteen years old and was the tiny rower who sits with a megaphone, shouting at the front of the boat. When she opened the door to her dorm, she was barely five feet in her socks and Birks. She was wearing a huge sweatshirt that came all the way to her knees, her white-blond hair scrappily tied back, and I could see she had unusually aqua eyes now she'd stopped crying. Behind her were cardboard boxes, half-full and chaotic with books. Her pinboard was empty and only one poster remained on the wall. James Dean, in a coat, walking down a rainy street.

"Payton?" I asked, though I knew it was her. Her eyes narrowed. "I'm Ivy. I go here. I'm a senior."

"Okay?" Her lips were so dry they were cracked.

"I saw you upset the other day coming out of Thatcher Kane's office." The instant I said his name, her grip on the door tightened, fingertips pressing white. "Can you tell me what that was about?"

"Nothing." She looked behind her, then back at me. *Please go now*, she meant.

"Are you leaving NYU? That sucks, I'm really sorry. Can I come in for a second?" There was more to this situation, I was sure of it. Whatever had upset her was more personal, more emotional, more Thatcher-based than bad grades.

"I'm choosing to go home." She chewed a flake of skin on her lip, and I saw a tiny bead of blood crest there. "I'm over this place. I want out."

I nodded, but I still felt that she was running from more than "this place." I suspected Thatcher had been two-timing me. It wasn't as if guys hadn't done it to me before. Eric Oleksow, case in point. He'd pretty much ten-timed me, and I was the last one to know. I'd sworn I wouldn't let that happen again. "Okay. But can I just ask you, how well do you know Professor Ka—" "He's an asshole." She crossed her arms, the baggy sweatshirt pinning to her tiny frame. "Why? How well do *you* know him?"

I lost all momentum right there. I hadn't come over to talk about me. Payton's energy was a blend of fatigue and aggression, and maybe I'd been wrong and her problems *were* just academic. Regardless, it was obvious she wasn't going to tell me anything, so I just shrugged as if to say *Sorry to bother you.* Then I turned to walk away.

"He's a complete fucking perv. Get out while you can."

I spun around, the slap of her words echoing down the hallway. But her door had already closed.

—

That night, I went over to Thatcher's place. He'd ordered in, and we were sitting on stools at the kitchen island, eating with chopsticks, a glass of crisp white wine in front of each of us. I hadn't touched mine.

"Can I tell you something, Ivy?" He was chewing, his mouth full. "You look lovely tonight."

"Oh," I said, jumping a little as he leaned over and kissed the side of my head. "Thank you."

"Are you going to tell me what's on your mind?" He took a sip of wine, smiling like he always did at my worries, as if they were all fluff and cuteness. But was this worry baseless? What was I supposed to do with Payton's warning? A perv *how*? There was nothing about Thatcher that warranted the accusation. Except for our relationship . . . he was a professor, in a position of power. He'd said himself he shouldn't be anywhere near me. But no, *I'd* chased *him*. Hadn't I? Round and round it all swirled in my head as I toyed with my Kung Pao chicken.

"Do students ever proposition you?" I asked suddenly, and he coughed, fogging the curve of his wineglass. "I'm serious! Do they ever, like, offer to blow you for a higher grade?"

"Wow." He dabbed at his mouth with a serviette. "This conversation took an interesting swerve."

"You can tell me, Thatcher. I'm a grown-up. And it'd be totally understandable if everyone on campus hit on you. Girls like Payton, especially. Struggling for grades." There was a pause while his forehead furrowed. "That's her name. Payton Nielsen. I ran into her today."

"Did you. No doubt she was full of stories. She's been kicked out, Ivy. She's setting fire to everything she can on the way out."

"No, I know, and it just occurred to me that maybe she tried something on with you. And you wouldn't go for it. And she's turned it around in her head?" The cadence of my words rose, and Thatcher reached over to touch my face.

"If I tell you that yes, students offer me all manner of sexual favors for grades, you'll feel threatened, destabilized, and I don't want that. There's no need. But if I tell you no, as a professor, it never comes up, I'd be lying. I can't win. Maybe don't ask the question? You know that we're a couple, Ivy; we're exclusive, and I value that greatly."

"You do?" I asked. The haze of my anxiety started to clear.

"I do." He pushed our plates to the side. "Don't you?"

We both stood at the same time, bumping into each other in our hurry to kiss, the urgency of our bodies surprising. Payton had shaken me, but I was back from the brink, the relief turning fast into desire, as I pulled Thatcher's shirt from his chest, gripped his neck as if floundering from a shipwreck. *Yes*, I thought, *everything yes*, and he carried me to the sheepskin rug, pressed on top of me, my nails in his back. When it was over, he rolled flat for a minute, then stood.

"See?" he said, fixing his jeans as he took off toward the bedroom for a shower. "We're fine. Don't listen to those girls. They're just bitches who're trying to ruin it."

I leaned up on one elbow on the rug, watching him move out of sight. *Bitches?* Why say that? Little fingertips of doubt crept back in. Payton was his ex-student. How unprofessional could he get? And who were "those girls"? As far as I knew, Payton was the only one who'd thrown any shade. I sat up properly. Or was she?

My summer after junior year, I'd decided to stay in New York instead of going home. I wanted to get a job, be with Thatcher, experience the city differently through July and August. My house share was done, the next one not set up yet, and I didn't want to crowd Thatcher by moving into his loft. But Regan had an apartment in the Village, one she shared with two other models, Umi and Harlow. Regan was already away shooting in Seoul, her room empty for a while, and she let me sublet for free.

"Only Harlow will be around," Regan said. "I don't know her, she moved in while I was out here. But go over, meet her. Umi says she's cool."

Thatcher came with me that first day. He was attentive

like that, concerned, invested. Regan's building was a beautiful old brick one, the apartment wide-windowed with original radiators and edgy art on the walls. Harlow opened the door in a Bowie T-shirt cinched into huge jeans. She was tall, sculpted, with blunt bangs.

"Are you a smoker?" she asked as soon as we were inside. "There's a rooftop terrace; it's where we always hang out."

Thatcher and I followed her up there, although neither of us smoked. The air was warm, the view dusky, and I figured I'd take a pic, send it to Regan, so I nipped back downstairs to grab my cell from my purse. But as I came back onto the roof, I caught a flash of Harlow stepping away from Thatcher, something hurried and furtive in the angle of her elbow. Something not right.

Later, when I asked him about it, he'd looked pained. "Okay, look. She asked me out. While you were gone. Wanted to know if I'd be into that, and I said no, I would not."

I'd believed him, taken the room, gotten a job in a coffee shop, and barely saw Harlow again. She moved out at the start of July, took off for a contract in London, the big apartment all mine for two months. At the time that felt great—major competition removed—but now, as I sit up on the rug, it feels uneasy. Regan said even Umi lost touch with Harlow. She literally dropped off the map.

I stood, pulled on my clothes, listening to the water of Thatcher's shower running. *He's a complete fucking perv. Get out while you can.* Was he as exclusive as he claimed? As honorable? I crept into the study, a small boxy white room in which I'd hardly ever set foot because Thatcher had asked me not to. *It's your classmates' work, baby. Off-limits. We can't blur every line we have.* There were no built-in closets, no cabinets, just an industrial-looking filing cabinet, a shelf above it displaying framed degrees and awards. Large mahogany desk, and a luxury office chair. I ran my fingertip over his laptop touch pad, and the screen came to life, but I didn't know his password.

Think, Ivy, think. If I was hiding anything about myself— or about a relationship I was keeping secret from my secret lover—where would I put it? The desk drawer was all paper clips and pens. I turned to the filing cabinet. In the top drawer were bank statements, documents, reams of paper I had no time to read. The second one, textbooks, a whole stack of NYU brochures, a pile of fat manila envelopes stuffed beneath. Above me in the pipes, the shower turned off. I closed the drawer, but felt an insistent, instinctive tap-tap-tap. Yanked it open again, reached down for the envelopes, and pulled out the first one.

10

THE SECOND I OPENED the envelope and realized what I was holding, I felt my lungs empty as if I had been punched. In my hands were three Fujifilm photographs, white bordered, the kind that have no digital trace. Each picture was of the same girl, about my age, passed out on a rumpled bed, the name *Veronika* written underneath in thick Sharpie. Horrible fleshy images of her legs spread wide, the angles varied but all equally vicious, exploitive, and obviously completely without consent. Dry-mouthed, I grabbed more photos from the envelope, found a different girl, Jordan, totally out of it too. My mind was reeling. Had Thatcher *taken* these? Jesus Christ, were these his students? Was *Payton* in one of these envelopes?

On rubbery legs, I hurried back to the kitchen, threw the whole envelope into my bag as Thatcher emerged from his bedroom drying his head with a towel. I couldn't look at him. What had he done? Who the hell was he?

"I forgot to ask you," he said, fetching a glass of water. "What are you doing for Christmas? Spending it in the city with friends?"

I couldn't answer him. *We're so proud of our voyeurism, our appetites*, I'd told him so cleverly when I'd first pitched my *Paradise Lost* idea. All this time, I was talking about *him*. He was the worst savage of all.

"What's wrong? You look strange."

"Do you *know* those girls?" I blurted. "Are they students? Did you roofie them and take photos, you sick fuck?"

He fluttered his head like I'd smacked him. "What did you just say?"

"I found your little gallery. The photos in your study. Don't deny it. I know what you are."

He gaped at me, face hollow. "My porn, you mean, Ivy? What the hell? They're not students—why on earth would you think that?"

"They're . . . they're all young and passed out!"

"They're actresses! Sex workers. Adults who have agency and are being paid. I ordered the photos online from a website, there's hundreds of them. It's a global industry, you fucking child."

I felt shaky, adrenaline coursing as I put one hand on the cool marble countertop. "It's still disgusting. You still jerk off to fake-comatose girls. That's not okay."

"Stop slut-shaming them." He shook his head, eyes full of contempt. "Why are you being so judgmental?"

"Thatcher, they're literally the same age as the girls you teach! I bet the dean would have something to say abou—"

He rounded the island in three steps, grabbed my bag, and

pulled me hard to the front door. "How dare you? We're done. Never, ever come back here."

The door slammed and I stood in his corridor, hot, terrified, feverish. I called an Uber, cried the whole way home. By the time I got there, he'd already emailed me from his faculty account.

> Ms. McGill, I have been approached by a student, in strictest confidence, who is bringing forth serious allegations against you of plagiarism and unsanctioned use of AI. Obviously, I have no choice but to take the matter to the Academic Integrity Committee. I felt you should know, however, that for the duration of the investigation, your scholarship status will be withheld, as will all recommendations for graduate school. Should you wish to discuss this, you may do so with your current supervisor. Yours, Thatcher Kane.

I read the email three times, numb with shock. It was total bullshit. There was no "anonymous student" whose identity Thatcher felt sworn to protect, I'd never copied anything, and I didn't even understand AI. But could I prove any of that? He had access to several of my old assignments. Could he feed one of them into a database, then claim that version had come first?

All I had was the bulky envelope in my bag. Thatcher had everything else.

—

In the silvery light of the upstairs cabin, a bigger wave passes under the boat. I sit up, lean past snoring Pearl, and grab my day pack. Inside is the manila package, the one thing I have over Thatcher. I couldn't leave the photos behind in New York. Even with plausible deniability, he knows those photos would ruin his career. A highly regarded prof who possesses porn like this? His reputation would be damaged enough, and maybe students who'd suspected his sexual tendencies (like Payton must have) would speak up. Thatcher would be canceled, his precious tenureship burned to the ground. And that's why he's here, manically chasing me. It's why he won't stop.

I open the envelope, tip out the twenty or so images into the empty chip bowl, trying not to look at any of them. A clump of tissue paper falls out, too, inside of which is a round brass stamp, the kind people use to press envelopes shut with wax. It's charred, tacky, with a swirly, pretentious letter *K* on it, some seal Thatcher probably ordered from Etsy to look important when he sends out letters. That's going straight in the trash. I throw it to the bottom of my pack, grab the barbecue lighter from the low shelf, and squirt fuel all over the photographs.

I need to be done with him. Fully, once and for all. The fetish photos he bought online are upsetting, even if consensual, and I want nothing left in my life that's his. I kept the envelope because it was the one shred of power I had: I could tell the dean, I could tell Thatcher's next girlfriend, or maybe, if I let him stew long enough, I could even get my scholarship back. That's why I haven't blocked him. It was an insurance policy, a bargaining chip, but it's turned into a dye pack, a scent he's trailing. And now, more than anything in the world, I want it gone.

The lighter catches the white edges of the photos, the images of those women curling with flame, turning to black. I carry the bowl outside, watch the smoke wisp as the fire dances a foot high, until nothing but flaked ashes remain. Only when the pictures are gone, when there's nothing left for Thatcher to chase, do I head back into the cabin and lie down on the bench again. I wrap my arms around my middle, try not to shiver.

Water laps, the boat creaks. Eventually, I fall back to sleep.

11

REGAN FINDS ME FIRST, coming through the galley gate, emerging up the steps wide-eyed.

"You slept up here?" she asks. "Why didn't you come down?"

"I didn't trust being inside without air. Plus it was super dark, and I didn't want to crash around and wake you up." I heave myself up to a sitting position, hugging my knees. The nausea has gone, just as Desh said it would, but my body feels stiff and tired.

"Shit, dude, you could have woken me. I checked on you three times before I went below, but you were out cold. Desh told me he brought you soup."

"He did, but . . . he didn't stay long."

"Did you sleep at all? Are you okay?" She stands stricken by the bench, hair wild, brow honest, all that effortless style, just like on the first day I met her. She'd been unpacking in our freshman dorm when I walked into our room with my dad. Her corner was already so artsy. Throw cushions, photos, plants. There was no way I could match her or keep up. We said hi, a clash of worlds. *You girls can have each other's backs*, Dad said, and after he'd gone and Regan helped me get settled, it was as if the deal had already been struck. *Here's everything I'm good at*, we each seemed to be saying. *Take whatever you want that'll help*. And what I learned as the year went by was that I had more currency than I thought. Not in style, but in solidity. Regan needed a real friend.

"I'm fine," I say as she sits on the opposite bench. "I just bunked here with Pearl for the night. She's super cuddly. We spooned." We both laugh.

"What's all that?" Regan points at the bowl of dark ashes on the floor. "You were burning shit up here?"

"Just photos outside. They were Thatcher's. They're all gone."

"Nice. Good riddance." She pauses. "You look like death, fyi. Like after Jason Hoefflinger's spring break party. The one where you threw up in his fridge." I groan at the memory, and Regan sits down next to me on the bench. "When did you last drink water?"

"God knows. Yesterday was gross."

"Tell me about it. Christopher finally cornered me in the evening with his knots seminar. He was very thorough and paternal. So, *that* was fun." She pauses, and I see the hurt in her that still crops up at any mention of a father figure. Her dad walked out on her family when she was only thirteen. From what she's told me, he just upped and left, barely taking a suitcase with him. I think it explains her defiance now. How dismissive she is of men.

I reach for her hand, and she lets me, even though mine's tacky with grime.

"Today will be better," she says. "You're on the mend."

"I really am." And deep down, in the most crucial way, I know it's true: I've been purged of a poison. The trick now is to let Thatcher know there's nothing left to chase.

"Come outside to the fresh air. I'll get you some crackers and cold water."

I let her help me along to my sun cushion, the shape of my hips and knees indented into the yellow fabric. Apart from that, no traces of my misery remain. Gulls shriek in the breeze, and the air is gentle. We're anchored in a sheltered bay, palm tree fringed, postcard perfect, completely deserted. How different it all looks in the light.

Regan deposits me in the shade, heads back to the galley to fetch supplies. While she's gone, Christopher wanders up on deck, spots me, and heads over.

"You're feeling better, I hear?" He sits beside me, fatherly with concern. "Bit of a rough start."

I smile weakly. "Sorry I missed your knots lesson."

He looks sharply at me, perhaps checking for sarcasm, but I'm too exhausted to have a tone. "Regan just told me you woke up alone in the dark. I'm so sorry. I thought you were settled, and that a starlit night might help. If you needed anyone, I felt sure you'd come down."

"I could have. It's okay."

"But you must have felt lonely. Again, I apologize. That was a real misjudgment on my part. Normally I don't make bad decisions."

I wait for a beat, gathering the strength for a conversation. "What do you do at home, Christopher? For a job, I mean."

"Until very recently, I ran an art cinema." He smiles, the creases around his eyes deepening. "The Rosebud. Seats you could lay back in, beautiful ice cream, only the best films from around the world. It was a hotspot. Really wonderful."

"You named it after *Citizen Kane*?" For some reason, I want him to know I'm more than just a weakling who gets seasick. I'm cultured; I get cultural references.

"I did!" He looks down at me, impressed. "I'm a huge Orson Welles fan. *The Third Man*. So great. All that shadow and misconception."

"Totally." I nod, even though that reference is beyond me. For a second, I'm back in Thatcher's tutorial, pretending I understand everything he's saying. "You don't run the theater anymore? What happened to it?"

He knocks once on the deck with a knuckle, closing the nostalgia. "It shut down six months ago. Tastes change—you know how it goes. People don't want to watch subtitled movies. They want Marvel heroes and not much else."

"That's a shame."

"It is, but there you go. So, listen: let's draw a line under yesterday. Today is a fresh chapter." He spots Regan coming to join us. "I'll leave you to it. Breakfast will be ready soon; it'll be good to get something back in your system. I'm glad you're out of the tunnel."

He passes Regan at the railing, and she turns to stare at his back, then moves toward me, handing me a glass and some crackers. "Everything okay?"

"He apologized. All good. Hey, did you find your phone?"

"No." She curls her lip. "And I hate not having it. Feels so weird. But everything's on the cloud, and we'll be in Bowen in about six hours. I can buy another one there."

—

After I've nibbled some crackers and had some water, I do feel better. Regan suggests a swim, and we head to the stern. We jump off the swim grid—a little platform at the back of the boat—the water cool enough to be refreshing, glittering like diamonds in the early light. I feel yesterday's sickness wash from my skin, bobbing my head underwater, rinsing my hair. When we climb back on board, we grab towels and find that Desh has laid out a breakfast of fresh fruit, yogurt, and granola. He's just showered, too; his shoulders are glistening with water and sun. The day is looking up.

We sit in a circle to eat, Lila passing me the plate of sliced-up banana, her light-brown eyes worried.

"I'm okay," I tell her. "Fighting fit."

"Nibble the food all the same," Christopher warns me. "We're sailing again after this."

"About that," Desh says. "What if we just had a fun day? Ivy's had a shaky start, and it's paradise here. There's not a soul to be seen in any direction."

Christopher's coffee mug stops midway to his mouth. But Desh is right. Around us, the bay glitters, sapphire and aquamarine. It's sand, ocean, and sky as far as the eye can see. Here I am with the warm sun on my skin. The backpackers of Airlie are well behind us; the slushy puddles, sirens, and socked-in skies of New York, a distant memory.

"Can't we just chill for a bit?" Desh presses. "You know, snorkel, relax, hang out? We'll get the music going. I'll do up some good nosh. Isn't that why we're all here?"

I smile at him shyly. He's really looking out for me. Regan nods agreement, leans forward to grab an apple, blocks my view.

"Yes, I want to do that too," Lila says. "Pleeease, Dad? You promised this would be a fun trip, and all we do is chug through the sea."

If Christopher is offended, he hides it quickly. "A unanimous vote! Far be it from me to go against my crew. There'd be mutiny!" He leans back on his cushion, but his neck muscles seem tight. "We can sail into Bowen tomorrow. No rush."

"Brilliant." Desh stands. "Let's have some fun. I'll get the tunes on."

I lock eyes with Regan, and both of us smile. Getting on this boat was the right choice. We're going to be fine.

12

ALL DAY LONG, we swim, zoom around the deserted bay in the tender, explore the shore with its bone-white driftwood, sun bake, do it all over again. I take an hour-long nap in the shade at noon, and feel restored. Christopher stays largely out of our way, letting Lila do bombies with us off the swim grid while he nods like a gently impressed uncle.

"Keep that hat on when you're out of the water," he warns her, clearly worried about her fair skin burning, and I swim alongside while she doggy paddles, puffing, not blessed with athleticism. Every time she dries off, she clamps her cap back on dutifully, happy to avoid sunburn and the (seemingly endless) attention of her father. But it's a perfect day for fun in the tropics: Desh's music is summery and upbeat, and I feel safe, relaxed, a million miles away from recent troubles and home. Desh brings out trays of appetizers that are so professional-looking it's hard to believe he whipped them up in the four-foot-square galley.

"You're an awesome chef," I say, after devouring a crostini. My appetite's back. "That soup you brought me last night was a lifesaver."

"No problem." He slides his sunglasses to rest on top of his head.

"Have you been a chef for a while?"

"I started out studying in New York—"

"Oh, that's where Regan and I go to school!" I say, with the overexcitement of a speed dater. If Regan was listening, she'd roll her eyes. "Where we went. Doesn't matter. Keep going."

"Once I found cooking, it suited me," Desh says. "I've been working my way around the world since I was twenty-two. So, five years. Mostly on bigger dive boats." He bends to pick up the tray, passes me the last crostini. "But tourism's tiring. There are only so many toga parties and conga lines I could take."

"Yeah, that sounds terrible," I mumble, having never participated in either.

"This boat will be way better. And now you're over your sickness, it's going to be lush." He grins at me. "Also, just so you know, I don't make soup from scratch for any old person."

I stare at my knees, my face hot. Why is he being so sweet to me, when surely he'd rather hit on Regan? They were playing cards together for hours. She's fun, and a model. Whenever we meet guys together, it's always the wingman who talks to me, as if it's planned and he's running interference.

—

At dusk, I help Lila set up her lanterns for our dinner outside.

"Mum would like these," she says quietly, threading the

wires around the boom. "She always hangs fairy lights on the patio. Bigger than this, though. Like light bulbs."

The depth of her wistfulness is obvious; even her fingers are shaking. "Maybe you should call your mom tomorrow when we're in town?"

"Dad says I can't. We're giving her space. She's on a yoga retreat right now." She nods, being brave, but even if their family is in transition, it doesn't seem right to put Lila through that. When my parents split up—I was eleven, and my mom had met someone new, moved out, created chaos for a while—the one thing they both really pushed for was open communication. Everyone needed space, but not a limitless amount of it, not without any connection. And what kind of mom wouldn't want to talk to her kid? I say nothing to Lila, but I want to figure out a way I can help.

Once it's dark, we sit under the boom like we did on the first night, Lila right by my side, watching Desh feed morsels of canned tuna to Pearl. The cat sits on a fringed cushion like the Queen Mother, regal and serene, enjoying the gold-star catering.

"Well done, Desh," Regan says, passing him a salad bowl. "Delicious food as usual. And today's been totally great."

"Thanks," Desh replies. "I had to work around Pearl. She's not adhering to industry standards on hairnets."

We all laugh, including Christopher who sits at the outskirts of the circle, pouring himself more wine.

"Today was nice, but tomorrow will be beautiful too," he says. "A calm early morning ride into Bowen. And then up to the shipping channel."

"How come we're motoring and not sailing?" Desh asks.

"Trade winds." Christopher sips.

Desh hesitates. "It's unusual to sail north at this time of year, though, isn't it? Lows in the monsoon trough. I mean, how far are you going? Aren't you heading straight into a tropical cyclone belt?"

"We'll be alright," Christopher says, and Desh shoots me a doubtful look, but I can only raise my eyebrows back at him. I only know a little bit about sailing, and we'll be out of the picture by Darwin. Beyond that, it's not really any of our business.

"When is Helen expecting you home?" Regan asks.

"This month. Or early February. Ivy, do you feel well enough to start boat watch tonight? I'd like to get some kind of patrol going."

"There's not very much to watch," Desh says.

"No, but we need to be comfortable in our roles by the time we reach Carpentaria." Christopher sets his glass down carefully.

"I'm taking first shift?" I ask, part proud, part intimidated. I wasn't even well enough for his prep talk yesterday.

"We'll do two-hour slots," he says. "Starting at ten p.m. It's a beautiful night. Why not go for a swim before boat watch starts?"

"Are you planning on doing that?" Regan asks quickly, sounding like a girl who's embarrassed to hang out with her dad.

"No, I'm off to bed, and so is Lila. But you youngsters should make the most of it. Be wild. Be free." Christopher stands and dusts down his shorts, his face a little sorrowful, as if such notions of freedom are no longer an option for him. *That's parenthood*, I think. And a tangled divorce. And being, like, fifty. I cross my legs, stay seated, and as sorry as I feel for him, I don't try to convince him to come swimming.

———

Once dinner is cleaned up, Christopher and Lila retreat below deck. Regan and I strip down to our bikinis and jump in together from the swim grid, whooping before we splash. The moon is blanketed behind cloud, and something about the darkness has turned the ocean thicker: it's warm and molasses-smooth against my body. I tread water, watching Desh stand above me, his chest and stomach muscle glinting in the shadows.

"Excuse me," he says. "No staring."

I turn away, my lips pressed hard together, but as soon as he's in, he swims over, and there's a moment where our calves entwine underwater that feels loaded, illicit, exciting. I swallow some saltwater, coughing, laughing, liking how he looks with wet hair. Regan grabs him and tries to dunk him, and we're just forming a pedaling, breathy triangle when Desh stops, frowns at the water behind my shoulder. Really frowns, so his whole neck and shoulders change angle.

"What?" I say, wheeling around, but the ocean is tar-black and a big wave bats my face, forcing my eyes closed for a second. At once, my legs feel dangly and vulnerable. What did Desh see? Was the water parting for something? A gray mass, a creature, a *fin*?

Regan grabs at my arm, murmuring, "Who the *fuck*?" while my vision clears, and I notice the back end of another vessel—dark-hulled, modern, and sleek—drifting in right on the other side of ours.

13

I START TO SWIM for the ladder, but Desh is faster, overtaking me as he cuts through the swell. Beside me, Regan splashes against the churn of displaced water.

"Is it Thatcher?" I sputter to her, my stomach spiking with adrenaline. "Is it him?" This cruiser has come in *so close*, and God help me, he could probably have hired a boat in Airlie Beach as easily as a cab. But how would he know which way to go? I reach the bottom rung, see a guy now climbing over our railing, and as weird as that is—as disrespectful—my heart slows down a notch. It isn't Thatcher. This man is rangier, thinner, much scruffier.

Regan grabs my arm again. "Is it—could it be pirates?"

Instantly, my brain flashes back to Milo outside the Airlie Beach hostel. *They'll take you, use you, throw you into the sea.*

"Get out, let's get out, it's just one man," I say, and we scramble our way up the ladder, crouching together on the swim grid. Whoever the guy is, he's not armed. In the lantern light, I notice his scruffy hair and his cheekbones, sharp, like he's chiseled out the flesh around them. Desh is talking to him by our boom, a towel wrapped around his waist, and the two of them laugh before Desh turns, gesturing us in.

"It's okay. This is Blake. Blake Colson, right?"

"Coleman," the man corrects him. "I saw you fellas moored here and thought I'd be neighborly. I didn't know you were goofing about in the water. Thought you'd have seen me coming. Apologies for the fright." He smiles at each one of us in turn.

"You're on vacation?" I ask, stepping forward, my shoulder brushing Desh's. He feels sturdy, like a wall.

"I'm retired," Blake replies, and both Regan and I frown. From what we can see of him, he doesn't seem old. Thirty-five at a push? Maybe he's loaded, but his silhouette is all baggy cargo shorts and bare feet. His cabin cruiser, though. It's not huge, but it's money. Similar height and length to our boat, but brand-new, glossy in the low light. Dad was always nervous about cruisers like this when we were out in the dinghy. *Wide berth, Ivy. That one's too rich to be scraping.*

"Are you traveling on your own?" Regan asks, beating me to it as I cast a look at the boat's name. The *Salty Dog.* Its lower level is dark, only the running lights on. No faces—no Thatcher—pressed to the window.

"All on my lonesome own-some." Blake nods. "How about yous?" He says it just like that: *yous.*

"We're five altogether," Desh says. "Us three are crew."

"Righto." He pauses. "Don't see many boats out here this time of year. Maybe we should team up?"

Regan catches my eye. Blake's clearly looking for company. But he strikes me as one of those guys who might push a little hard. Who'll rush into a crowd, eager for buddies, only to watch it scatter. Also, we've had such a nice time all day—such a *private* time—and the thought of joining up with another boat, with a stranger, feels invasive. Disconcerting. Uncool.

"You'd probably need to speak to our skipper," Desh says. "He's below deck with his—"

But just as he says it, Christopher emerges from the covered cabin, stands tall by the door.

"Gosh, we have a visitor." His smile looks forced. "I see you've met my crew."

"G'day, sorry to intrude." Blake steps toward him, shakes his hand, then wipes his own on the back of his shorts. Below the strap of his G-Shock watch is a tattoo I didn't notice before. Something flagged and feathered. Vaguely military. "Blake Coleman. The *Salty Dog*'s my boat. She's out of Mackay."

"Christopher Edwards." Another gritted smile. "South coast."

"You're a long way from home, Chris."

"Christopher."

"Heading north? I was just saying to these guys that we should go in tandem. Safety in numbers. And it doesn't hurt to share a laugh or two." Blake shrugs, as if he already senses the idea is unpopular.

"Maybe. Although, to be honest, we're kind of a solo operation." All the charm has gone out of Christopher.

"Maybe we could have a beer, though? A sundowner on the *Salty Dog*?" Desh turns to us, somehow not realizing that the sun went down ages ago, or that he's the only keen one in our group. Why is he so open to teaming up? "Sundowners are a boaters' thing. Drinks and appies at around five p.m. We could just be a bit late to the party."

"Yeah, I'm actually going to have to say no to that," Christopher says, and Regan nudges me. *Look at that*, she's saying. *Our skipper's more of a boss than I thought.* "I'm sorry, but I've just got my daughter to sleep. I can't leave her alone on the boat."

"We could do it here," Blake suggests, looking around. "Yous have got more room up on deck anyway."

"Well, no," Christopher says. "Then it's a noise issue. I really don't want to disturb her." There's a long, difficult silence.

"Fair enough," Blake says. "No worries."

"Perhaps we could join up for breakfast tomorrow?" Desh says, blithely oblivious to the fact that Christopher is glaring at him. "When are you off, and how far are you headed?"

"Flint Beach is the end of the line," Blake says, almost as if it's a decision he's making for all of us. "Should be there in three or four days. And breakfast would be great. I'm not an early bird, not in a hurry. No wife to push me around. Are you married, Chris?" He shifts his focus to the sunroom.

"Yes and no."

"How old is your daughter? You didn't say."

"She's young." Christopher walks forward with his right arm outstretched, herding Blake toward the railing. "It was a pleasure to meet you, and we'll see you in the morning. Say around nine?"

"Beautiful. My boat or yours, doesn't matter." Blake straddles the railing, steps across the gap between the two vessels.

"Also, maybe you should anchor further away? I'm not sure how firm the seabed is, and I wouldn't want you to drift and slam into us overnight."

"Ten-four. Roger that." Blake salutes, but there's something else in it, some kind of rejection or sarcasm.

We make a half-hearted show of being sociable as he heads inside his cruiser, but Christopher's knuckles are white as he grips the railing, all the muscles in his neck rigid like rope.

"Bit of a weird dude," I say, and Christopher looks at me, his wolf-gray eyes intense.

"Why? He didn't seem—" Desh begins, but Christopher push-pulls the railing like he's trying to rattle it.

"He could be anyone!" he says, his voice reedy with the need to shout and be quiet at the same time. "A bad guy, a liar, we don't know! At sea, you can't take chances, Desh. You might want to think about that before you sign us all up for drinks and brunch."

"I was just . . . trying to be friendly. Extending a simple hello."

"Well, friendly could get us all in real trouble. So, until you know who you're dealing with, I'd suggest you don't extend anything at all." He turns and walks back below deck, the menace in his warning settling over us all like an icy chill.

CHRISTOPHER EDWARD FARRIS
RECORDED INTERVIEW
Date: January 8, 2020
Location: Cairns, Northern QLD
Conducted by Officers from the Queensland Police,
Far Northern Region

POLICE: Mr. Farris, let's talk a little bit more about your life in Hobart.

CF: I don't see how that's relevant.

POLICE: Well, you're in the unique position of knowing everything that happened before, and everything that happened after.

CF: After what? After Lila fell in the water?

POLICE: Did she fall?

CF: [Silence.]

POLICE: So let's talk more about before. In Hobart, you ran a movie theater. Is that correct? The Rosebud. It closed down in August of last year.

CF: June, July, August. Somewhere around there.

POLICE: Thank you. Why did it close down, sir?

CF: There were some funding issues.

POLICE: In August of last year, your wife, Helen Farris, disclosed to the police that there had been some inaccuracies in the theater's bookkeeping. Were you aware that she filed a report?

CF: She reported some funding issues, yes.

POLICE: She reported embezzlement, Mr. Farris. By
           you. The Rosebud shut down as a result.

CF: That's not how I remember it. Charges
           weren't brought. If there were inaccuracies
           in the bookkeeping, the gaps were tempo-
           rary. It was all figured out.

POLICE: Were you angry with your wife for reporting
           you?

CF: No.

POLICE: You didn't find it disloyal at all?

CF: Yes, I found it disloyal. I felt betrayed.
           That's not the same thing as angry.

POLICE: The two of you separated last September.
           Helen filed for divorce. You moved out of
           the family home.

CF: That's correct.

POLICE: Thank you. Now, jumping forward a few
           months, you've got ahold of a boat, and
           sailed off—unregistered—into the sunset.

CF: We've already addressed the registration
           thing.

POLICE: Does the name Blake Coleman mean any-
           thing to you, Mr. Farris? You're nodding, but
           could you please respond for the recording?

CF: Yes, I've met Blake. He boarded my boat
           without asking.

POLICE: When was that, sir?

CF: I don't know. January 3rd? It's all a bit of a blur.

POLICE: I'm sure. I'm sure it is. Was that the first
           time you'd ever met him?

CF: [Long pause.] I'm not . . . I don't see how any of this is needed for whatever you're doing here. Whatever you're trying to prove.

POLICE: It's just that three days later, on January 6th, a severed arm washes up on Flint Beach, just south of here.

CF: What? That's got nothing to do with me. Or my boat. There are sharks in the water, crocodiles. That arm could be anyone's.

POLICE: It could be. Except that Search and Rescue did a sweep of the area. They found the person the arm belonged to. Dumped on an atoll, dragged there by currents.

CF: Are you saying it's Blake Coleman? That he lost a limb and drowned?

POLICE: [Silence.]

CF: Because if that's the case, if that's what this is all about, I swear to you *on my life* I know nothing about it. I mean, the guy was dodgy as hell, helping himself to whatever he wanted, breaking rules, boarding boats. I don't know. He might have had enemies. I could see that. I could. And he was a drinker, he liked to drink, he kept inviting us over for—

POLICE: The person we found is female. [Long pause.] So, I don't know, Mr. Farris. Who could it be? Would you like to have another guess?

14

CHRISTOPHER HAS GONE to bed, but Regan, Desh, and I are in the cabin, keeping our voices low. It's past ten—so officially I'm on boat watch, even though I can't see much of the horizon. A hundred yards away, the *Salty Dog* glints in the moonlight, every window dark. Regan's lying on the cushioned bench with her head on my thigh, while across from us, Pearl has curled up next to Desh. Her tail twitches against his ribs.

"Christopher didn't have to rip into me like that," Desh says, pincering his thumb and forefinger to pull cat hair from his tongue. "I get that there are rules about boarding another man's boat, but Blake didn't seem like he meant any harm. Or did I miss something? Did you pick up a criminal vibe?"

"No, just a pushy loser one." Regan shifts, leaving a tacky smear of salt and suntan lotion on my skin. "But I didn't want to hang out with him."

"Me neither," I say.

Desh gets up and sticks his head out of the door, a soft breeze moving in around him. "Well, it looks quiet over there. I don't think he's coming back."

"Coming *back*?" I say. "Is that likely?"

"Anything's possible at sea, Ivy." Desh mimics claws, his fingertips coming to a stop on top of my scalp. "Weren't you paying attention?"

I wriggle out of his reach. As much as I don't mind him touching me, there's something off-putting about a joke where I'm the prey. I didn't like Christopher's warning. The whole thing has me on edge, especially since I understand being in real trouble. It's what I'm running from already, after all, and I haven't sent Thatcher word yet to call off the chase.

"You'll be alright." Desh withdraws his hands, puts them in the pockets of his board shorts. "I'm heading to bed, but make sure you shut the stair gate properly whenever you go back through it. That's rule number one on these shifts, according to Captain Uptight. Regan, you want to do the next one?"

She shrugs from my lap. "Why are we even being night watchmen? There's literally no one out here except Blake."

"We have to do *something* work-related," I say, and Regan groans. "We are getting paid. Christopher is our boss."

"I'll do the ugly shift, the two 'til four," Desh offers. "But if you need me at all in the night, just holler."

"Thanks, hero." Regan watches him coolly. "What would we do without you?"

Desh falters. "No, I wasn't being . . . I'm not saying you couldn't—"

"I'm just messing with you. Sleep well. I'll wake you at two a.m."

He throws me a stilted wave, then heads into the galley, Pearl following him. As soon as he's gone, Regan sits up, her hair flattened on one side where it's dried salty with seawater.

"He is so. Totally. In love with you."

I feel an immediate rush of heat when she says it. A good heat. A nice rush. Still, I push her shoulder, shake my head. "What? No, he's not."

"He's all jokey-jokey, touching you as much as he can. Offering to be your personal bodyguard." Her tone is conspiratorial, like we're twelve at a sleepover, but I can't tell if there's a sliver of annoyance in it. Or surprise. Guys fall for her left, right and center, and as far as I know, she's never had one as a buddy. It's date them or dismiss them, never anything in between. "Don't look so worried. Desh is hot. *I would.*"

Hit on him back, she means. Or sleep with him. Is she interested herself?

Once, when we were newly roommates, we'd gone in a group to a club that was so loud and hot, and I didn't feel comfortable. My clothes weren't right, my shoes were clunky, all our friends were doing lines of coke off enamel toilet lids in the washroom. Regan took my hand, pulled me into the corner. *This place is crusty. You want to get out of here?* As we walked home, I asked her if she'd only left the club because of me. *Yup,* she said, and her honesty surprised me. *I'll never lie to you, Ivy, about anything. Just ask me.*

As months went by, it became clear that Regan didn't trust many people. Men, definitely not, but it went deeper than that. Girls hated her, she said, and boys wanted to bang her. Adults—parents, cops, teachers—they all singled her out. As charismatic as she was, she felt judged by her looks, pigeonholed in two easy seconds. *Nobody's straight with me, Ivy. No one except you.* So, it became our rule. *Just ask me.* Between us, direct questions could never get lies in return. So I take a deep breath and ask.

"Are you into Desh?"

"No. *You* are."

"I'm— I really don't think it's me he's after. Or . . . not *only* me."

"Aha." She reaches up and taps my chin. "You think he's a player. Not every guy's a villain or a jerk, you know."

She's referring to Thatcher, of course, but maybe also to Eric, whom she met when he came to visit me freshman year when he was still my boyfriend. He was a tall, fleece-wearing, Nordic-looking boy who aired his opinions willingly, which seemed so dazzling to me in twelfth grade, when most people hid what they felt.

We never slept together. Eric's family was religious, and our dads worked together at the feed mill. Perhaps Eric worried I would tell. Instead, he liked me to undress in front of him while he watched from a chair. He touched me in ways that weren't sex, he said. They didn't count. I was never allowed to touch him. When he showed up to NYU for the weekend, Regan came out for dinner with us at TGI Fridays. He questioned every food and drink choice she and I made, until Regan "accidentally" spilled a full glass of water into his lap. He swore at her, calling her a "dumb whore," and I broke up with him right there in the restaurant. Later, I found out he'd been sleeping with the entire debate team. Anyone without a direct link to his dad.

"Do you know who I think might be a jerk?" I say, keen to shake the memory of Eric. "Blake Coleman. Super keen to hang out, then kind of mad when we wouldn't."

"Totally. Did you see his feet? I met a casting director once who said you can get all the information you need about a person from their toes. I love that guy; his Instagram feed is the best." There's a long pause because I have nothing to add to that. "Wait here. Back in a second."

She slips downstairs into the galley. The wind picks up, rattling the sliding door to the covered cabin, and I glance again at the *Salty Dog*, rubbing my upper arms. All of a sudden, I'm not sure I want to be up here alone. Is there any way Blake could come back without us knowing? Surely he wouldn't swim? I'm just picturing that, his adamant entitlement for company as he slices through the water, when Regan returns, pressing her thumb to the side of my cell phone.

"What are you— No, don't switch it on!" I throw my hand out, as if the cell is a ticking time bomb. Doesn't she get it? Thatcher's on there, and as much as I need to message him, I also need more time to prepare.

She hesitates. "I was going to check Insta. I can't take it—I hate not having a phone, it's driving me nuts." She sits down beside me, tents her sweater over her knees. "And don't you think we should check in anyway? What if our families have contacted us? We've been out of communication for three days."

I bite my lip, think about my dad. Is he missing me? Does he know I've ruined my scholarship, that I'll have to drop out? NYU must have sent a letter home by now. He'd been so proud of me when I'd been awarded a full ride, the first McGill family member ever to make it to college. But maybe it's time to deal with all of that. *Wherever you go, there you are,* Dad used to say to me as a kid, and I always thought it was the most redundant expression. But I'm starting to get it now. I am my own inevitable companion. It's time I made friends with that, learned I'm my own north star. Besides, Thatcher *has* to be told that his precious photos are gone. Otherwise he'll just keep hounding me.

Regan reads my uncertainty. "He'll have gone back to Sydney by now. Or flown home. Whatever. We hate Thatcher Kane. Good riddance, remember? We've moved on." Her thumb hovers over the screen as she waits for the go-ahead, and I nod, tell her my passcode.

"Is there even a signal?" I ask. "We're pretty close to land but I don't know if there's a cell tower."

"Let's see. Hey, we can also google Blake. I bet he's the son of an Australian mining tycoon. Millionaire, hiding it in bad haircuts and no pedicures so he seems more relatable."

"Yes," I say, trying to laugh, although I'm still wary, can't take my eyes off the phone. "That's a good guess. Although I'd put him as ex-milit—" I'm cut off by the sound of a text coming in, that telltale drag of foreboding. The tone coats me like a waft of ammonia. There's another text. And another. Regan and I stare at each other, mouths clamped shut, as the cell dings eighteen times.

"Holy shit," Regan says quietly. "It's him, isn't it?"

15

"READ THEM," I say, the stress going straight to my stomach, just like it always does. My insides feel slippery, as if I've swallowed a liter of grease. "Out loud. Please?"

She braces and sits down next to me, scrolls to the first one. "'I'm here. You're not at the hostel. Where are you?' How the fuck did he know which hostel? Did he visit them all?" She licks her lips. "Are you sure about this, Ives? Maybe we should just delete these and not give him a voice."

"No. Keep going." Because isn't it the key to outwitting our enemy—knowing him as well as you can? I think Sun Tzu said that, although he might have been full of shit, because I feel so sick, I can barely get a clear thought.

Regan takes a deep breath. "Okay, next. 'I've come all this way. I thought we'd spend a nice day together.' Jesus, he's insane." She checks my face. "Are you doing okay?"

"Yup. Go ahead."

"'There's no reason at all to avoid me.' 'I'm not angry

anymore.' 'I simply wanted to talk things over, bunny.' 'What you've done is very unfair.' He calls you 'bunny'? That's disgusting. What does he mean by 'unfair'?"

"It's a long story," I say, my throat dry as she studies me. "Do they get worse from there?"

On she scrolls, her eyes widening. "Wow. Holy shit. Okay, no, I can't do this." She passes me back the phone, her face distressed.

Hands shaking, I read the next texts. They're all variations of 'Where are you?' sent on January 1st—the day we got on the boat—but by the tenth message, he's writing in capitals, jerky half sentences that read as if they're shouted, drunk.

U THINK I WONT FIND YOU?????

I KNOW WHO UR WITH

IVY

IVY

IVY

IVY

GIVE IT BACK

FUCKING BITCH

I WILL DESTROY YOU

I throw down the phone onto the cushion, and Regan puts her arms around me.

"Destroy me?" I say, my sob muffled by her shirt. "What the hell? Hasn't he done that already?"

"Take a breath. He's a monster. But remember he *cannot* find you out here. Three days is a ton of distance. That's why he's so angry." She waits a few seconds. "Ives, what did you take from him?"

"Photos." I'm really crying now, pawing at hot tears as they spill. "He had gross photos in his study, and I stole a whole fat envelope of them. It was porn off the web."

"Oh, I . . ." She doesn't know how to ask the next question. "Like, so . . . what kind of porn? How bad?"

"He gets off on young women pretending to be spiked. Likes to imagine they're passed out, or fucking dead while he . . ." I can't finish the sentence. Beside me, Regan has covered her mouth with her palm. "I just saw two girls: Veronika and Jordan. There were a ton more envelopes in his drawer. I told him I'd found them, and that the dean might be interested in his sexual habits. He threw me out of his loft and made up all this shit about me, so now they're withholding my academic scholarship."

Regan sits up. "*He* did that? No! Can't you get it back?"

"I thought I could. That was my grand plan. I knew if I just took the envelope to the dean, though, she'd never believe it was his. But he'd be way jumpier. So I was going to blackmail him with the photos I stole, the envelope he must know by now is missing."

"Wait, what? The photos are where? Here, in your *bag*?" I hang my head. Poor Regan. All the things I brought on this trip without telling her. "Show them to me. Let me see." She swallows, readying herself, but I shake my head, downcast.

"I can't. They're what I burned last night."

"You— Okay. Right. Okay." She's thinking fast, like me. Thatcher's in a huge country—if he hasn't flown home yet— and were he to guess we are on a boat, he'd figure we're sailing south, not north. Not into the cyclone belt. And he doesn't know who I'm with. He barely knows what Regan looks like. She was never his student; she took media and marketing before she dropped out, and she wasn't home last summer when I sublet her apartment. But the ugliness of this whole situation is horrible. I thought I was climbing out of the muck, yet here I am again, right in the very middle.

"I know I have to reply, have to tell him the truth." I pick at a loose strand of stitching on the bench cushion, my shoulders slumped. "Right? There's no ignoring him, even though he's the fucking worst. But he doesn't realize there's nothing left to reclaim."

She puffs out her cheeks but nods. "I like that he's suffering. But, yeah, plan A is never see him again. That's all you want."

"Exactly." How pleased I'd been when Thatcher first noticed me. Now I can't think of anything I want less.

"I'll go to bed, give you some space. Or do you want me up here while you message him?"

"I got it. Thanks, Regan. I'm sorry it's such a mess."

"It's not *you*," she says, leaning in and giving me a hug.

Once she's gone, I stand, press my forehead to the cool glass of the cabin's sliding door. I hate Thatcher with every fiber of my being. He's broken my heart, ruined my academic credibility, and stolen my scholarship and chances for grad school. My parents will be so ashamed of me. We're blue collar, not thesis folk, and when NYU accepted me, my dad threw a party. *My daughter, the scholarship kid. You're the best one of us all.*

My thumbs quiver over the alphabet on my phone. *Do it, and stay safe*, a voice says in my head. The clear, sensible version of myself, that person I haven't heard from in a while. I take a breath, start to type.

I burned the envelope. Nothing here. Go home, I don't
want a war.

I press send, then screenshot his eighteen texts, just in case.
I'm not an idiot. If it comes down to it, we'll see who destroys
who first. But as I'm shutting off my cell again, there's a piercing scream from below deck. A child's terror, wild and deeply
afraid. I rush down into the galley—which is empty—then
into the corridor. Another scream. It's Lila, it's definitely Lila.

I fumble my way along the dark passageway, Regan joining me from our room.

"What the hell was that?" she asks, flustered, just as a door
slams behind us.

We both whirl, press ourselves into the wall. But it's
Christopher, stepping out from the bathroom, his elbows in
our ribs as he tries to get past. He squeezes by us, opens the
door to his cabin. We crane behind him, seeing Lila in her
bed behind the muslin curtain, her body facing away from
us, curved like a little cashew.

"Pumpkin? You were dreaming, are you awake?"

"Is she okay?" Regan asks.

Christopher turns to face us, light from his bedside lamp
cutting the room behind him into shards. "No real drama.
She's had a bad dream. I told you she's prone to them. Thanks,
though." He shuts the door partway, as if we're bothering
him now, unwanted room service, or the kind of people
who'd jam their foot in the gap. "She's still asleep, girls. It's
late. Shouldn't one of you be on boat watch, and the other
one heading to bed?"

"Yeah, yeah, we're going," I say, my belly tweaking
because something is not right in this room. "Is Lila—?"

"All good. I'm here now. Thanks again for checking in."

The door shuts abruptly, throwing Regan and me into shadow. *That's it? That's all we get?* The slam feels symbolic— the nervous press of a palm onto a lid that's starting to rise— but Christopher wasn't in the room when Lila screamed, and she's gone right back to sleep. It was—it must be—a night terror. Still, we stand silently for a minute before turning and feeling our way back along the dark spine of the corridor, my fingers jittery against the damp of the wood.

16

I SLEEP FITFULLY, wracked by terrible dreams. In all of them, someone's scaling the boat, creeping up over the railing, leaning down through the hatch into our room. Every time it's Christopher's zinc-striped face I see first, but as he smiles, his teeth and bones morph and leak into Thatcher. Thatcher who's smarter than me. Thatcher who found me halfway around the world. Thatcher who's intent on destruction. *See, bunny?* he whispers at three a.m. *Told you I'd find you.*

When I finally properly wake, I'm dry-mouthed and vaguely aware that we've been motoring for a while. Regan's still asleep. We'd sat up together until two, merging our boat watches, both of us wrung out and stressed.

"Did you think— Was there anything going on in there?" I'd whispered in the spectered light of the covered cabin. "Christopher seemed really keen that we leave."

"Hey, I don't like the guy, I find him super annoying, but I don't have him pegged as abusive." She shifted as she lay on the bench. "Mind you, parents mess us up more than anyone."

I nodded. Regan and I had bonded over our parents' divorces. Her dad was to blame for the collapse of her family, but she also had a beef with her mom, who'd talked her into going to NYU in the first place. *It'll be so good for you, honey*, Regan always mimicked. Her heart had been set on staying in San Francisco and being a runner on a low-key film set, before making the jump to LA. It wasn't "an adult plan." NYU was prestigious, and in the end Regan did what her mom had wanted. My mother had done her fair share of steering the ship badly, too, although I've let most of that go. I was eleven when she had an affair, broke Dad's heart, and abandoned everyone she was meant to love and protect. I was so mad at her I wouldn't speak during our weekly ice cream dates. Even now, I can't stomach the stuff.

"I think Christopher feels bad for Lila, and he's being territorial," Regan said. "Guilt parenting. He needs to be the *only* one who can help her."

"That scream, though," I shivered. "What a blood-curdler. Must have been a doozy of a nightmare."

"Yeah, but if you ask me, he and Helen have been at each other's throats, and Lila's seen all of it."

I considered that for a minute. "We should look out for her more. Make sure she's coping okay. We both went through the same kind of stuff at her age."

"Totally. We'll be her big sisters for a while, whether Christopher likes it or not." The way she said it, I knew she was taking him on. She'd be watching him closely now too.

We stayed huddled, getting up every now and again to check the emptiness of the horizon, murmuring reassurance, drifty and slightly dazed. By two a.m., we were both so exhausted that we didn't stop and chat with Desh; we just knocked for him and fell into our beds.

I still feel haggard, but I get up and tiptoe out of the cabin. Desh is already in the galley slicing tomatoes at the table. He must have taken Christopher's time-keeping complaints to heart after all.

"Is Blake here?" I ask, my voice sounding scratchy.

He stops chopping and looks up at me. "Blake's nowhere. Don't worry. Get a coffee."

I must look as haunted as I feel, so I pour myself one, my hands a little shaky. "How was your shift? Was there any more commotion?"

"Commotion?" He goes back to slicing. Measured. Practiced. Precise. "It was fine. I slept all the way 'til two, barely heard you knocking. I put in earplugs. Christopher starts up the engine at whenever-he-wants-o'clock and it's like lying next to a bear that suddenly roars."

"Oh, right," I say, surprised. I'd thought he was vying to be the boat's heroic protector. *If you need anything in the night, just holler.* Apparently we'd have to holler louder than Lila did to get past the earplugs, and her scream was like the world was ending.

"What did I miss?" he asks.

"Night terror. Lila." I sip my coffee. "It sounded like a bad one."

He pauses, the knife limp and wagging. "Is she okay? Are you?"

"Yeah," I say distractedly, "I think so."

I'm not, though, and as I leave my coffee and head up on

deck, I take a huge gulp of fresh air, trying to steady myself. We're a ways out from the coast, chugging through a graying sea, the sky overhead moody and hooded. I take another calming breath, try to rid my head of a horrible night. Maybe Thatcher has calmed down since he sent those ugly messages. Or he might have replied to me overnight, apologized, embarrassed he sent the other ones in the first place. Still, I don't want to check. He'd devolved so fast to ranting, it was as if he was hammered or on something. He liked liquor, for sure, always had a bourbon going. But is he more dependent on it than I thought—more dependent on all kinds of things?

It doesn't matter, I think. I've sent the truce text; I can wash my hands of him. Around me, the sea is wide and empty, a total absence of people and boats. Even the *Salty Dog* is nowhere to be seen. We must have ditched Blake before breakfast and just taken off. Not that I care. If anything, I'm happy about it.

Christopher stands at the bow drinking a cup of coffee. Lila sits at his feet, rolling a pebble for Pearl, who isn't interested.

"Hi, guys." I move across and lean down, put my hand on Lila's shoulder. "How are *you* this morning? Feeling okay?" She looks up, freckles crinkling as if she's confused by the question. *That's good*, I think. She's fine, she's totally fine.

"I'm trying to make Pearl play." She rolls the pebble again, but it bounces past the cat's paw and skips over the edge of the deck into the water. Lila's arms slacken in her lap.

"Put that bloody cat somewhere else," Christopher says. "She's getting fleas all over the cushions."

"Dad, she doesn't have fl—" Lila begins, but Christopher tilts his head. He watches as his daughter gathers up Pearl, her balance off-kilter as she carries her back to the sunroom.

"Bloody pain in my arse, that cat," Christopher says, rolling his shoulders. "Sorry."

I stare at him. He's pretending to relax now, leaning against the railing, but there's fresh tension in him today. Something new. Something jangly.

"I had no idea you didn't like Pearl," I say.

"She's Helen's pet. Clearly one she stood by with more permanence than she did me. Anyway. Doesn't matter." He sips from his mug, the tip of his thumb white where it grips the handle.

"Are you alright, Christopher? I see you managed to escape coffee with Blake Coleman." I hold onto the railing, trying to absorb the pitch and sway of the waves pummeling the boat as we push through them. *Please*, I think, *please don't get sick again.*

"I made an executive decision." Christopher leans forward, looking out over the ocean. "I felt we should get going. I've set a course, and we're on autopilot."

"Fine by me," I say. "How long until Bowen?"

"No, we went by it already. No need to stop."

"What?" The shock is immediate. He just blew by the town, didn't even ask us if that was okay? "But we . . . I thought we were— Didn't we need to refuel?"

"We can make it further, no problem. I checked with Desh. We have plenty of supplies." He moves off the railing, and I follow as he walks inside to the cabin, sets his coffee cup on the table with the nautical chart. "I mean, unless you were planning to get off?"

"No, it's not that," I say, sitting down with a thump. "It's just . . . What about the locks for our door? What about Regan's phone?"

"Next stop's not far. Townsville." Christopher busies himself with a mathematical compass, checking our direction, but the chart is long, and his knee traps a section of it. As he leans, I see the paper tear at a fold.

"You've—" I stand, pointing at the rip by his thigh. "You tore the map."

"Bloody oath! That won't do, will it?" He grabs at the paper, muttering. Looks around manically. I watch him, his energy skittish and strange, and a creeping realization threads up the back of my neck: *This man is in charge of your safety. This tweaky guy, the one ripping Papua New Guinea clean off the map. Look who you're dependent on now.*

"Christopher, how far is it to Townsville?"

"I thought we might head for Magnetic Island instead. It's just off the Townsville coast. Much smaller. Prettier. The whole island is only fifty or so kilometers square." He finds some Scotch tape and tears a huge strip, tries to fit two sections of the chart back together. But his fingers keep catching on the sticky side, and as he flicks them, the tape bunches, frustration starting to cloud around his brow.

"Do you need some help?" It's not comforting in any way to watch him make such a mess of the fundamentals. Our nautical chart is now missing a full inch of reef.

"No, I've got it. I can manage. And to answer your question, it's two days' sail to Magnetic. No time at all."

"Right." I hesitate. It isn't that we wanted to jump ship or stop crewing; it's just that Bowen felt like a stepping stone. A landmark. Some kind of reward. I know we're just employees and our jobs aren't difficult—so far it's been pretty much money for nothing—but even so, I was looking forward to

standing in a store, walking on solid sidewalks, buying a treat
for the next leg. I feel a little robbed, and Regan will too.
She's been counting the minutes until she can replace her cell.

"I apologize." He drops the Scotch tape, and it rolls to the
floor. He doesn't pick it up. "You're right. It should have been
more of a team decision, even if it was at four a.m. You
checked in on Lila like a good team player last night—thank
you so much for that—and now I've rewarded you by blazing
on without so much as a cursory heads-up."

"It's okay," I mutter.

He grabs the mathematical compass again, splits the two
chrome legs, walks it forward across the chart like a child
playing make-believe legs with straws. "You're very caring,
Ivy. You're a beautiful person with a lot to give. I'm sorry if
Lila's nightmares disturbed you."

He bends so low to draw a line from A to B on the map
and presses so hard with his pencil that he literally looks five.
Jesus, I think. *Our leader is losing it*. This isn't a good place to
unravel.

"I would add, though"—he stands straight, forehead
creased with compassion—"that I've done a lot of reading on
children's nightmares. What they mean, how they affect the
child, cognitively, developmentally. Socially. Emotionally."
There's a pause. "All the top psychologists seem to agree that
it's best not to mention the nighttime difficulties during the
day. Better to ignore and press on."

"What? That can't be right."

"Lila doesn't remember her bad dreams, and pointing
them out only makes her upset." His gray eyes pin me, and I
realize why they've always seemed wolfish to me. It's the

wilderness in them. The isolation. "Like I say, I've really read up on it."

"Okay, got it," I say, getting up. "I won't bring them up."

"Attagirl. See? I knew you were my employee of the month." He smiles paternally, then goes back to whatever inaccurate line it is he's drawing for us all to follow.

17

REGAN'S IN THE GALLEY on her own, pouring herself a huge coffee. She always takes it black, no sugar, another way in which she's effortlessly sophisticated. She turns at the sound of my steps on the stairs.

"What's happening? You look like you saw a ghost."

"Just . . ." I glance up toward the cabin, unsure whether I should fill Regan in. After all, she's only on this boat because of me. I can't very well announce that now I have doubts. "Just helping Christopher map-read and set a route." *Basic tasks that we'd all assumed he could handle.*

"Nice." She misses my apprehension and slips onto the wooden bench, moving a mesh bag of apples to a different overhead hook. "Where are we?"

"Beyond Bowen," I say, wincing.

"What? We sailed right by? Are you joking?" She's about to say more, but we notice Lila hovering at the periphery of the galley, still holding Pearl around the middle.

"Sorry," the little girl mumbles. "I'm not eavesdropping. I just don't know where to put my cat. It's too hot in our cabin."

"In our room, if you want," I suggest, waiting until she's headed away down the corridor. Then I lower my voice to a whisper. "Look, Christopher said he made an executive decision. That Bowen was an unnecessary stop. Between you and me, though, he seems a bit . . . frazzled."

"Frazzled?" Regan snaps. "What the hell does that mean?"

"Like, I'm starting to wonder . . ." I pause, struggling to phrase it right. It's so delicate. As much as I want her input, she'll jump all over anything Christopher does that seems even slightly questionable. "I'm starting to wonder if maybe Christopher's decisions might need a second opinion. You know, maybe Desh could weigh in?"

"Christopher's decisions need overruling. He can't do that! Can't just *miss out* towns. Hell, no, that is not okay." She moves to get out from behind the table. "We're . . . we're at the mercy of choices he makes. Like, he has us completely imprisoned as long as he's sailing. We can't ever get off if he doesn't stop."

"He's not . . . I don't think he's trying to imprison us." *Here we are again*, I think. I knew we'd go straight to red alert. "He's not threatening. He's just a bit clumsy and tense. And he will stop. At Magnetic Island, in two days' time. He has to, for fuel and supplies if nothing else."

She blinks rapidly, as if inside her head there's a whole volley of thoughts going on. "I don't like it, Ives. Seriously. I think this is a really big deal."

"Okay, but I'm sure you could broach it with him. He's a guy who likes to communicate." Is that true? I think of him slamming his cabin door last night. It wasn't a great sign of easygoing openness.

"Good. I *will* broach it. I'll tell him we're getting off the boat at the next stop." She watches me, her jaw set. "I'm not doing this anymore if he takes away our options. That's total bullshit."

"Can you calm down for a minute? It's just shopping we've missed out on. Christopher hasn't done anything to us. We don't need an emergency ejector button just yet."

She looks at me sharply, but I stand my ground. I can't get off the boat this soon. Even if Thatcher's planning to fly home now he's read my text, I don't want to be on land in his domain, somewhere he could potentially find me before he leaves. Maybe there's a benefit to blazing past towns. If I stay on the boat, Thatcher's only an issue when I turn on my cell.

"You do know that Christopher's more than frazzled, right?" She leans out, checks the corridor, but Lila must still be settling Pearl in our room. "He's been dumped, Ivy. Helen obviously dumped him. She probably met someone new. There was nothing mutual or amicable about it."

I grimace because what she's saying feels right. He is a man who seems like he's inching toward a breakdown. Desperately trying to hold on to his dignity, or some kind of normalcy for Lila.

"It's why he's in such a rush to keep moving," Regan says, "but he doesn't even know where to, or for how long. He's desperate for motion. Anything to not think and keep traveling. He's on the run from his life."

She's aiming to spark my distrust, but instead I feel a jolt of sad recognition. Because isn't fleeing the wreckage exactly what I'm doing too? And there's *loneliness* in that. Bottom line, I empathize with him. At some point, the handful of people you take with you through a trauma will tire of your melancholy. It's always your mess to untangle.

"I know he's not quite the champion he promoted himself to be in Airlie," I concede softly, even though her lip still curls with contempt. "I can talk to him. And we're locked in now for a couple more days. So there's that."

"Talk to him or don't." She sits back, the apples beside her head swinging crazily. "But in two days' time I'm getting off this boat. You can come with me or not. It's totally up to you."

I turn, take a few steps down the corridor to join Lila and Pearl, stopping when I'm out of Regan's view. What a blunt, cold ultimatum. *Come with me or not.* I can't help thinking, as I steady myself against the curved wall, that if *she* was the one who'd been chased all the way to Australia, there's no way I'd suggest anything that might jeopardize her sense of safety.

—

The wind soon picks up, and we both throw ourselves into crewing. Perhaps if we stay busy, work together like the team I thought we were, we'll find some common ground again, and she'll realize she's overreacting. Together we raise the mainsail, heave ropes, tie them to cleats, shut off the motor. The quietness that comes after is mesmerizing: there's only the push of the waves, the creak of the boom and the snap as the sail tightens above us, smooth like a laundered sheet. It's powerfully calming. By noon, Regan appears way more relaxed, and I dare to hope that she'll just let the whole Bowen thing go.

In the afternoon, she and I lie out on cushions with Lila, reading in the shade of the spinnaker. Every now and again, the little girl reads sentences out loud because she likes how the words in them sound. I used to do that, used to be excited in that way about books. Regan and I manage a smile at each other: regardless of how Christopher feels about it, how jealous it makes him, his daughter wants to spend time with us. And if he can get over the notion that we're somehow his competition, he might see that our company isn't harmful to Lila. It's quite the opposite.

"Did Thatcher text you back?" Regan asks me, in a lull, putting her book down. "Or is it radio silence?"

"I shut off my cell." I don't want to talk about this, especially not in front of Lila. It's too dark a subject, and the kid's too clever for codes.

Regan nods once. "Hey, Lila, we'll be at Magnetic Island soon. Why don't you call your mom when we get there? Surely she's waiting to hear from you?"

Lila bookmarks her page. Sits up, readjusting her ball cap. "I want to. But Dad might be funny about it."

"She's been told to give her mom space," I explain, adding a raised eyebrow that only Regan sees. *Christopher's idea*, I'm saying. *Keyword: territorial.*

"Right." Regan ponders it. "But maybe you get to have a say, too, Lila. How much space do *you* need?"

"Less than this," Lila whispers. But she presses her mouth shut as soon as she's said it.

"Did your mom agree to you and your dad just sailing away indefinitely?" Regan shifts onto her elbow, her body casual but her eyes sharp. Where is she going with this one?

"Your mom's not going to get home from her yoga retreat or whatever and be, like, 'Hey, where *is* everyone?'"

Regan mimes it out and Lila laughs, we all do. But I know Regan isn't only joking, and in my head, I'm noting how deep her distrust of Christopher goes.

"No, they talked all about it," Lila says. "Dad thinks I need a proper break, and that Mum will feel better after a rest." She pauses, and Regan catches my eye. *He wants to get back with his wife. Good luck with that one, buddy.* "I'm homeschooling for this semester. Dad's great, he gets me, he really listens. We're planning this whole big surprise for Mum's birthday. It's at the start of February, so we'll be back in Hobart by then."

"Where's Hobart?" I ask.

"That's where we live. Don't you know that yet? It's the capital city of Tassie. Tasmania."

"Okay. Right on." Regan lies flat again. "That's good you have a plan. Just . . . you know. Make sure you're getting what *you* need in the meantime."

"I . . . I will." Lila stands, takes her book and her cushion, and heads back toward her dad at the helm. *Poor little push-pulled thing,* I think, watching her go. But then I catch Christopher's eye. He's been monitoring us the whole time. He gives me a thumbs-up, then waits to see if I'll return the gesture. I do, but half-heartedly. Quickly, I turn and lie back down on my cushion.

At around four, Desh arrives up on deck holding a bundle of canvas. Regan's taking a shower, so I'm the only one here by the racing sail.

"Look what I found under my bunk," he says, tottering toward me as the boat leans. "Christopher can't have known it was there." He pulls the long roll of fabric from its plastic wrapper and unfolds a hammock—striped, wide, and a little dusty. It's easily big enough to hold two people.

"I bet it came with the boat."

"Well, here, help me set it up." Desh scans the bow for a good spot to tie it up. "Sleeping up on deck would be way better than down below in that noisy sweatbox."

I can feel Christopher watching us from the helm, but he can't leave his post to come see what Desh is doing. Desh loops knots like an expert sailor and pulls on them until they're solid. The hammock fits perfectly between the railing and the spinnaker's pole. He sits down in it sideways so it's more like a porch swing, motioning for me to join him, and once we're in, the curve of the fabric blocks the entire stern from view. We're in our own little crescent moon.

Desh pushes us back and forth with his toes, exhaling peacefully. Our shoulders and hips are thrown together as we sway, and I'm aware that my heartbeat has picked up.

"Ivy, are you happy you got on this boat?"

I turn my head, his face so close I lower my eyes. The neckline of his T-shirt is sun-worn and frayed, and I can see the top curve of his chest muscle.

"I think it was a smart move," I say.

He nods, picks at a fleck of salt on his shorts. "And the people you left on land . . . are they . . . happy about it too?"

I smile. He's asking me if I have a partner. He's fishing. "I didn't leave anyone nice."

"No?" He smiles while his head lolls back, a strand of his hair kicking up and tickling my ear. "That's good. You sailed away from the garbage heap."

"Yeah," I say, smiling back. "I really did." He's all dark hair and cheekbones, a picture of laid-back, outdoorsy health, and it strikes me how comfortable I am in this moment, how long it's been since I truly felt that. "What about you, Desh? Are you glad you got on when you did?"

"As decisions go, it's looking better and better," he says, and I laugh. We rock together in a lazy, contented silence, until a new thought strikes me, spikier as it takes shape. Does Regan still want off this boat in two days' time? Seriously, how can I leave? This mood, this sense of well-being, this peace—none of that exists on land for me right now. I'll be edgy wherever I go from here. I'll have to fly home. To my dad's house in Michigan.

I sneak another peek at Desh beside me, at the way his bicep rounds out when his arm is behind his head. If it was Regan he was smiling at in a hammock, I'm pretty sure she'd be wanting to stay. Will she understand that, though? Will she listen? Something tells me it'll make her angrier, as if it's a contest of some kind. If I'm honest with myself, there are a lot of reasons why I don't want this journey to end. But in a way that I'll need to keep to myself for a while, Desh is becoming one of them.

18

WHEN CHRISTOPHER CALLS DESH away to make dinner, he scuffs his heel on the deck to slow the hammock, then leans forward and clambers out.

"Meet here later?" he says. "When it's starry out?"

I nod, liking how every article of clothing he owns is sun-bleached, how he'd rather sleep outside than in. The way he jogs more than walks and rarely ever wears shoes. Nice toes, and isn't that all I need to know? More than all that, though—more than anything—I like that he's pledging his choice. Picking me over Regan. When does that *ever* happen? I set the hammock swaying again, hug myself around the ribs.

By seven, the sunset is in full force, and everything's lit up in a gilded bronze. The sky sets everyone's skin aglow as we sit around eating the last of Desh's pasta. We're full and lulled and luxurious. Regan's had three glasses of wine and seems mellow. She hasn't mentioned leaving the boat all day. Christopher is back at the helm, steering with small corrections that take thirty seconds to be felt, like a secret whispered down a line through a tin can. *Does he know what he's doing?* I wonder, my mind casting back to that torn nautical chart. But so far, nothing's gone wrong, and maybe I need to trust that more. I probably shouldn't even have said anything to Regan. Lila lies with her head on my thigh, and I let her, even though I know Christopher's probably envious. He needs to relax too. We all have our work to do.

Above us, the mainsail creaks. Regan watches it.

"Are we sailing all night, Christopher? Round the clock?" she asks, the tiniest hint of confrontation in her tone, although it's unlikely anyone hears it but me.

"Just 'til ten. 'Til boat watch."

She nods once, gives him a wink. *I see you,* she's saying. *I know what you're all about.* And even though he's oblivious to the fact that they're not getting on, it worries me. I feel prickles of tension rising after the calm of the day.

"I'll get the speargun going when we next stop," Desh says, gazing down along the hull as we cut through the water. In this light, he's beautiful. I swear he could get a contract at Regan's agency. "That food was tasty, but we need some fresh fish."

"Sounds good, but watch out for crocs in these waters," Christopher says. "Don't go at dawn or dusk."

Lila shifts, turns her head on my knee. "Saltwater crocs can grow to seven meters, and weigh around a thousand kilos. That's massive."

"It is," I say, as in my mind I see a dark scaly *S* shape slither along the surface of an after-dinner swim. A beady dinosaur eye, a devastating thump. "God, I wouldn't want to meet one on a dark night."

"Dad, are we in danger? Could they smash the boat?" Lila sits up, picking at the hem of her shorts.

"No, sweetie. They're not big enough to hurt the boat, although I don't want you swimming anymore. We're in their territory now, and in three days or so we'll be at Flint Beach where there are estuaries and river inlets. They'll be marked on the charts. You should be careful, Desh—of sharks, too—especially if you catch any fish."

"What kind of sharks will there be?" Lila asks, her fingers fidgety as she ties a thread around the tip of one finger, watches the flesh turn purple.

"Bull sharks are the deadliest. They like to swim up the rivers," Christopher begins, while I shake my head at him. Why terrify the poor kid? He gave me a whole speech on not mentioning her nightmares, then fills her head with images like this?

"But we're safe on the boat," I cut in, noting the irony of how many times I've told myself the exact same thing in the past couple of days. Sharks or Thatcher. What little difference there is.

"Totally safe," Desh agrees, likely picking up on Lila's nervousness, although it's me he's looking at. "Hey, you know what, guys? Why don't we play a game? It's nice out here. Let's throw in some post-food entertainment."

"What kind of game?" Lila brightens, while Desh stands and jogs to fetch something from inside the cabin. He returns, steps over my legs, catches my eye for a second.

"How about *Who Am I*? We'll write names of famous people on the backs of these playing cards." He opens the pack, hands one out to each of us. "Then you hold the card on your forehead where you can't see it, and have to guess who you are within twenty questions. Only yes or no answers. You've played this before, surely?"

"No, but I can learn fast. Can they be cartoon characters?" Lila sticks out her tongue, no doubt running through options in her head, and it's good to see her so quickly diverted.

"Sure, if you want." Desh hands me the Sharpie he's brought, holding on to it for longer than he needs to so that I'll look at him. I tug it away, smiling, feeling the chemistry crackle. "Christopher, are you in?"

"Of course," he says, one eye on the horizon. "I'm always doing two things at once."

"Okay, pass your card to the person on your left once you've written on it," Desh says. We all do as we're told. "Nobody look. Everyone lift them at once. Ready?" In unison, we raise a playing card to our foreheads, press it there with a forefinger. Regan is SpongeBob SquarePants, Desh is Kylie Minogue. Lila is mine: Maya Angelou, and I'm just realizing she's too young to have read any of her work when I notice Christopher, standing proud at the helm, holding Richard Nixon flat against his brow. Regan gave him that one, but from the look on her face, there's a hidden meaning in it.

"I'll go first," he says, "then I can steer two-handed again. Okay, am I a man?"

"Yes!" we all shout, even though I feel uneasy. Nixon wasn't *only* a controversial politician, and yet something tells me that's the only reason Regan has picked him. She's using the game as a message board, something specifically for Christopher.

"Am I famous?" He adjusts the steering wheel slightly, smiling.

"Yes," Regan says quickly. "Very. You were President of the United States in the seventies. A very memorable one."

"Huh," Christopher says, his eyes twinkling. "When was handsome old Ronnie Reagan in office?"

"After," Regan watches him. She's the only one answering now. Desh and I exchange nervous looks because her tone is off. "You were doing okay until you started this giant cover up. Everyone busted you, and you had to resign."

Immediately, I get what she's doing. *You're a liar, a man on the run*, she's telling him. *I know what life you've left in the dust.*

"The nineteen seventies?" Lila pipes up. "That's ages ago. It's not fair if I haven't heard of him."

Regan sweeps on, raising both of her arms above her head, her fingers in peace signs. "*I am not a crook!* But you were, you totally were. You were selling your people one thing and doing another."

There's a difficult pause while Christopher looks at me— at *me*, as if I'm any part of this—then lowers his playing card. Turns it around, smile tightening. "Nixon. I see. Righto."

"Was he the Waterga—" Desh begins, but Christopher cuts him off, his voice quieter than I've ever heard it.

"You gave me this one, Regan? You're on my left. Are you a politics expert?"

"Not especially." Her shoulders are square, and I turn to her, frowning. There's no need to pick a fight like this.

"Isn't that man good?" Lila asks, looking from face to face. "Why is everyone so upset?"

"Let's ask Regan. She's full of political opinion." Christopher lets go of the wheel. It jolts and spins freely, carving a fresh pathway to who knows where.

"It's just a broad comparison. Nixon had everyone hood-winked while he made choices to suit himself." She looks around. "What? I'm not even allowed to say that Christopher's got us all where he wants us, trapped out here—"

"Regan!" I shout. "What are you doing?"

"*Trapped?*" Lila repeats, and Christopher's head jerks in her direction. I can feel the anxiety coming off him: he's terrified that Lila will get the wrong idea, change her view of him, think less. He's so gripped by the need to be her guiding light. To remain the favorite. It's heartbreaking to watch.

"Richard Nixon ended US involvement in the Vietnam War. He was a good leader. Nobody seems to remember that." He puts both hands back on the wheel, grips tight. "So thank you, Regan, for choosing him. He was a man under pressure, doing his best. What a fun game, everyone."

He's part furious, part willfully missing the point, and nobody says anything. After a few seconds, Regan stands, tosses her card to the deck, and grabs dishes to take back to the galley.

"I'm done playing," she says.

19

"I'M SORRY," Regan says, turning as I follow her down into the galley. "And also I'm not."

We stare at each other, likely thinking the same thing. *Are we really about to part ways?*

"Reags, why would you do that? You blew up the whole night."

"Because he's out of line!" She crashes plates into soapy water. "And we need to call him out on it. People like him probably get away with shit like this all the time, gaslighting everyone into accepting it. But I don't buy him, or his whole sob story. I don't care."

"He's not dangerous, though! And he's not like Thatcher." My voice is hard. "He's shook up and lost, but he's not trying to hurt us."

She stops, hangs her head for a second. "Okay, he's not Thatcher. That's true. But it doesn't mean we should stay on the boat. He's a liar; this whole trip he's on isn't admirable.

It's desperate! His world's gone to shit, he's not getting any of it back, and he's gone into control freak mode. Including controlling our access to land! Why don't you care? It's like he's holding our heads underwater, deciding whether or not we can breathe."

I say nothing, unsure why it's still so life-and-death in her mind, when Christopher comes down the steps into the galley, holding the pasta bowl and an empty wine bottle.

"I should have informed you that I was skipping Bowen, Regan. It was a real-time decision at four a.m. I felt you wouldn't want to be woken." He waits, but so does Regan, leaning there against the sink.

"The decisions are all on you," I say, because somebody has to try to make things better, release a little tension from this space. It feels like any minute now the whole boat will blow sky-high. "You're dealing with a lot."

"I am. Thank you for saying that, Ivy. I really am." He sets the bowl gently onto the counter. "But you make a good point. I am in charge here. I'm the skipper, and I'm your boss. Navigational choices are mine to make. I thought I'd been clear about that from the get-go."

Regan's arms cross. The two of them lock eyes. *Oh, no,* I think, standing to the side of the conflict, remembering what she was like in college. If she feels there's an injustice, she'll cut to the chase, go right to the middle of the conflict. One time in freshman year, she found out that our senior res adviser had sent dick pics to a girl in our building. The girl hadn't reported him, she'd been too scared, but Regan went straight to the NYU head of admissions and scrolled through each pic right there at the front desk. The adviser was kicked out the same day. Regan doesn't care about process or hierarchy. Christopher telling her who's boss is like throwing down a gauntlet in her world.

"I don't trust your leadership," she says. "I think you're unraveling."

I take a breath to defend him, then stop. Because there's some truth to what she says—even though she's driving too hard at it. But Christopher gulps as if her statements are viscous, like sludge thrown into his mouth and face. He takes a breath so deep that his ribs press against his T-shirt. "You chose to get on my boat."

"That's true." *And I'm choosing to get off it*, she means.

"So while you're here and being paid, I expect a certain level of respect. And compliance." He pauses, no doubt wondering if he'll get either. "I'm lowering the sails now and dropping anchor for the night. All. Hands. On. Deck."

"No. Problem." Regan still stands with her arms crossed. She'll help, but only for me, Desh, and Lila. She won't do another thing for Christopher now.

He hesitates, then heads back up the stairs. Regan raises her eyebrows at me, but I can't return the solidarity. I don't align. It's not helpful to tell a drowning man that he's drowning. I turn and leave her in the galley alone.

—

Outside, the sunset has long faded, replaced by a musky indigo dark. Lila is playing Solitaire near the swim grid, squealing with frustration, having to flatten cards before they fly off in the breeze. Desh is steering, his hair mussed and curly, but Christopher takes over and heads us into the wind. I go to the bow, where Desh's hammock lies in a crumpled heap on the deck. Christopher must have made him take it down when they lowered the racing sail, and I feel a beat of sadness. I was looking forward to meeting him there.

Regan comes outside and joins me. She yanks on the anchor line, her hands definite. "I know you're not coming with me tomorrow. You're too into Desh."

Shit, I think, *busted*. But I'm not going to spill everything like a lovesick kid. "Desh? I am not." I watch him douse the mainsail, heave on ropes, the muscles in his shoulders straining. Christ, he's literally like something out of a romance movie.

"Yeah, right. It's funny, though. I thought you were off guys."

I feel a plunge of disloyalty. She's right. She invited me to Australia to get over what she thought was a fling, not start another one while I'm here. The deal at the start was clear: *forget all the weak-ass guys*. But Desh isn't either of those things. He's different. "Reags, listen—"

But she's busy releasing the chain, while Christopher starts up the engine, backing us away so the anchor will set. For all the discord between the two of them, they work together like well-rehearsed dance partners.

"Nice," I say, impressed. "You're like a pro out here."

"I'm like a pro everywhere." She picks at a blister on the pad of her hand. Keeps her eyes down.

Christopher cuts the engine and the quiet is almost shocking. He hurries up to watch the anchor line. "I think that's got her. Are we dragging? It's hard to tell."

"I don't know," I mumble, still wanting him to feel certain of these things on his own, rather than having to ask. He's oblivious to the fact he just lost a crew member. And backed me into a corner with his I'm in Charge speech. Now I have to choose either land, where Thatcher is, or sea, where Regan won't be much longer. Both feel wrong.

Christopher stares at the offing, almost catatonic, and Regan and I wait for direction. Her body language is wary, like she's anticipating a sudden move from him, doesn't know which way it'll go.

"All good?" I ask him. "Job done?"

"Job done," he replies softly. "Thanks for your help."

Desh arrives behind us, picks up the mound of his hammock from where it's been dumped next to Christopher's hatch. "Hey, skip, can I hang this again now we're stopped?"

"No, I don't think so," Christopher says.

Desh's shoulders drop. "I . . . How come? Is it in the way?"

"It is, yes. Just in case we need to access this part of the boat in a hurry. I can't have that giant thing swinging around. And also you might rock over the railing and fall in."

"Fall in? But I'd tie it here, to the—"

"I said no." Christopher smiles. "Thank you."

Desh drops the hammock again, stamps it flat listlessly with his feet. Definitely no late-night porch swing for us, then. Nobody says anything for a minute.

"I'm also switching up the night watch schedule," Christopher adds. "Seems unfair to make Desh take the two a.m. shift every time."

"What did you have in mind?" I ask, already knowing. It's a duel. They're locked in. This is all part of it.

"Desh, then Ivy, then Regan," he says, and Regan laughs drily.

"It'll rotate?" Desh asks, hands on his hips.

"Yes, and in fact I'd like the early shift—yours—to start now, Desh, if that's okay."

"Wow," Regan snorts, staring up into the blurry sky. Beside her, I get a pang of anxiety in my stomach. I hate this. I hate that they're so at odds.

"All good?" Christopher smiles grimly and puts his hands in his pockets. "That's settled then. Regan, I'll relieve you at four. And now I'm going to put my daughter to bed." He strides away and gathers up Lila from the stern, glancing back darkly every few seconds.

"Jeez, I thought you were meant to be chilling him out," Desh says once he's gone, poking me in the ribs. "You promised you would at the start."

"I think that was a 'we' thing." I bend sideways, his fingers tickling. "You and me."

"Well, you're fired. You had one job to do, and I'm afraid I'm going to have to let you go."

I bat his arm away, part amused, part stressed out, and while we wriggle and banter, Regan turns.

"Guys?" she says. "I'm heading in. Have a good night."

"Wait," I say, following her to the cabin. "You're going straight to bed?"

"I was just going to read for a while up here. Grab a little alone time." She won't look at me, as if I'm the one who's ruined everything, and I feel a sudden surge of anger.

"Fine. You do that." I call back toward Desh on deck. "Night. Sorry about the hammock. See you at midnight."

Regan sits down and opens a James Patterson book I know she has no intention of reading. She's hates crime fiction; she's just trying to make me feel bad. I roll my eyes and head to our room, where I lie down fully clothed on my bed.

Where does Regan get off? It reminds me of January in our first year, when we were just back from Christmas vacation. I'd worked the whole break and had four hundred dollars in my pocket, which she told me we should spend on clothes. I should have spent it on groceries and books, but we went shopping all the same. Regan styled me, helped me, told me what would look good. We walked arm in arm down the sidewalk, our cold breath mingling behind us like a shared scarf. It was so freeing, the kind of fun outing I never got to have with my mom. But the next day, when I saw her in the cafeteria after class, Regan was wearing my brand-new sweater.

"What?" she'd said when she caught my look, as if I was being weirdly possessive. "You wear my stuff."

And I'd let it go, because it was true—she had tons of clothes she lent me, even though none of them were unworn, with the tags still on, fresh from the store. I toss and turn on my bed, too upset to sleep. She's manipulative. She just expects me to fall in line with whatever she thinks, as if I can't have an opinion (or a nice sweater) of my own. Sure, she bought my ticket to Australia but I'm paying her back, so this is my adventure, too, and she doesn't get to dictate when it's over, at least not for me. And as for Desh, he's calming in a really soulful way, not just some random guy, a backpacker whose name I don't know, who I'll hook up with and bone in the top bunk of a busy hostel dorm. Also, didn't she just spend the evening mad at Christopher for being domineering? It's one rule for her and another for everyone else, and

I'm not playing along this time. That's not real friendship. She doesn't always get to be leader. I lie on my back, my hands in fists. Finally, at around eleven, I give up on sleep and decide to go hang out with Desh until his shift ends.

I expect Regan to be snoring on the daisy-print bench seat in the cabin, but she's nowhere to be seen. The Patterson novel is on the floor, tossed aside like the stage prop I always knew it was. But as I move to the doorway, I see her sitting next to Desh at the railing, laughing at something he's saying, pushing him on the knee like she just can't handle any more of his fun.

I swallow, my mouth acrid with bile. There's my friend, the one who's so against liars and frauds. Regan didn't want alone time at all: she wanted two hours on her own with Desh. She's taking what she wants. Just like she always has.

20

I TAKE A STEP BACK, withdraw to the darkest part of the cabin. Anger scribbles under my skin like fire ants skittering. I feel hot. It's not even Desh I'm maddest at. He's a player! I should have known he was too good-looking to trust. But Regan. Her sneakiness is so unexpected. I know she's smart and tough—she outmaneuvered every professor with a deadline she ever met— and that on rare occasions when the universe didn't drop gifts in her lap, she'd adapt and go after them. But I'm talking drinks, food, clothes, names on the list for a club. Never anything big. And we're meant to always tell each other the truth! *Just ask me.* She's never snaked me on a guy, never, but maybe her loyalty's only good if the guy's unattractive.

The galley is quiet as I creep back downstairs, tiptoe back to our room. With the hatch open, I can hear the two of them up on deck: Desh's low voice, rising as he gets to the punch line of a story; Regan's easy laughter in return. I imagine her sighing, so laid-back, so platonic, but she's not sitting up there to be friends with him. She doesn't know how to do that with men. She knows how to wield power, how to out-dazzle, how to win. And I realize that her inevitable, natural supremacy has always underscored every part of our friend-ship. She *is* like a pro everywhere.

Has there ever been a room I've stepped into with Regan where I haven't been acutely aware that everyone is looking at her and not me? I lie back on my pillow, staring up at the blank white curve of the ceiling. Being best friends with someone stunning brings with it the unavoidable role as sidekick. Freshman year, I was an also-ran, forever secondary to the main attraction. Guys would approach me to ask about her, and at the start, I didn't mind—I was shy and still dating Eric anyway, didn't want the focus on me—and I liked being linked to Regan. My social standing went up by association. But after I met Thatcher, everything changed. My confidence grew in my second year, and I could feel myself unfurling like one of those tropical flowers in the night. I spoke up more in class, took time over how I looked before I left the house, bought myself sexy lacy underwear that hugged against my skin like a secret. In the rare times after Regan dropped out that she and I met up—where our versions of New York City intersected—I had more to bring. A glimmer of a power that was separate from hers. A status that now needed defending.

In May of my junior year, more than a year after Thatcher and I had started seeing each other secretly, I'd arranged to grab dinner with Regan after a university fair at a convention center downtown. Thatcher had asked me and a couple other juniors—his *brightest and best*—to run the NYU stand, promot-ing the English faculty to possible applicants. It was a day-long event—same spiel over and over, with Thatcher doing most of the speaking and charming—and by five, I was excited to see Regan and catch up, hear her headlines, get a change of scene.

She'd come straight from a casting call, walking into the stale air of the foyer in a tight T-shirt dress that stopped mid-thigh and a pair of Doc Martens. Long beautiful limbs, wild hair, perfect sunglasses. *Look at her, look at my friend*, I thought, smiling around, until I caught sight of Thatcher's face. He was transfixed by her, as if she was lit on stage, and everyone else had been thrown into shadow.

"Professor Kane," I said, hurrying to break his trance. "Is it okay if I head out now? Regan's come to get me."

He put his hands in his pockets, tilted his head, watched her. Whatever tractor-beam power she had, she'd even gotten *him*. And I was thankful, so thankful that she stopped at the doorway, waved at me, and never made it across to our table. What would have happened if she had?

Pearl slips into the room, jumping up onto my bed with a trill. She paws at my sheet repeatedly, as if dragging something upward from a drain, making the fabric pock. *Hi, old lady*, I say to her, stroking the broad bone at the top of her skull. *We're staying here, you and me, where it's comfy.* On this boat, I mean. All the way to Darwin. Without Regan. Because, seriously, why keep being undermined and overshadowed, especially by someone who doesn't even consider my feelings? She can press on; I'll be fine on the boat. I'll be fucking *fine*. The cat concurs by lying down, her back so close to my face that I have to shift to accommodate her. But we hang out like that for a while, unlikely bedfellows, until it's midnight and time for me to take over Desh's shift.

Regan has stayed on deck for the duration of it. Of course she has. I run into her as I round the corner into the galley. "Hey," she says, stopping at the bottom of the stairs. "I was just coming to wake you."

"Nope. Got it." I start to move beyond her, reaching for the handrail.

"Are you okay? Can you wake me up at two?"

"Sure," I say. "Or Desh will. Whatever's easiest."

I keep my tone steady, but all the same, her mouth opens and shuts like a fish's. I say nothing more, climbing up into the sunroom, relocking the gate.

Outside, Desh turns as he stands beside the boom, brushing something off the hem of his T-shirt. "Nice, you're up. Did you want me to hang out with you for a bit? I don't mind staying—"

"I'm good," I say. "Thanks."

He stretches and the fabric of his shirt catches against the line of his chest muscle. *No*, I think. *Don't look.* In fact, when he steps toward me in the jaundiced light, I find myself backing up. Doubt crosses his face, the tiniest frown of it, and he wraps his hands under his armpits.

"Okay, well, night then. See you in the morning," he says.

"Yup. See you then."

I walk to the bow, climbing onto the fiberglass roof of the covered cabin, laying back against the hard white shell. Above me, the sky is blank, not even a single star twinkling. It's silent out here, big, and empty. *This is where you're at*, I think. *You're on your own. No friend on the boat, no love interest, no reliable ally. Wherever you go, there you are.*

21

CHRISTOPHER STARTS THE ENGINE at four a.m. again, so by the time I wake up, we're almost at Magnetic Island. From my bed, I look across at Regan, still sleeping. I woke her after my shift last night with a cursory prod, got into my sheets with a sigh that denoted exhaustion, so mad at her that I didn't want to speak at all. But this morning, right now, as I look at her, I feel differently. It's as if I've somehow slept some of that heat away, like a muscle that was cramping and now feels rested. She needs to explain herself, acknowledge that she was being a bad friend. But as I sit up, place my bare feet onto the cool of the cabin floor, and stand, it's very clear to me that the residue of last night isn't really annoyance. It's worry.

Up on deck, Desh is helping Christopher fix a bolt on the steering wheel, Lila with Pearl by the front sail. The sky is dark, brooding.

"Morning!" Lila waves at me, adjusts her ball cap. "We're nearly at land."

I head toward her, clocking the fact that she needs a break from the boat too. Perhaps we all do. But the thought of doing that *without* Regan, or having it be the destination where we separate feels fluttery in my belly. As pissed off as I've been, I don't want her to leave the boat. I don't want to face the coming weeks alone. I need to talk to her.

"It'll be good to be on land again, right?" I say, wobbling a smile. "We can go shopping. Buy a stash of chocolate for the next leg."

She nods, pleased. "Will Regan come too?"

I falter. "I'm not sure. I think it's possible Regan's about to do her own thing. But maybe I can talk her out of it."

Lila's mouth makes a perfectly round O, like she's reading between the lines. She struggles for a second with something, and when she speaks again, her voice sounds raspy, like the very first time we met. "I know what it's like when your best friend lets you down. When they turn shady."

"Shady?" I shake my head at her. "What does that mean?"

"At school, I told my best mate, Vicky Danvers, that my mum and dad were fighting a lot and my mum threw things, and I thought she'd keep it a secret because—"

"Wait, your mom *threw things*?" That's new information, a new part of their puzzle. So, Regan was right: that breakup wasn't amicable in the least.

"She threw a wineglass that smashed. And sometimes a cup. Always at Dad, because he kept saying she was seeing someone else. And I told Vicky, thinking she wouldn't, like, blab it to everyone. Turns out I was wrong." She fiddles with the cushion fabric.

"She told everyone?"

"Yeah, put it all over her socials. Even after she pinky swore. She was a shithouse friend."

"I hate that," I say, noting that it's the first time I've heard Lila swear. "That's the worst. Vicky Danvers sounds like she double-crossed you."

She pauses. "But Regan's doing that too. I'm sorry, but she is. She flirts with Desh all the time, and she knows you like him."

I feel my face redden, in spite of myself. Lila's eleven: it's unlikely she's fluent in flirting, and yet her intel is spot-on. I think back to Regan's prop of a novel last night, the fake solitude, the scampering the minute I left. My skin starts to feel hot again.

"I just think best friends should have your back," Lila adds quietly.

"They should. It's a basic fact." Is Lila right? That the bottom line is Regan's untrustworthy and overly competitive, and I shouldn't be feeling so distressed about her leaving? I close my eyes for a second. Whether Lila's preteen perspective holds weight or not, maybe it's better if Regan goes and I stay, just brave it out. We'll get a break from each other, space we need to recalibrate.

"I'm not friends with Vicky Danvers anymore," Lila says, as if offering me a template.

"No? Well, friendships can be complicated. Sometimes it's hard to know whether to work at them or cut them loose."

"Dad says it's about toxicity. Nobody should hand a loved one poison and expect them to drink."

I stare at her in shock—how is she so adept at understanding metaphors, especially dark ones like that?—but it strikes me she's not that different from me at eleven. Watchful. Thoughtful. A little too introspective. She's probably grasping more about the world than anyone realizes.

"Girls!" Christopher shouts from the stern, and we both stand. "Look!"

The coastline of Magnetic Island is in sight. For the next twenty minutes, Christopher steers while Desh yells directions and I run around the deck, tying off ropes and lowering bumpers. The closer we get, the more lovely the island looks, its tiny coastline dotted with a hub of homes in the hills.

Regan emerges just as we sail into a little harbor, leaning her backpack against the starboard rail and jumping off the boat with the stern line, tying it expertly to a metal cleat on the edge of the dock. I follow her, liking the solidity of the wooden boards underfoot, their silky wetness. It feels so strange to be standing on something that isn't in motion, and I laugh as I realize my body now feels off-balance when things are still. Regan doesn't smile.

"Are you staying, then?" she asks, so brusque. There's so much we have to talk through that the whole thing feels pointless already. Besides, it's obvious I'm not leaving the boat: my bag isn't packed. I nod stiffly. "Right. Fine. See you up in Darwin, I guess."

Another robotic nod. The tension between us is turning my muscles to lead. I don't want to leave it like this, but feel stuck. Why should it be me who apologizes? While I'm grappling with the sense that I'm being handed poison and expected to drink it, Desh passes up Regan's bag, his face flat with disappointment. He raises his hand in a limp wave that clearly doesn't match how much he wants her to stay.

"I owe you wages before you go." Christopher steps forward and hands her a fan of bills, almost dropping them into the gap between the rail and the dock's edge. So he knew she was leaving—she must have told him below deck. His tone is curt and professional, while behind him Lila kicks one sneaker against the side of the boom.

"Good luck, guys. Look after each other." Regan stares pointedly at Desh as she stuffs the bills into her pocket, and he nods as if a secret message has been received. I don't know what that was, but they're making me feel like some kind of project being transferred. When Regan turns to me, I jam my hands into the pouch of my hoody. She reads the body language, turns, and walks away along the wooden platform, pride in her shoulders. I stare after her, but she doesn't look back once.

BLAKE COLEMAN
RECORDED INTERVIEW
Date: January 9, 2020
Location: Cairns, Northern QLD
Conducted by Officers from the Queensland Police,
Far Northern Region

POLICE: Please state your full name for the record.
BC: Blake Coleman.
POLICE: No middle name, Mr. Coleman?
BC: No.
POLICE: Date of birth?
BC: September 9, 1986.
POLICE: Thank you. Okay, first off, could you tell us what happened to your forehead, just there? You have a sizable bruise.
BC: This? Just a whiskey incident. Night got away from me. I took a spill in the dunny.
POLICE: When was that, sir?
BC: Couldn't say. Bumped my head. Minor.
POLICE: Right. Moving on, then, how many times had you met the crew of the *Alone at Last* prior to the events that took place on the night of January 6th?
BC: Met them? Once or twice.
POLICE: Which is it?
BC: Twice.
POLICE: Thank you. And where were you on the night in question, sir? That of January 6th?
BC: Don't call me "sir," please.

POLICE: January 6th, Blake.
BC: You've checked the *Salty Dog*'s GPS system.
           You know exactly where I was.
POLICE: On the night in question, your boat was
           moored outside of Flint Beach harbor.
BC: There you go.
POLICE: Were you on board the vessel?
BC: Yes. All night. Next question.
POLICE: Did you know about the party happening on
           the *Alone at Last* between the hours of six
           and midnight?
BC: How could I? I wasn't on their boat.
POLICE: Don't you own a paddle board, Blake? We
           have an inflatable one in evidence that we
           believe is yours.
BC: [Audible sigh.]
POLICE: So you could have attended the party with-
           out GPS logging it.
BC: Look, I wouldn't call whatever they were
           doing a "party." You might want to check
           your facts.
POLICE: What would you call it?
BC: Heavy drinking. For reasons you clearly
           don't know.
POLICE: Isn't that why we're here, though? So you
           can tell us things?
BC: [Silence.]
POLICE: At what point did you realize there'd been a
           serious accident on board the *Alone at
           Last*?

BC: When you told me there'd been one.
POLICE: But you'd met everyone on the boat in person?
BC: Some of them. I don't know their names.
POLICE: And none of them ever boarded *your* boat?
BC: Nope.
POLICE: Are you aware of an arm being recovered
           from the waters around Flint Beach? A sev-
           ered female arm?
BC: The girls I met had arms. Two each.
POLICE: [Long pause.] What do you do for a living,
           Blake?
BC: Nothing. I'm retired.
POLICE: You were a member of the Royal Australian
           Navy from 2005 to 2015.
BC: I know.
POLICE: Thank you for your service. Why did you
           leave?
BC: I developed an attitude problem.
POLICE: It's hard to imagine that you'd have
           emerged from ten years in the Navy with-
           out the requisite skills to observe a boat in
           distress, or identify key people aboard it.
BC: Is that a question? [Long pause.] Look, alls
           I'm saying is you're barking up the wrong
           tree. It's the same thing every time. All you
           fellas in uniform running around like head-
           less chooks. Slow it down. Look properly.
POLICE: I don't think I follow.
BC: You haven't got the first clue what you're
           dealing with here. For starters, you

shouldn't be calling what happened on board the *Alone at Last* an "accident."

POLICE: So, tell us. Tell us what we're missing.

BC: Well, how hard are you trying? How far have you dug? Do you know about the detention center records? You've found those, I assume.

POLICE: Detention center records?

BC: Yes, the juvenile crime. What he did to that poor girl before. Back when he was a youngster, a teen. [Pause.] How can you not know about this? You're going in circles.

POLICE: [Long silence.] We weren't aware that the subject of our enquiry had ever been detained as a youth.

BC: Christopher Farris? No, he wasn't. I'm not talking about him.

22

FIVE MINUTES AFTER Regan has gone, Christopher finds me sitting quietly in the sunroom.

"Shall we crack on?" he says, rocking from heel to toe in his boat sneakers. "If it's okay, I'd like you and Desh to do a quick stock take of supplies and come up with a grocery list. Let's get going."

He doesn't seem remotely upset by Regan's departure; if anything, he seems reenergized. Perhaps that's to be expected.

"How long are we staying? Can we explore the island for a while?" Maybe a walk around the town will make me feel better, get me ready mentally for how different this next leg of the trip will be. Lila and I can hang out. It might be fun, like having a kid sister. Even without Regan, I can be there for Lila.

He zips up his fleece to the throat. "We'll take the day. Lila and I are going to the Forts Walk for a picnic." He pauses, noticeably not inviting me. "You and Desh need to be back on the boat by five p.m. They're calling for squalls later tonight, and I'd like to outrun them."

"Outrun them?" Desh walks into the sunroom, squeezing behind Christopher. "Good luck with that." He carries on down to the galley.

I grab paper and a pen and follow him. Desh is squatting with his back to me, pulling out supplies from cupboards, and I stack them into rows on the Formica table.

"Pasta," he murmurs, passing me the last of the bulky packages so our fingertips touch. "And write down fresh fruit—we need limes—and we'll pick up some shrimp and avos."

There's something intimate in his manner, but I don't want it. Instead, I scribble dutifully, aware that he's watching me. I underline *avos* unnecessarily. Straighten up, face him, my neck hot. "Is that everything?"

"Are you doing okay?" He's standing so close that I can see gray flecks in the green of his eyes.

"Yes, thank you." *I'm not your project. I'm not anyone's.*

"What's happening with Regan?"

"With *me* and Regan? Nothing. Do we have tea and coffee?" I move to the cupboard, wrench it open, ferret inside the packet of tea bags.

"Ivy." He takes the box, sets it down onto the table. "What are you so mad about?"

"I'm not mad. I'm trying to do a stock take."

"Is it because Regan and I hung out last night?" He stares at me like I'm a puzzle to be solved, but why is it so difficult to fathom? Desh was hitting on me in the hammock. It's insulting to be switched out for something better.

I take a deep, self-protective breath. "I just find it hard to be compared to Regan. You know, to always be thought of as second best."

He laughs. Actually laughs. "Do you have any clue at all what's going on here?"

I stare at him, then mumble, "Here in this kitchen?"

He throws out his arms, as if there's some epiphany available to everyone that I'm not seeing. "Regan spent two hours last night trying to persuade me to get off the boat today."

He might as well have lit a fuse in my head. I feel the spark of fresh rage, the fizz. "With her? She wanted you to leave together?" How *dare* she? That's about as backstabbing as you can get—

"No, you banana. She asked me to leave so that *you would come.* I guess she figured I was a factor in your wanting to stay." He waits, his mouth pursed as if a little bit pleased, while inside my brain, the fire sputters out. "What I'm saying is, she only hung out with me last night for *you.* She said the two of you have different thresholds for Christopher's behavior. She gets that; she knows she's more easily triggered. But she didn't want to leave without you today. That was the whole thing."

"She didn't . . . she wasn't trying to . . . ?" A rolling great wave of dismay washes over me from head to toe. She wasn't being shady or snaky. She just wanted us to keep traveling together.

"There's nothing going on with me and Regan." He puts his hand on my shoulder, the weight of it as heavy as the guilt. "You two had a shitty goodbye. I really think you should go find her."

—

I move quickly once I've gotten my head straight. According to Desh, who helped with the timetable, Regan is aiming for Townsville and the mainland. Bigger, faster, more her style. She'll be walking to the Nelly Bay ferry terminal right now. Boats leave hourly; if I run, I might make it in time.

"What are you— Are you off to the grocery store?" Up on deck in the shade, Christopher's filling Pearl's food bowl with a mound of kibble.

"No. Desh has it covered. I need to go fix things with Regan." I clamber onto the deck bannister. The gunwale. Whatever.

"You're coming back, though?"

"Yes. Don't leave without me."

He nods in the way parents do when they consider their grown child to be wildly misdirected. I ignore that, leap from the side of the boat, and set off at a jog through the harbor.

The island is steep and winding, a rabbit warren of forested national park. There's no time to get lost, and I run, scanning road signs frantically. The midmorning air is clammy and damp, the asphalt spongy underfoot. After days on the boat, my body feels like it's swaying even on land. The sensation is bizarre, slightly dizzying.

I can't believe I thought so poorly of Regan. Discounted everything our friendship ever meant without even asking her a question. What the hell is the matter with me? All the good instincts I have I ignore. And the bad ones I act on immediately.

At the top of a big hill, I'm panting and out of breath when I spot the main ferry terminal sitting below me, a little outpost with a slope-roofed office by the water. The metal handrails along the jetty shimmer as I descend at a sprint; I imagine them damp to the touch. There's a boat two hundred yards from shore, but I can't tell if it's coming or going. A cluster of backpackers hang around the main building, and I slow to a walk, throat burning from exertion and the thought that I've missed her, I'm too late, she's already gone.

But as I round the corner of the ticketing office, there's a gray bench in the shade. I spot her flip-flop first. Her ankle. She's stretched out with her back against the wall, sipping from a can of Lift Lemon. She coughs at the sight of me, wipes her mouth with the back of her hand.

"I'm so sorry," I blurt, stopping right in front of her, hair sticking to my face. "I got jealous and I'm stupid and a moron."

"What? What are you doing here?" She stands, checking my shoulders, hoping for the sight of a backpack.

"Last night, I thought you were . . . It doesn't matter. I just needed to get here and say that I love you, and you're my best friend—my *real friend*—and I'm sorry the crewing can't be longer for you."

"No, it's okay, it's not . . . your fault." Her backpack tips from where it's leaned against the bench and she grabs it, steadies it. "I'm sorry I'm so touchy about Christopher. I just can't be around him."

"Are you mad that I can? That I'm staying on the boat?" I wipe my brow, feel the sweat at my hairline. "If we're friends, we need to let each other go, because sometimes our tracks don't run parallel—"

"I'm not mad at all." She smiles, pulls me into a hug, strands of her hair tickling against my cheek. "I'll miss you, but it's only four or five days 'til I see you in Darwin. It'll be good for us. We'll have stories."

I nod, so relieved I press harder against her, my forehead

scraping against the bony jut of her clavicle. "I'll text you as soon as I get near the city."

"Good." We step back, both of us squinting happily. "I'll be there waiting. But for now, I need to get on that ferry."

There's a boat docking behind us, the crew lowering a walkway onto the jetty. An imminent goodbye sweeps us toward silence again, and we hold hands as we walk down to the dock. Passengers are getting off, filing past us—day-trippers in sensible hiking shoes, clutching sunscreen and hats. There's the sense of a clock running out.

"Stay safe, Reags. You're the greatest." I hug her with my back to the water, but even as I speak, I feel her entire body tense up, as if she's just turned to stone in my arms.

"Holy fuck!" she hisses, lurching away from me, grabbing at my wrist and yanking me toward her.

As I stumble forward, I look back just in time to see Thatcher Kane step from the ferry onto the walkway.

23

REGAN YANKS AT MY ARM AGAIN and I stagger, my legs slow-motioned and heavy like in a nightmare. "Go!" she pushes me through the gaggle of tourists lined up behind us, but her voice is muffled. A car horn through a window in a tunnel. "Ivy, move! Quick!"

The urgency snaps me out of my stupor, and we flounder back up the path, hurtle around the corner to the road. Regan's backpack bounces against her shoulders as we run uphill, our breathing high-pitched and ragged. A couple of cars go by us, and I flinch each time, expecting brake lights, the sudden fling outward of a passenger door, a cornering awful chase.

But we reach the top of the hill, and Regan steers us toward a clump of gum trees. We crouch behind a burl of scabby papery bark.

"What the fuck!" Regan pants. "How is he here? How the fuck is he here?"

She looks as scared as I am, eyes as wide as they'll go. I can't think straight, my vision a series of snapshots, my head clicking every time I blink. The jetty is empty now, the walkway removed. Where the hell has he gone? Into the ticketing office? The bathroom? The cafeteria? He's like a spider I've lost track of when I looked down for a second. The truce text I sent him has done nothing at all.

"He didn't see you. It's okay. We're okay." Regan's fingertips shine white as she grips the tree. "Ivy! Do you think he went past us in a cab?"

"I don't know." I swallow. "No, he'd have spotted us. I don't know."

"We can't go back down there. How has he guessed right? Have you fucking switched on your cell?"

"*You* did! *You* switched it on! To look at some goddamn Instagram feed." It comes out far too harshly, but I grab her hand, squeeze it. "We were so quick, though, and it's been off since I messaged him back."

Her eyes glisten, and for a horrified second, I think she might burst into tears. *Jesus*, I think. *Look what I've done!* I've dragged her into this nightmare, this retaliation that should never have included her.

"The boat," I stammer. "Our boat. He can't know about it." Because this has to have just been a terrible coincidence. Or a choice that has nothing to do with me at all? Thatcher has flown miles to Australia; maybe he's seeing the Great Barrier Reef before he goes home. There's a second, only a second, where Regan and I stare at each other. After that, we're flying along the road toward the little harbor where the *Alone at Last* is moored. We sprint past road signs and trail maps, my journey in reverse, and with every pounding step I pray that Christopher will be there, he hasn't gone on his picnic, they're behind schedule, they're disorganized, they haven't left yet.

Two hundred feet from the jetty, the yacht looks quiet. No signs of movement on board. Sliding door to the covered cabin gleaming and glassy as if shut tight. *We need to leave now*, I think as I run. *Now*. We can't hang around until five. The old wood of the dock shudders under our feet as we pound along it, toss Regan's backpack on board with zero indecision, any reason she had to leave irrelevant now. She knows what I'm up against, has seen him in the flesh. And what would have happened if she'd run into Thatcher on that jetty? Would he have remembered her from when he'd gazed at her across the foyer of that convention center, or from my old Instagram posts? I'm not at all sure he'd have just walked on by. Guilt floods me, and a sob builds in my throat. We're now *both* better off on the boat.

We jump from the dock, stumbling onto our knees near the boom with a thud that brings Christopher to the door of the covered cabin.

"You're here!" I shout, manic and jubilant, hefting the door sideways at the same time as him, our hands palm to palm each side of the glass.

"What's this?" he says, shooting Regan a dark look. "Changed your mind?"

"We need your help," I blurt. "We ran into trouble. Is everyone on the boat?"

Christopher's eyes widen but he doesn't move. *Start the goddamn engine!* I feel like pushing him aside, doing it myself.

"What kind of trouble?" he says.

Regan stands a cool distance from him, her eyes on the jetty, at the swathe of paved accessibility beyond it. "Can we please go? Like, right now?"

"We need to at least get away from the dock," I say, and Christopher looks right at me, his pale eyes piercing into mine. "Please." For a second, there's a moment of recognition in him, as if we have something very fundamental in common. But then Lila comes up the stairs behind him holding Pearl.

"Dad, I can't find my rain jacket—" she says, then stops short. I watch happiness, confusion, and then concern fleet across her face as she notices Regan on deck. "Why are—?"

"Get back inside, Lila. Picnic's canceled." Christopher's voice is low. "Right now."

Wordlessly, she turns and does as she's told. Christopher steps into the cabin, starts the engine. "Desh hasn't left yet; he's below deck," he says, factual and swift as he moves to the gunwale, climbs over onto the dock, undoes the stern rope from the cleat. He tosses it at Regan with such force that it clips her on the side of the neck, but he doesn't say anything, doesn't apologize. Instead, he moves along the jetty, pushes the boat away with his foot, jumping on board again at the last minute.

He pulls in the bumpers, heads back into the cabin, and throws the engine into gear. Not once does he hesitate. I stare at the back of him, at his steady hands on the throttle. How is he able to process this emergency so calmly?

"Did anyone follow you back to the harbor?" He turns as he steers.

"No." Regan's skin is blotchy with stress and running.

"We don't think so," I add miserably, while Regan avoids looking at me. What a terrible teammate I am.

"Did you buy anything on the island?" he asks.

"What? No," I say, just as Regan cuts in with "A soda. But I paid with the cash you gave me."

She doesn't catch my eye and seems to be keeping up with Christopher's questions better than I am. To me, his precision feels strange. *He's done this before*, I think suddenly. *Left in a hurry, fled in a panic.*

"This is a family boat. A family vacation," he says, pushing the boat into a higher gear.

"I'm sorry," I say, edging back toward the railing. "We'll . . . I'll figure it all out so it doesn't land on you."

He exhales, shaking his head, as if it's a bit late for that. "You could have been honest in Airlie Beach. You ought to have told me there was a situation you were trying to avoid."

My eyes dart to Regan, expecting her to counter, to fling back all the things she's pretty sure he failed to mention too. But she's quiet. Internally analyzing. I can't tell who's the maddest, or at whom.

Christopher returns to navigating, his neck and shoulders tense as we pull out of the marina. And as much as I'm grateful for that, I find I'm holding on tight to the starboard railing. Relief washes over me, curdled with guilt, but there's something else there, too, something deeper and more uneasy. A pinched feeling, ominous in my head like a hand raised. Here is a man who knows what it means to flee. Before, we'd thought he was just avoiding reality, the loneliness of his own failures. But now it's starting to look a lot more specific.

Why doesn't he want to be found?

24

AS SOON AS WE'RE out of port, Regan and I go down to our cabin, passing Desh who has every half-used food item out of the cupboards, and is trying to steady a tilting bag of flour.

"Oh, hey," he says, mostly to Regan, as he wipes his hands against his shorts. "You're back! That's great. I wondered why we were on the move. Everything's falling over."

"Hey," we say in unison, but our tone doesn't match his in the least and we don't offer to help him clean up. Instead, we hurry along the corridor, push our door shut with Regan's bag, sit down on opposite beds. She leans forward onto her knees, threads one thumb over the other. *Here we are again*, her body language is saying. *Right back where I didn't want to be.*

"We need a plan," I say. "I know this isn't our solution."

She nods quickly, a bird's response, fast and jerky. "I'd say direct to Cairns on whatever fuel we have left, taxi to the international airport, fly straight home."

I murmur agreement, while all the fear and the adrenaline—the shock of actually *seeing* Thatcher—thrums in my veins like I've had too much coffee. And now there's this odd uncertainty circling around Christopher like a storm warning. Has Regan been right this whole time? Is there something threatening about him?

I want to go home. Where it's safe. Where my dad is. "Cairns is totally our best bet. It's two days' sail at the most. We can change our tickets, pay a fee, whatever." I wait, watching her wretched face. "I'm so sorry. I never meant to drag you into this. I don't know why the hell Thatcher's still coming after me. I mean, why won't he stop?!"

"He's obsessed and always has been." She pauses for a minute, thinking. "Ivy, did you look closely at those photos of his before you got rid of them?"

My head flashes awful splayed legs, slack chins, hair stuck in strands to necks. "No, I-I . . . couldn't. Why? You think there was something I missed?"

She clears a clag in her throat, face grim. "Maybe there was a detail in them he wouldn't be able to dodge."

"What, though? His handwriting on them?" There's a long silence. It feels rational, possible. Did he write—or make up—the girls' names? *You name them, you claim them,* my dad always warned whenever I rescued some half-dead field mouse, or put a snail in a Tupperware with holes in the lid. But was Thatcher doing that? Going for ownership? It feels likely. Before I can stop myself, I picture him whacking off, grunting out the name he'd assigned.

"Ivy? I said whatever it is in the photos, it's a direct link to him. Has to be. And he doesn't believe for a single second that you've burned them."

"But how did he know where we'd be?" My left foot is tapping, my stress levels peaking, because I already know the answer, and there's only so much more dread I can take.

"Somebody's tipped him off," Regan says.

I grab my pillow, hug it to the front of me. She's right. Australia's huge, and him being on that ferry cannot be coincidence. It was naïve to even consider it. As if on cue, we both stare at the loosely shut door.

"It can't be Christopher," Regan says. "I don't like him— I've made no secret of that—but I've been racking my brain for a way he and Thatcher connect, and I just can't come up with one. Same goes for Lila." Her thumbs stop rotating. "Desh, though. You told me he went to school in New York before he switched to cooking."

"But—what? He said he started out there. You think that he knows Thatcher?"

She runs a palm over her face as if exhausted. "No, it's dumb and totally unlikely but *what the hell is going on*? Your phone has only been on for ten minutes this whole time. Thatcher can't have tracked you. And mine is gone, probably at the bottom of the ocean."

"Plus he doesn't have your number."

Her eyes are still closed, and she squeezes them, as if intent on a mental checklist. "There's no GPS on this boat. We're totally analog. So, the only way he could track us would be . . . *if he knew the name of our yacht*. Could he be calling the coast guard?"

She looks up suddenly, and we lock eyes. I try to calm

down, stop the shouting in my brain, think for a minute. Who other than us knows the name *Alone at Last*? We didn't even tell it to our parents. That Blake guy, I guess, but he was nothing and we haven't seen him since that one night. Was there anyone else along the way? In my mind are a tangle of faces, a fairy-light string of characters we've met on this trip, and as I start to tease them apart, one of them snags and lights up.

"Oh, my God!" I say. "Milo. The Swiss boy you hooked up with at Airlie Beach. He knew about the boat. What if Thatcher ran into him at the bar? The crew poster was still on the wall. He might have pointed it out."

Regan sits up straighter. "In which case, Thatcher could have gotten Christopher's phone number."

"Shit, Regan, I feel ill. Could he track Christopher's cell? I haven't even seen him use it. How does that work?"

"Surely he couldn't." She's clearly not certain either, though. We're completely lost. "Especially not if it's out of range. Or does he have some kind of Wi-Fi booster he hasn't told us about?"

"Jesus! I don't know. How do they work?"

As we're fretting, there's a knock at the door and Christopher pushes it open, his toes hitting the barrier of Regan's backpack.

"It's just me." He stands in the doorway. "Can we have a chat? For starters, you should know that we'll likely motor until sunset, then head for an inlet I've found on the map. I reckon we might need some shelter overnight."

"Are there towns close by?" I ask quickly. "Any main roads?"

He pauses as if unclear whether I want them or not. "No. It's entirely deserted. Kangaroo tracks."

"Okay, thank you." I clear my throat. "And could anyone call the coast guard to find out where we are?"

His brow furrows. "The coast guard? Oh, no. No, that's impossible. They wouldn't have any record of us."

"Good," I say, although even as I speak, another dark passageway opens up for me, creaky like a door in a horror movie. *No record of us.* He hasn't registered the boat. From the little I know of sailing, I'm sure that's a legal requirement.

Regan sits back against the wall, hugging her knees. "Do you keep your cell phone switched off, Christopher?"

"No. It's on, for emergencies. Even though phones are the demise of modern civilization. Humans aren't meant to be reachable twenty-four-seven. I'm trying to opt out."

"Could you completely opt out for a little while?" I ask, my smile tight. "Switch your cell off until we leave?"

He leans against our doorjamb. "I could do that. But look, this is what I mean. Whatever happened on Magnetic Island—whatever you're ducking—you've involved us all now. I need you to be honest with me. Is Lila in danger?"

"Nope." Regan grips her knees.

Christopher's gaze switches to me. "Can you give me any more detail than that?"

"I'm having a problem with an ex," I say, and Regan's eyes start to signal alarm. But it's okay, I know what I'm doing. I watch Christopher's expression intently. "His name's Thatcher Kane. I came to Oz to get away from him, but he's come after me. He won't leave me alone."

Christopher's face remains concerned, but it's placid. No twitch of recognition. Unless he's a brilliant liar, he's never heard of Thatcher.

"Why haven't you reported him?" he asks.

"She didn't know he was like this." Regan's voice is flat. "He hid it from her."

His bottom lip protrudes, and he nods, as if it's the most common thing in the world to be pursued by someone you've underestimated. "So, what's next? How will you get away from him?" His composure continues to be unsettling, and I get that sense again of a backstory he hasn't offered, a key fact or two he's keeping very well concealed.

"We need to get to Cairns as quickly as possible," I say. "We haven't decided beyond that." It's a lie—Regan and I know exactly what we're doing—but something tells me not to hand him a full itinerary.

"Righto." He claps his hands together. "Straight to the city, phones off, no messing about. When you get to there, obviously don't use credit cards." *He's already guessed it all. He knows we're going, that he'll lose crew. Why isn't he more upset?* "Pay the taxi driver in cash, and don't be memorable. Sleep at the airport if you need to—not at a hostel or hotel—but don't bunker down at your gate. Go to a wrong one, then scan your own from a distance when it's time."

Regan looks as perturbed as I feel. *Jesus*, we're both thinking. This guy sounds like a pro. I've just told him I'm being stalked and hunted, and he doesn't seem the least bit thrown. In fact, he has a vetted day-to-day plan for situations like this. Is it just that he watches too much true crime on TV?

"Okay, thanks," I say, trying to keep my face relaxed, but once he's gone, I turn to Regan, who's still staring at the doorway.

"Let's get a lock set up for tonight," I say. "We can rig one up ourselves."

"Totally." Her face is bleak. It's what she's thought all along: something is not right about Christopher.

"Is he . . . Do you think he left Hobart in a hurry?"

"Yeah, as fast as he could sprint, but I think Helen knows he's gone. She dumped him. All their friends would be in on it; they'll all be talking. He'll have been super humiliated."

It's true, I think. When my mom left Dad, his pride was hurt, and he didn't even want to go bowling anymore in case he was seen.

"It's what I've always said: this trip isn't Christopher being heroic and fatherly. It's about him licking his wounds."

"He was . . . different just now. Not in a tailspin."

"I'd say he's falling apart *and* adapting. People can do both at the same time." She rubs her eyes, exhausted. "He's probably got it in his head that if he fully disappears for a while, then sneaks back for Helen's birthday in February, she'll go, 'Oh, I've missed him, what was I thinking? My husband is such a thoughtful, worldly adventurer. Not this giant dork after all.'"

"Right," I say, wondering if all heartbreaks are like that. A slightly delusional rebuild. A scramble to reinvent yourself. Like flying to Australia on a whim.

"It doesn't change anything I think about him," Regan says. "He's volatile, desperate, and trying to counter it by controlling everyone. This isn't safe passage, Ives. But right now, it's the best we've got."

25

WE HEAVE CHRISTOPHER'S TOOLBOX out of the bathroom, and I leave Regan to rifle through it for anything that'll make us a lock. I move to the galley, to head Christopher off if he comes back down. He's up on deck with Lila, but we're not sure how he'll feel about us helping ourselves to his things.

At the table, Desh is peeling shrimp for dinner. Translucent curves of pink-gray shell stick to his hands like torn fingernails.

"Fixing up your door?" He motions for me to sit beside him, and I squeeze in along the bench. "Was that one of Regan's conditions?"

"Conditions?" The smell of the shrimp is mild, but still they look sweaty on the cutting board, their eyes too beady and ink-black. I tug at the neck of my T-shirt.

"For getting back on the boat." He rubs his nose with his wrist, his skin tanned against the pale-blue fabric of his hoody. "She was dead set on leaving. You must have been very persuasive."

"No . . . I . . . I don't know. In the end, getting back on the boat was what we both wanted. At the time." I hesitate, stare at the table. How much detail should I give him? If today's taught me anything, it's that information is worth protecting. But I need a few answers from him—because what if Thatcher *didn't* meet Milo? Doesn't know the name of the boat? *Wasn't* tracking Christopher's cell? The only other possibility is Desh. I don't know how to get his story without handing over all of mine.

"Okay," he says, smiling as if he can hear me battling inside. "That's all good, then."

"Desh," I edge, my voice wavering. "You know when you went to college, before you changed it up to train as a chef?"

"Yup." He focuses on peeling another thin scab of shell.

"Where did you study?"

He stops, frowns. "I told you. I was in New York."

"No, but . . . It definitely wasn't at NYU?" There's a pause while he scrapes at a shrimp with his knife, almost as if ignoring me, and I feel a tweak of impatience. "What did you study? Did you have, like, a favorite teacher?"

"Why do you want to know all that?"

"It's just . . ." I trail off, my finger toying with the wiry antenna of a discarded shrimp head before I realize what it is that I'm doing. "I don't know very much about you. I'm . . . making conversation."

"Huh." He slices open a shrimp, drags out what looks like a long blackened vein. "I was in an emergency medical tech program. Community college, not NYU. I wanted to be a paramedic. Until I really didn't."

"EMT?" I'm unable to hide the rush of relief in my voice. "Wow, I wouldn't have guessed that."

"No?" Another slice. "Why not?"

"You just seem . . . I don't know. Too mellow."

He laughs, one nasal shunt of breath, as if I couldn't be more wrong. He doesn't offer anything more and keeps his eyes low, his hands busy. It occurs to me that we're back to his fact sheet again, where he won't say anything that's off script or superfluous.

"What's your family like?" I ask, trying to coax him out. "Do you have brothers or sisters?"

"One brother. Rafi. He's a dick. Sells hot tubs to millionaires in LA."

"Really? That sounds . . . lucrative. What about pets? Or best buddies? Or, I don't know, *girlfriends?*" I deliver the last line with a nudge, jokily—*Go ahead, break my heart, I can take it*—because after all, I still suspect that he might be a player. But the moment the question's out of my mouth, Desh drops his knife, the handle skidding into a puddle of shrimp slime.

"What is this?" he says. "The fucking third degree?"

I gape at him, shocked. "No, I wasn't . . . I'm not being nosy, I'm just—"

"Can you move? I need to dump this out." He stands with the cutting board and bumps me with his hip, encouraging me to stand, and we move along the line of the cushion in an awkward side-by-side shuffle. For a second, I watch while he scrapes shards of shell into a bag. Why is he being so hostile? These aren't overwhelming questions I'm asking him. They're not unusual at all.

"Desh, I'm not trying to interrogate you. I'm just being . . . chatty."

"Yeah, well, I'm just being private." He keeps his back turned, his tone hard like the metal of his knife.

"Fine." I raise both my palms, even though he can't see them. "Don't tell me anything at all."

"I've told you plenty." He turns, his eyes so much colder than usual. "Did you get it all? Do you need to go and write it down?"

I stare at him, at this man whom I suddenly don't know even a little bit. I say nothing, but turn and stumble back along the corridor as the boat pitches. The squall is gathering. With every minute that passes, the waves feel bigger and bigger. I press open our door, steady myself for a second, the sailboat groaning like it's climbing uphill.

Regan is kneeling just inside, grinding a hook into the doorjamb, a little off-balance. Her tongue peeps out the side of her mouth with the effort. "I can't find a lock plate, but here, let's try this." She shuts the door behind me, and it holds. "Nice, we've— What's wrong?"

"I don't know. I just had the strangest conversation with Desh. I asked him basic stuff about himself, and he got all mad like I was invading his privacy."

"That's weird. He was so chill when I sat up with him on deck."

"Right." I feel my shoulder muscles stiffen, but try not to succumb to comparing myself. The chat they had last night was probably lighthearted. Nothing to do with family or girlfriends. Nothing that hit a nerve. "Anyway, I found out he didn't go to NYU. Couldn't have known Thatcher."

"Thank God for that." She leans toward the toolbox, trying to jam the screwdriver back into its spot. "So it has to have been Milo, then, most likely."

I nod, watching as she pulls out the tray that separates the top section of the box from the bottom, tosses the screwdriver in. But from where I'm standing, a sliver of something else catches my eye. Something rectangular. Rose-edged. Out of place.

I crouch down and halt her as she tries to replace the tray. Reaching in, I dig past hinges and bolts to the very bottom, my fingers connecting with a rubbery flatness. I pull the object out and hold it up like the worst prize from a lucky dip, while Regan's jaw drops in disbelief. It's her cell phone. Dark-screened, dead, and dusty. But not lost at the bottom of the ocean. Not lost at all.

26

WE STARE AT EACH OTHER, both of us motionless with shock. Christopher had Regan's cell all along? He snuck into our room, stole it from her bed that first night, stashed it, and has lied about it every day after.

"What was he . . . Was he trying to hack into it? Or he just didn't want me to post anything? He didn't take yours. Was he punishing me?" Regan keeps tucking a strand of hair behind her ear, then it bounces back again.

"I don't know! But put it back, put it back in there so he won't know we know!" I try to snatch the phone from her, because now we may have two villains to deal with, and we've just put our lives in the hands of one of them. *Are* we safer here on the boat?

"No! I don't want— He can't have it, he doesn't get to take anything that's mine." She evades my stretching hands, like an older sister keeping a treat out of reach. I can smell the strain coming off our skin as we grapple, pungent with everything we've had to go through today.

"Regan!" I hiss, urgent, while behind me, there's a tiny tap-tapping on the door, like a baby bird pecking at a twig. I stop and turn, and Regan rams her cell phone into the back pocket of her jean shorts, then quickly bends to shove the toolbox tray back into place, kicking shut the lid.

"Just a second," she calls out, as she unhooks our lock, then stands back. I press behind her, my breath on the back of her shoulder blade.

The door pushes slowly inward. Lila steps in, gripping Pearl around the armpits, the remainder of the cat's body hanging like a weighted pendulum.

"Is it okay if I come in? Dad said your cabin's off-limits, but . . ." she heaves Pearl onto my bed, but the cat springs away, settles beside my foot, disdain coming off her as she cleans her front paw. Lila notices the toolbox on the floor, the thick atmosphere in the cabin, and looks from face to face. "Are you two still having a fight?"

"No." I shake my head at Regan, who copies me, tries a smile. "We're good, we were just chatting. Fixing up a hook to keep the door from swinging open."

"That's what Mum and Dad always said." Lila bunny-ears quotation marks. "*Just chatting.*"

There's a pause while Regan and I struggle for some kind of response. So much has happened today and all of it so harrowing that it feels too sudden to be back in the presence of a child. Especially one who's referencing her own trauma.

"Are you doing okay?" I ask finally, a question that's about as complicated as I can manage. "Why did Christopher say we're off-limits?" To my left, I can see Regan's mind is racing too. She's fidgety, doesn't know what to do with her hands.

"He says you're crew, not my friends, but I don't think that's true." Lila's chin looks a little wobbly as she lowers herself onto my bed.

"Of course it isn't," Regan says. "Your dad's not always reliable."

I flash her a horrified glance. *Easy*, I think. *She's eleven. Even if he's creepy to us, he's still her safest place.*

"Can I talk to you about . . . him?" Lila seems to be looking mostly at me. "I might have . . . I think I did something bad."

I feel myself expel the last of my lungs' air. Oh, God, I'm at maximum capacity. I fight the urge to lie down and curl into a fetal position. "What did you do?" Her forehead creases with worry, and she shoots a scared look at Regan. "Would you rather talk to me alone?"

As Lila dithers, Regan grabs the toolbox, steps toward the doorway. "I'll leave you girls to it. Ives, let's catch up as soon as you're done."

I nod, let her go, take a breath once the door is closed. "Okay, what's up?"

"How come Regan came back? Did you two figure things out?" She gestures toward the corridor.

"When you're really friends with someone, you might have ups and downs, but your baseline will always be solid." She nods unhappily, perhaps thinking about her friend, Vicky Something, again. Is Pearl really Lila's bestie now, like her dad said? I sit down next to her on the bed. "Lila, what is it? What's on your mind?"

What the hell could it possibly be? Whatever secret she's stowing, it's pressing outward at every part of her face. I wait while she takes a few runs at it, tries to muster the courage. She grinds her fingertips into her eyes.

"I called Mum from Magnetic Island." It comes out as a wheezy exhale. "I shouldn't have done it. Dad said not to contact her, but I snuck his mobile and did it anyway. And you guys asked me how much space I could handle, you said I get to have a say, you put all that in my head, so it wasn't my—"

"Hey, slow it down. It's alright to want to talk to your mom." I put my arm around her, feel her lean into me. "It's the most natural thing in the world. I still tell my mom tons of stuff—I mean, she lives in a different house, and I'm closer with my dad—but moms are important. You can't replace them. What happened when she picked up?"

"She didn't." Lila's eyes brim with tears. "I left her a message. I told her the towns we're nearest to—Magnetic today, Cairns the day after tomorrow—and what the boat's called. Even though Dad told me not to."

I open my mouth to speak, but nothing comes out. *Christopher didn't want Helen to know the name of the boat?* But hadn't they talked the whole thing through? He'd said the trip was a family decision, whether or not it was last minute or came out of a marriage ending. Is Helen's big birthday surprise tied up in not knowing about the *Alone at Last*? Maybe he's planning to hand it over as a gift. I imagine the little girl rattling off facts in a flurry at the sound of the beep, muddled by the emotion of hearing her mom's voice on the outgoing recording, knowing there was a time limit. Would the message have been too garbled, or would Helen have gotten all the details? And now that she has them, what would she do?

"I'm such a traitor." She shakes her head, dislodging fat droplets of tears that spill down her cheeks, splashing onto the linoleum. "Dad's going to kill me."

"No, he's not! And anyway, whatever's going on between him and your mom isn't your deal. You should never be expected to pick sides." What is with these parents? One of them cordoning her off, the other completely unavailable? "Sweetie, are you really homesick? And just not telling anyone?"

She nods, her shoulders drooping.

"Okay, let's think of something that will help." I pause, dig deep for some energy. "What's one thing your mom does for you that you kind of miss?"

"Braids my hair." She sniffs wetly. "And brushes it. For school."

I reach into the side pocket of my backpack and pull out my hairbrush, hold it up to her, smiling. Shyly, she takes off her ball cap, slides off the mattress, and sits below me on the floor with her legs crossed. *At least*, I think, *at least I can do this*. Not everything today needs to be a terrifying cat-and-mouse chase.

"So, tell me more about your mom. Her name's Helen. She lives in Hobart. Likes yoga. Teaches art. But what does she look like, what's her favorite color, favorite food?"

Lila's head tugs to the left as I start to work out the tangles. "She's tall and thin like a willow tree. Her favorite color is butterscotch. She likes designer cardigans, figs, dates, and expensive tea."

"Wow," I say. "She sounds very stylish."

"She is, but she's aggro a lot. All the kids in our school hate her. She goes berko really easily." I stop brushing. Below me, Lila picks at a scuffed fingernail, staring down into her lap. "They call her the Atomic Bomb. Sometimes she just blows up."

"She does?" *Christ*, I think. Shouts at school, throws cups at home. I'm about to ask Lila if her mom ever blew up on her when I notice something strange about Lila's hair. Peering lower, I'm right: there's a quarter inch of hair at her scalp that's a different color to the rest. Lighter brown instead of dark auburn.

"Have you dyed your hair recently?" I ask.

She puts her palm to it, startled, as if I've just set it on fire. "What? No."

"It's cool! I like the color, I just didn't know you'd—" But she scrambles to her knees and stands, brushes herself down. "What are you doing? I haven't braided it yet. I wasn't judging—it's just new information, is all."

There's a long, gaping silence while she stands knock-kneed, pleading at me with her hazel eyes. But I don't know what's happening, why she's so upset, what the big deal is about her hair.

"Please, please don't say anything to Dad," she whispers.

Chills creep up the back of my neck as I blink at her, dumbfounded. She turns and runs out of the cabin, leaving Pearl on the floor beside me.

CHRISTOPHER EDWARD FARRIS
RECORDED INTERVIEW
Date: January 9, 2020
Location: Cairns, Northern QLD
Conducted by Officers from the Queensland Police,
Far Northern Region

POLICE: Mr. Farris, can we talk about your wife
            for a while? Your ex-wife, Helen. How
            would you describe her? [Long pause.]
            It's not a difficult question. One adjective.
            Give it a shot.
CF: Cold.
POLICE: That's . . . that's the one you'd choose?
CF: Or gone. Is that an adjective?
POLICE: You sound upset.
CF: I'm very upset.
POLICE: Would you have picked such negative words
            to describe her at the start?
CF: No, of course not. But you weren't asking
            me about the start. Newness is always
            inaccurate.
POLICE: What an interesting thing to say.
CF: Well, marriage is a long game.
POLICE: Was it a surprise to you when Helen filed
            for divorce?
CF: It shouldn't have been, I suppose. Fifty per-
            cent of marriages end that way. I often
            think that wedding ceremonies should be
            held on skydiving planes. If the stats were

the same on the parachutes opening, none
of the couples would jump.

POLICE: You often think that?

CF: I'm saying commitment should be worth
more. We all know the risks up front.
Getting out once you've already agreed to
them shouldn't be a thing.

POLICE: Loyalty. It's big for you, isn't it?

CF: Yes.

POLICE: Like when she betrayed you over the
Rosebud. The embezzlement claim. That
must have been a major turning point for
your relationship.

CF: Why do you keep asking questions like this?
You don't know me. This isn't therapy. I
haven't paid for your opinion.

POLICE: Is Helen seeing someone new, Mr. Farris?
Does she have a new bloke in Hobart?

CF: We're separated, not divorced.

POLICE: [Pause.] Okay, let's stick to the facts. You
took on the management of the Rosebud
aided by Helen's inheritance money, left to
her by her folks when they died in 2016.
Correct?

CF: Yes.

POLICE: Thank you. So you can understand why
she'd guard it so ferociously.

CF: No, I can't. It's not like she guarded me
with the same ferocity.

POLICE: [Pause.] Was she nice to you?

CF: *Nice?*

POLICE: The thing is, we're trying to better under-
             stand Helen's character.

CF: Why?

POLICE: We'd like to know whether you felt
             harassed by her. Examined. Under attack.

CF: I'm sure I felt all of those things at some
             point. As would every married person you
             ever asked.

POLICE: But did she evolve into someone you felt
             you had to . . . contest?

CF: Look, I don't like the inference that I was
             weak in my marriage, or useless, or . . . or
             what? Are you asking if I was *afraid* of her?

POLICE: Were you?

CF: Yes! Terrified! But aren't we all? On some
             level, every husband is afraid of his wife.
             [Pause.] What? Why are you looking at me
             like that?

POLICE: Were you aware that your daughter told
             Helen where you were on January 5th?
             Giving her exact map coordinates?

CF: No, that didn't happen.

POLICE: We have phone records, Mr. Farris. A voice-
             mail message left by Lila. Would you like
             me to play it for you?

CF: No, thank you.

POLICE: Why not? Would it upset you to hear the
             tone of your daughter's voice?

CF: I don't want to hear Helen's.

POLICE: [Long pause.] Search and Rescue have found human remains in the waters around Flint Beach.

CF: You said. You said that already. On the atoll.

POLICE: No. This is different. This discovery is without question a crime.

CF: Where were the remains found, then?

POLICE: Twenty feet from where your vessel was moored January 7th. And do you know what's interesting about that?

CF: No. Nothing.

POLICE: This body was already dead when it hit the water. Head and hands removed. Time of death: close to midnight, January 6th.

CF: [Silence.]

POLICE: Head and hands, Christopher.

CF: Stop. Please stop.

POLICE: There's blood spatter on your boat.

CF: Fish blood. From fish. From the speargun.

POLICE: We have the speargun in forensics. There's human blood on it.

CF: I want a lawyer. Right now. I'm saying nothing else. Not one word.

POLICE: We can sort that out for you. But for now, can you tell us who owns that speargun, Christopher? Is it yours? [Silence.] If you know anything about it at all, now would be the time to tell us. [Silence.] Okay, mark it down. Interview halted at 1:06 p.m.

27

I RUN OUTSIDE ONTO the deck, assuming Lila's come up here. What did she mean, *Please don't say anything to Dad*? It can't be a secret she's keeping from him. Any father would notice if his daughter's hair color changed. Or does she just mean don't bring it up? He's angry that she did it without his approval. To him, it'd be a big deal—she's young to put such harsh chemicals on her head. Christopher wouldn't like that. They must have had a big fight, and she's been wearing that baseball cap the whole time not just as sun shade but also to placate him.

The squall is blowing harder now, following through on its threat. I hold on to the frame of the covered cabin. Above me, the sails strain and I wonder if we should lower them, if at some point they'll rip. Christopher is at the helm, but there's no sign of Lila. She must have squirreled herself away in her cabin.

"Isn't it amazing out here with Mother Nature?" he yells,

his white T-shirt billowing madly, sticking to his ribs. "Even though Mummy is *very mad*!"

I don't laugh at his joke. Given what Lila's just told me about Helen, it's not in the least bit funny. Where the hell is Desh? Here we are in a storm, being led by a man who rips maps and steals cell phones, whose daughter is tiptoeing around him while he remains preoccupied with the speed of the boat. But then suddenly a new thought drops into my head like a pebble, its ripples spreading out wide.

What if Lila's hair isn't rebelliousness, or some sore subject she doesn't want to revisit with her dad? *Holy shit, what if it's neither of those things?* My knees buckle as I realize why she might have reacted as she did, why Christopher doesn't want us talking to her, why he tried to fob me off with bullshit child psychology. He already knows about Lila's dyed hair because he *did it to her.* Then he swore her to secrecy, and he's terrified we'll catch on.

"Come have a go at steering!" he shouts, as if inviting me onto a roller-coaster ride, but I shake my head at him, everything inside me rattling. I need Regan. She doubted him in exactly this way earlier, hedged at this very scenario. She has to be up here. I peer around the side of the cabin and there she is at the bow, trying to gather a rope, staggering every time the boat lurches into a new trough of swell.

"Reags! Hey!" I yell, my voice cracking as the wind whips away most of my syllables, flinging them elsewhere. Why is she even out here? She's tied herself to the railing with a metal fastener, but it's too wild, and she's too close to this man I've misjudged.

"You should clip in." Christopher is suddenly behind me, in a tiny pocket of quiet where the wind drops, a strange lull in all of the tumult, as if the storm is taking a breath. "We don't want you swept off the boat, never to be seen again."

His desolate eyes watch me, and I nod but feel myself backing away. Does he know that I'm onto him? Everything he's saying sounds like a threat to me now, and I get that same rush of time running out that I had in Thatcher's study, when I found those photos and knew he was finished his shower.

"Regan!" I shout again and this time she hears me, pushes back the hood of her jacket. She moves along the railing toward me, unclipping as soon as she reaches the edge of the cabin. I beckon her inside, heave the door closed, shutting out the din of the storm.

"Are you okay?" I ask. "Why are you out there with him?"

"Not *with him*. For fresh air. If I'm too cooped up, I feel frightened."

Frightened? No, she's the strong one. She can't be the one to come undone. I reach for her hands, grip them in mine. Her skin is damp and chilled. I want to tell her about Lila, about what I think Christopher's done, but beside me the glass pane shudders as the wind picks up again, and I feel the weight of everything bearing down.

Should I spare her this latest layer of stress? She looks wrung out, and my heart plunges with guilt. On land or at sea, she's not safe, and it's entirely my fault.

"What is it, Ivy? You look terrible. Are you getting sea-sick again?" She pulls me into a wobbly hug. I can feel a pulse hammering, but I can't tell if it's hers or mine. I exhale into her jacket, loving her for asking after me, when clearly she's so low herself. As long as I've known her, she's been triggered by people with hidden agendas. *Nobody's straight with me, Ivy. No one except you.* And here we are, surrounded on all sides by people with secrets, men we can't trust. Even Desh now seems undependable, almost aggressive. Regan and I will be better off, safer, stronger, if we both know everything.

I pull out of her hug and quickly check the stairwell down to the galley, make sure it's empty. "Listen to me. I could be wrong, but I think Christopher has stolen Lila."

"He's what? The fuck?" She sways and sits down on the bench seat. "But I asked her! I asked her about that—"

"I know, but I don't think Lila realizes. The whole big birthday plan, or whatever, I think Christopher's made all that up. You were right—he's adapted, he has a plan, but it's not about going *back* to Helen. She doesn't have any idea where her daughter is. Or she didn't, until today when Lila called her." I lick my lips, taste the dried salt on them, hating how much deeper I'm dragging her in.

"How the . . . Do you know this for sure? We're accessories in a fucking kidnap situation?" She looks about to pass out.

"I don't think he's, like, knocked her out and put her on a boat. I think he's tricked her. Talked her into it. Confused her. She's keeping so much in, I don't know."

"Where are you getting all this from? From *her*? From *Lila*?" Her tone suggests the little girl's testimony might not be totally watertight, and I get that. Lila has been through so much—more and more, as I'm realizing—and a little drama in the telling is understandable. And didn't she already lie about the ongoing night terrors? But the look of pure fear on her face when I noticed her lighter roots—I don't think she could have faked that.

"He's dyed her hair, Regan. I think he's *altered* her."

"Jesus Christ." She puts one palm to her chest.

"And it would explain why he's in such a hurry," I add. "Doesn't want anyone anchoring nearby or taking pictures, hasn't registered the boat, won't stop anywhere he doesn't need fuel . . ." Regan's shaking her head, quick little tremors that make her curls quiver.

"I *knew* this. I called it in that Who Am I? game," she says finally. "He *does* have her trapped out here, just like the rest of us."

I breathe out anxiety in a straight, steady stream because this time, I can't disagree. He's controlling everything. I should have listened to Regan before, at the earliest signs of Christopher's oddness, all the things she flagged. "Should we tell Desh, or turn on our phones, or maybe see if we can get anyone on the radio?"

"No!" She grabs my shirt, pulls me down beside her on the bench. Her voice is hushed, breath hot, her whole body taut. "We say nothing. Keep our heads down. Get off this horrible boat in forty-two hours. We get away from them all and go home."

I nod, but I know I'll need to figure out a way to help Lila. I can't just abandon her. Outside, through the sliding door, Christopher is gripping the wheel, his head thrown back in the wind. Is he singing? Howling? He's King Lear in the storm, bedraggled and in exile, a total lunatic.

28

REGAN AND I TEAM UP for watch tonight. Of course we do.
We're not spending any time apart until we land back in
America. By one a.m., we're deep into the second of our
combined shifts, huddled at the prow with the hoods of
our jackets up. The squall has settled, blown itself out,
leaving in its wake a steady hiss of hard rain. Christopher
is asleep—thank goodness, since fatigue is only adding to
his manic state—but he set a course, and we're chugging
slowly on autopilot. He asked us to sit outside tonight for
better visibility, even though our view has been nothing
but smeared darkness in every direction. We agreed without argument, though.

"I still can't believe he's making us motor at night." Regan
grips my knee under the worn blue tarp we've tented around
us as the boat lurches. "It's so dangerous! And the way he
tried to sell it like he's doing it for us. *I'm sure you want to keep
moving.*" She mimics him, fear laced into her outrage. "How

dumb does he think we are? Like we're not calling the cops on him from the airport. We know he's just racing away from his wife."

"Totally." My teeth grind as we churn through another wave. The sails are down and we're in low gear, but we should have been moored in the sheltered inlet he'd mentioned hours ago, safe in our cabin with the door locked. We're completely shattered. All the muscles in my legs keep tweaking, and each time I blink, my eyeballs sting. The sky is swampy and thick, as if we're looking down, not up. "Thirty-six hours to Cairns, Reags. At least we're getting there faster."

She sweeps water from her forehead, staring at the wet sheet of black horizon.

"I've been thinking about the start of the trip," she says quietly. "Other things Christopher did."

"Like what?"

"I'm pretty sure he never checked in at the Airlie marina." Regan shakes her head and the tarp crinkles. "The office was closed, and he left before it opened again. I bet he didn't even have a fob for the gate. He just opened it from the inside and kept it wedged."

"God, you might be right," I groan. "Why didn't I catch any of that?"

"It wasn't just you." Regan nudges me. "I know you think it was, but it wasn't. Some people are too good to catch."

Like Thatcher, she means, though I know neither of us wants to say his name out loud. But I can't help wonder where he is now, what he's plotting.

"You know what we should do?" I force an energetic tone,

even though I'm in danger of spiraling too. "Picture Cairns airport in bright sunshine. The cab we get into. The shiny floors of the departure lounge."

"Yes," she says, leaning into that image, her head against the flat of my shoulder. "That's better."

"And we'll get there, Reags. We can do it. We'll be okay." My confidence is questionable, but regardless, she seems bolstered as she tightens the tarp around us. But in the lull of conversation, I hear footsteps behind me and turn, rain spiking my cheeks like darts. As I squint across the deck, I can see Desh at the railing, threading hand over hand, making his way toward us.

"Hey." He hunkers down next to Regan, rain spattering the pale fabric of his sweatshirt darker. Regan doesn't respond, doesn't offer him any kind of cover. She was mad at him through dinner, at the way he'd served his shrimp dish in silence, then retired straightaway to his cabin as if punishing me. Whatever nerve I'd hit with him earlier, he was still sore about it, and she could tell it bothered me. As he'd walked away, Regan had rolled her eyes at me. *Such a baby*, she meant. It didn't make me feel any better.

"Hey, Desh." I shuffle aside, making room for him. "You're up late. You want out of the rain?"

"No. I'm good." The curve of his hood blocks his face.

"Are you here because you realized you owe Ivy an apology?" Regan asks, and he turns to me, as if the idea hadn't occurred to him.

"No, I came to see if you wanted me to take over. Christopher's on at two, but I can sit out here 'til then if you guys need some shut-eye."

"That's nice of you." I can't help it. I like him. I like the shape of his shoulders, his throat. Underneath that hoody, he'll be all muscle and warm skin. I think back to sitting next to him in the hammock, how happy I'd felt there, before everything went wrong, on the boat and off.

"Whatever. I'm awake anyway." He catches my eye but only for a second. It's as if he won't let himself smile.

"Desh, I'm sorry if I—" I begin, but Regan cuts in.

"We don't need your help," she says, her tone hard like a mean girl's pinch. Desh's head tilts. "With anything. Off you go, hero. You're pointless."

"What does *that* mean?" He frowns, his expression as cold as before, when he'd bumped me out of the way with his cutting board.

"You don't know what the word means?" Regan doesn't waver. "Or you don't know why we're applying it to you?"

"Regan!" I say, because that wasn't my word, I didn't choose it, she can't speak *for* me to Desh. *Don't listen to her,* I want to say. She's just worn out and overprotective. For a second, he glares at her, then at me, but I only shake my head. Then he stands, puts his hands in his pockets, bare feet planted on the rainy deck.

"Fine, then. Sit in the rain. What do I care?" He heads back toward the covered cabin, and I watch him disappear, all the muscles in my neck straining.

"Christ's sake!" I push Regan's shoulder. "Why did you do that?"

"We don't trust him. He was a dick earlier, a dick just now, and we haven't got time for it. He's the least of our worries." She seems to be gathering strength, but in entirely the wrong direction.

"Regan, I can handle my own—"

"No, you can't!" She takes a breath, steadies her voice. "No, you can't. You think he's hot and you'll make bad decisions." *It's not like you haven't made a career of it*, she might as well add.

"He *is* hot!" I yank the tarp so that less of it covers her. Who made her officer in control of my relationships?

"Ivy, we're in a predicament. We've unwittingly joined in on a child's abduction, and have you noticed how Christopher can't get rid of us fast enough? The quicker we leave, the less we'll figure out, but Desh is just a guy, just a—"

"You think I'm not freaking out too? You don't have to pick on Desh or be so sarcastic."

"Okay, but can you see that there's no point pursuing anything with him? Or, at the very least, it's not top priority?"

"Fine. But that doesn't mean you get to be a complete bitch to him. And definitely not on my behalf."

She recoils at that one, and I can tell she's struggling not to snap. In the old days, when we'd fall out as roomies, she'd have yelled by now. Then we'd have been silent for an hour. Then we'd have figured it out. Something about this is different, though. It feels deeper, more layered, more charged.

She exhales through her nose, like she does when she's being principled. "I'm sorry, but you don't know men like I do."

I laugh at that, although it's in no way funny. "Wow, what are you basing that on? Eric Oleksow and TGI Fridays? I've moved on a little since then, Regan. I've had experiences you don't even know ab—"

"I'm basing it on Thatcher."

Everything I was about to say disappears. A blip that drops out on a radar. I stare at her, at the flecks of gold in her brown eyes, searching for crowing or arrogance. But if anything, she just looks sad.

"Trust me," she goes on. "There's a lot you don't know about him."

29

MY MOUTH SLACKENS. What is she saying—she knows *more than I do*? She knows *him*? But they've never even met. She considers herself such an expert, and yet there's nothing she could possibly tell me about Thatcher that I haven't already had to painfully acknowledge. I'm about to tell her I get it—he's repulsive, and who knows what else he's into—when suddenly the whole boat shudders, and with an abrasive grind of metal against grit, I'm thrown hard into Regan's shoulder. We freeze, horrified, as we hear a loud scraping noise from the starboard side.

I scramble up and lean over the railing, trying to see down to the hull, but the whole yacht is listing, and I can't tell if we've hit a rock, run aground, or been bumped by something alive, something huge, under the water.

"What the hell is happening?" Regan shouts, grabbing the back of my jacket. "Be careful! Don't fall in."

"I think he's steered us straight into the reef!" I picture Christopher's torn map, his child-like inability to use that compass. Is there a goddamn hole in the boat? Is seawater flooding into the bedrooms already?

Regan grips my forearm, maybe thinking the same thing. "We're still grinding, we need to shut everything off." Another awful scrape, like nails down a chalkboard.

"Keep watch, hold on to the railing," I shout, reeling back toward the covered cabin, flinging myself in through the door.

Should I just fetch Christopher? But I don't trust him— he's the one who's motored us straight into this nightmare. Beneath me, the hull groans along shingle. We're on a sandbar, I'm almost certain of it, and there's no time to run down and get Desh.

I pivot with indecision, entirely overwhelmed. I don't know what I'm doing; I want to go home. Back to Michigan, where even if I've ruined things, it's familiar and safe. A bad day isn't being hunted, or kidnapped, or sunk. *Ivy*, I hear my dad's calming voice in my head. *You're the best one of us all.* I stop for a second and take a big breath, then step further into the cabin, pull the gear stick to neutral, and kill the engine. The air hums with the sudden absence of sound.

Okay, I think, looking around. Is that better? It doesn't seem like we're drifting, but as I peer at the screen of the depth gauge to see how much water's below us, I hear the tiniest of noises near the stairwell. Something soft. A catch in a throat behind me.

I spin around, expecting it to be Desh or Christopher, but behind me is a ghostly whiteness, and I step backward onto the bench with a gasp.

Lila stands watching me with her arms limp by her sides. Her baggy T-shirt drapes around her in folds like a cadaver's skin.

"Jesus, Lila, you gave me a fright!" I swallow, the light around us uneven and skewed. "Are you okay? Did the jolt wake you?"

"Don't let her in," she replies, hair dark against her cheeks. "You can't let her, don't let her."

"Who?" No reply. I wave my hand in front of her face, but she doesn't register it. She looks automated but upright, like kids I've seen in horror movies, demonically possessed beside the bed in a Victorian nightdress. "Lila, are you asleep? Oh, sweetie, we need to get you back to bed."

Regan fumbles her way into the cabin. "The scraping's stopped. Did you manage—" She pulls up short as I put my finger to my lips. "What's happening? Oh, hey, Lila—"

I shake my head, mouthing *Sleepwalking*. The little girl continues to stare at me, pan faced and vacant.

"She made it all the way up here in that state?" Regan hisses. "Holy crap, Ives, the galley gate's open. Desh was the last one through it. What if we'd still been out by the bow? We'd never have seen her."

I swallow, wishing away the image of Lila's little feet drifting all the way to the swim grid. If she'd fallen in, it would have been hours before we'd even realized. "Let's get her back to bed. Then fetch Desh and see what's happening with the boat."

"We should put Lila in our cabin," Regan whispers. "We can look after her. We'll do a better job of it than Christopher. How did he not hear her get up?"

I agree, then second-guess it. "Wait, though, what if he wakes and Lila's not there? Can you imagine how crazy he'd go?"

"Okay, we can play along, I guess, but I think we should pledge to look out for her, like, *all the time*. She's in real danger. He's so obsessed with stealing her, he's missing every-thing else."

I nod, a pang hitting me when I think about how lonely Lila's been on this boat. How homesick she is. He controls her when she's awake, neglects her when she's sleeping.

"Let's walk her back super carefully," I whisper. "You're not meant to rouse sleepwalkers. Something about the shock to the brain, but also she'll be embarrassed."

Every joint in my body feels rubbery as we inch Lila toward the galley steps like a precious vial we can't drop. Regan goes down a few stairs first, but as she turns, Lila reaches out, grabs for her shoulder. Their heads are at exactly the same height.

"Don't hurt me!" she gasps, her arm like a twig in the folds of her sleeve. "No, Mum, don't do that again."

"*What the hell?*" Regan whispers.

"She's dreaming," I say. "She doesn't mean you."

"No, I know, but what *does* she mean?" In the stairwell, Regan's face is sallow. "Why is she scared of her mom?"

"No!" Lila burrows her head into my side. "Don't let her in!"

"We won't," I reply gently. "You're safe, Lila. It's okay."

She whimpers, an animal in pain, and neither Regan nor I move a muscle. A high-pitched tone has started in my head, as if I've turned up the volume on a bell that's always been ringing. What if I've gotten this all wrong again? I put a hand to my cheek, my skin hot. Is Christopher *not* the bad guy?

"Regan." My voice wobbles. "Maybe he's taken Lila away from her mom for a different reason?"

"Dude, I was just thinking exactly the same thing." Her whisper is intense. "What if *Helen's* the dangerous one?"

I scroll back through everything Lila has told me about her mother. All those extra little details she threw out without meaning to, a whole story taking place in the footnotes. The violent cup-throwing at home. The explosive shouting at school. The Atomic Bomb. Everything slides topsy-turvy. "Is this a *rescue* situation more than a kidnap?"

Regan shakes her head, a fluttering bird in the stairwell. We don't know a single thing for certain. Suddenly, I remember the cryptic message Lila put in that cowrie shell, the one I haven't even asked her about that she raced to deliver at the marina gate. Was it this? *My mother is a wolf at the door. Don't let her in.*

"Why would she call her, though?" Regan whispers, checking that Lila's still totally expressionless. "Why do that if she's scared?"

"Because it's never straightforward. It's her mom. It's messed up." I know this, I know it because I've been there too. At twelve, I exhaled hatred whenever I thought of my mother. She was an agent of chaos in my life. And then I needed her desperately with every breath in.

"Let's go wake Christopher," Regan says, her tone surer about him than I've ever heard it. And I feel that way, too, as if finally we have the missing piece of the puzzle. We move Lila down the stairwell and along the corridor, shadows filtering across his door as we knock on it. Glancing down, Lila stands quietly between us, her face as patient and trusting as a child waiting in line at the library. She's still fast asleep. I reach out, move a strand of her bangs softly from her brow, while inside the cabin, we hear her dad roll over in his bed, then his feet hitting the floor.

30

"BLOODY OATH, where did you find her?" Christopher's hair is a muss of deep sleep. It's close to two a.m., and I realize I've never seen him this late at night before. His cheeks are stenciled dark with stubble.

"She's sleepwalking," Regan gestures toward Lila's bed, and Christopher widens the door quickly and guides Lila in. "She wandered all the way up to the covered cabin."

"Wasn't the gate latched?" His movements are flappy and too fast. He keeps tangling the sheet when he should be smoothing it back. "Oh, my God, did I forget to lock it? I'm so exhausted lately. Just dog-tired. Thank goodness you saw her in time! I can't believe I slept through her leaving. You idiot, Christopher, you stupid bloody—"

"It wasn't you." Regan stops his dark muttering, helps Lila crawl onto her mattress, while he wrings his hands.

"Well, here, let me tuck her in," he says. "Jesus wept."

Lila curls up facing the wall as if it's nothing, as if she's just gotten back from the bathroom. Along her bedside shelf is her little trail of polished shells, still in ascending order. Christopher strokes her head. Once, twice. Leaves his hand hovering there, reverent, as if she's a newborn, his other hand covering his lips.

"It's okay," I say, reaching out and touching his arm. His skin is dry as a husk, slightly reptilian. "You're doing everything you can to protect her. Regan and I have been talking about it. You've already done a lot." He looks at me sharply, pale eyes suspicious. *No*, I want to tell him, *we're on your side. Don't worry, we figured it out.*

"She's my little girl," he says.

"We know." Regan nods. "We get it."

He grabs a fleece, zips it up tight, studying us. Obviously he's not going to admit what he's done, the rules he's broken to save Lila. Not outright, and not to us. But *we're* arriving at it differently—the whole dynamic between us has changed—and I'm hoping he can read it, that he can tell.

"Christopher, there's something else." I touch him again and he jumps. "We had a problem on our shift and were just dealing with it. I think we've hit some kind of sandbar. I've had to shut off the engine."

"You've done what?" His neck tendons jerk as he suddenly listens hard. Has he only just noticed the motor's not running? *Poor man*, I think, *he's gone from deep sleep to this horrible shock.* I still can't even process what could have happened to Lila. Had she gone into the ocean, she'd have died treading water, on her own. There's not a chance in hell we'd have ever found her again. "We've stopped moving? No, that's not an option. I have a job to do."

Regan reaches for my hand, squeezes it. Christopher's alarm is only confirming what we already suspect. He's a father who's terrified his ex-wife will catch up and overpower him, clawing Lila back to whatever trauma he'd intercepted.

"Maybe come up and see?" Regan suggests.

"Right," he says. "Yes. Every problem has a solution." He pushes past us in the doorway, checking back at Lila asleep. "Should I lock her in? In case she sleepwalks again?"

"N-no," Regan and I stammer in unison. Strange that he's asking us. But at least it shows he hasn't been imprisoning her as a habit.

"Shall I stay down here with her?" Regan says. "I don't mind. I mean, we can all come up and latch the gate properly, but maybe it'd be good to make sure she's peaceful?"

He nods gratefully, and as I follow his stumbling gait out to the galley, Regan gives me a small smile. *He's not great in a crisis*, she's saying. But we're alright. We've got this. And it's better that she's rallying a little, that for now we can shelve whatever fight we were having.

In the covered cabin, Christopher starts pressing buttons on the depth gauge, then looking out toward the stern, as if trying to read the lean of the boat. He keeps running his hand through his hair, his movements getting more and more anxious.

"Christ!" he shouts suddenly, wheeling around with his hands on his hips. "What the shitting hell am I supposed to do now?"

I flinch. It's literally the first swear word he's ever uttered, and it sounds so out of place. "Are we totally stuck?"

"Completely!" His voice breaks like a teenager's. "We can't move until the tide changes. We're at the mercy of forces beyond our control, plum in the middle of a bloody great sandbar. Which, by the way, was not on the map."

"Okay, so how long does the tide take?" I ask, one hand outstretched. He needs to calm down. I don't want to be stuck, either, but it's likely only a few hours, and neither Helen nor Thatcher can board the boat. We're on a sandbar, in pitch darkness, in the middle of the Coral Sea. It isn't no-man's-land. We're not about to be ambushed from all sides.

"We're sitting ducks until sunrise." He steps outside, fists tight at the dark horizon. "Three hours? Four? It's not good, not good at all."

"I'll sit up with you," I offer. "Let's hang out until dawn. I won't sleep anyway, I'm too wound up."

Even as I say it, I realize that a few hours ago, I wouldn't have helped Christopher with a thing. But I've discovered a strange kind of unity here, an unlikely bond. The truth is we're running from bad people together. Christopher, Lila, and I are a ragtag bunch of fugitives, and there's no reason at all not to team up.

"Really?" Christopher dips at the knees, amazed at my generosity. "I'd love that. Thank you, Ivy. I'd love the company."

—

For the next couple of hours, the two of us sit in the covered cabin, although Christopher can't really stay still. Every ten minutes, he's out on the deck, checking knots, tightening ropes, readying himself for the moment of escape when it comes. I think of Lila downstairs on her pillow, little upturned nose, quiet snuffly breaths. Regan doesn't come up on deck, so all must be well, even though I'd like the chance to talk to my friend, ask her what she meant by my not fully knowing Thatcher.

Did she just mean generally? Was she being speculative? *If you found photos in his filing cabinet, Ivy, it's pretty likely he has more secrets in other vaults.* I think of the third drawer I didn't open, the laptop I couldn't unlock. She's right—he manipulated and outsmarted me—but I can't face the idea that the Thatcher abyss goes even deeper.

Around four-thirty a.m., pummeled scuffs of pink start to streak the sky. I stand and head onto the deck, which feels slimy underfoot. Heat will soon start to gather, but the dampness of everything is already suffocating, the new day foggy and dense. Regan appears, looking pale and worn out.

"All quiet. She's still sleeping," she tells Christopher, who's standing on the swim grid, dipping to the ankle with each wash of the tide, even though neither of us can see ten feet past the edge. "I latched the stairwell. I need some fresh air."

"That's great. And things up here are improving." He's going for optimism, although his face is jaded and drawn. "The boat's starting to sway again. No critical damage to the keel." His feet disappear into the water, the murky soup of it. "Oh, look, and here's the last of the night watchmen reporting for duty."

I turn to see Desh struggling into his surfy Hawaiian shirt, lines of stomach muscle on view for a few seconds before he does up a button.

"Why didn't anyone wake me?" He seems to direct the question at me, as if it's my fault, or we've all been at a party without him. "I was due on at four. I thought someone would at least come down."

"Didn't we go over this already?" Regan says, joining us at the swim grid. *You're pointless*, she means, and I groan inwardly as Desh scowls. Why is she hell-bent on fighting with him? I get that her nerves are frayed—everyone's are—but she's dejected one minute, lashing out at him the next, and there doesn't seem to be any kind of medium level. I step between them.

"We ran aground," I explain. "We've been stuck here watching the tide."

"We—really?" For a second, it's as if he forgets to be sullen, like there's still a supple, easier version of him underneath all this hard crust. "Can I do anything?"

"You could fetch your speargun." Christopher points at the water around his toes. "Heaps of fish here. You could catch one, make yourself useful."

Desh pauses, although it's unlikely Christopher realizes he's playing into Regan's insult. Then he shakes his head and heads back toward the cabin. I force myself to look away, back out across the water, just as a ridged, swampy curve rises in the water ten feet away. I stare in disbelief as it surfaces in a slow, menacing slither.

"Croc!" Regan screams, tugging Christopher back off the swim grid with such force that he staggers and falls backward. "Ivy, did you see that? It's huge!"

I nod, petrified, just as an almighty thump against the stern throws us all off-balance. Christopher leaps up, and we cluster at the railing in a sudden burst of fear, all of us watching the water. Fog swirls like smoke at its surface.

"Can a saltwater croc break the boat?" Regan voice sounds young, a scared child. "Jesus, Christopher, can it climb up the swim grid?"

Christopher can't seem to answer her. He has both hands on his head, his belly pressed to the metal bar.

"Do something!" I shout. "Get us out of here!"

"I— How?" He licks his dry lips, as fresh out of ideas as we are, and while the three of us brace for the next thump— *Where is the monster? Where has it gone?*—behind us on the port side, out of view, there's a horrible splash of something hitting the water. Something falling from the height of our boat. *Lila.* We all turn at once, a trio of ashen faces.

31

WE STUMBLE TO THE portside edge, bumping into each other in a frenzy, as displaced little droplets of ocean scatter over the deck like dark jewels. I reach the railing with the others, my heart pounding, imagining the top of Lila's head, a fan of hair around it, her arms flailing as she coughs and chokes awake, while a prehistoric hunter cuts up from beneath her with its jaws wide.

"I thought you were watching her!" Christopher yells at Regan, who seems paralyzed.

"She locked the gate—" I volley back, while both he and I shimmy as if we might jump in ourselves, our eyes set on the foam of bubbles, the little dented circle where she must have hit. But when a body surfaces, limbs pedaling, panicked and pencil-straight in the water, it isn't Lila we're looking at. It's Pearl.

I stare in dismay at her ears, flat back, the usual puffball of her fur slick against her as if she's fallen into a vat of grease.

She's paddling for all she's worth—eyes huge, paws splayed, panting frantically—and it can only be a matter of seconds before that crocodile circles back, opens its jaws, drags her down to the deep. It'll happen in a flash. She'll be gone.

"Grab her!" I shout, looking wildly around for a plan, when suddenly Desh shoves me aside and leans over the railing, a long-handled net in his hand.

He doesn't take his eyes off Pearl, his jawline tight as he concentrates, dipping the net underneath her tail. Thank God for him and his steady, unflappable coolness. He got here so fast. I exhale for the first time in a while as he levers Pearl out of the water, brings her deftly back onto the deck.

"Bloody oath, mate, well done," Christopher murmurs, crouching to help him untangle Pearl, whose face is smushed against the netting, everything about her bundled and miserable. "Poor old girl. She must have mistimed a jump or just doddered in."

"What's happening? Why are people crashing around?" We all turn to see Lila standing at the entrance of the covered cabin, a big crease of sleep down one side of her face. She rubs her eyes, gets her balance.

"Pearl took a quick dip." Desh bends with a towel—*Where did he get that from?*—and traps the cat, ruffling her before releasing her out of the net. She hurries away, darts for the sunroom. "But, hey, she's all good. I saved her." He enunciates his last words coldly for Regan as if to say *Who's pointless now?* Her eyes narrow.

"She fell in? Like, just toppled over?" Lila looks puzzled, bending to try and stroke Pearl as she slips past down the galley stairs. "Do cats do that?"

"Yeah, Desh. Do they?" Regan stands opposite him, feet planted, but he pushes past her to look over the railing.

"Are we good, Skipper? Looks like the croc has gone. I can't see it anywhere." He and Christopher strain to check on damage to the keel, but it's lifted from the sandbar enough that it's now fully submerged in water.

"Croc?" Lila's voice is reedy. "What croc?"

"It's okay, it swam off," Desh repeats, heading back to crouch beside Lila, but Regan blocks his path.

"As if you saved anything. This was *your* doing," she says.

His shoulders straighten. He's not much taller than Regan, but he's using all his height now. "What d'you mean?"

"Regan—" I warn, putting my hand on her arm, because I don't understand what she's getting at, either. Is she just pointing out it was *his* mistake with the gate—just now and last night? The blame Christopher threw at her in the heat of the moment might have stung. But it sounds like more than that, as if she thinks Desh had a plan here, and she's determined to expose it.

I've seen her like this before, seen her lock on to an opinion, and argue it against a more likely scenario. Like the time she accused a girl in her lecture group of stealing exam papers the night before midterms. She and Regan had done the bare minimum all semester, and then the girl had suddenly aced the class. *Cheater*, Regan surmised, but when she cornered her classmate in the cafeteria, it was obvious the girl had just smartened up and decided to study. Regan backed down and apologized, of course, but this outburst feels reminiscent. The same fiery need to reveal something, the same knee-jerk vigilantism. And sometimes she doesn't get it right. Pearl's accident was simply that: an *accident*.

"You pushed the cat in," she says to Desh, shaking me off. "So you could run up here and rescue her. You just didn't know about the croc."

"What the hell?" he says, and I feel myself inching to stand alongside him. Regan can't be for real. "Why would you even—?"

"Wait," Lila cuts in, eyes teary as she looks at each of us in turn. "Pearl swam with a saltie? But they're huge! What if she'd been eaten?"

"She wasn't," Desh snaps, and Lila's mouth presses shut.

Christopher holds up both of his hands, his fingers wide. "It's okay, pumpkin. The adults got scared just now, and everyone's recovering. Right, guys? Pearl is safe. Let's all take it down a notch."

"I'm telling you. Look at his face. He's hiding something," Regan says.

I choke out a laugh, the idea is so ridiculous. "That he threw a cat out the window? Can you hear yourself? You're losing the plot."

"Like *you* know what's real and what isn't." She turns on me, dark eyes flashing. "You're crushing so hard on Desh, he could set fire to the whole boat and you'd call it twinkly and romantic."

I gasp. She knows me so well, she can slice to the most vulnerable places. Is it true—is Desh as manipulative as Thatcher? Maybe dangerous? Before I can stop it, an image of Thatcher and me in bed looms into view, his face above mine, the ecstasy in the squeeze of his eyes as he climaxed with both of his hands round my throat. He'd choked me until I was frightened—actually clawing at his fingers to let go—but afterwards, he'd been so sweet, murmuring with his back to me as he drifted toward sleep that I was so sexy, so sophisticated, so unlike other girls my age. *You're a woman, bunny. You make love like a femme fatale.* I'd lain awake on his pillow, smiling in the dark at the specialness of it all. I put my fingertips to my neck, try to will the memory away.

"Wow, Regan." Desh shakes his head beside me, his eyebrows amazed. "Turn on us all, why don't you? Pick us off one by one. Have you ever had a friend you *didn't* sell out?"

"You shut up!" She pushes him, her palm snagging in the opening of his shirt so that the button pings off and scatters away on the deck.

"Get the hell off me!" he shouts. When I try to pull her to one side, Regan yanks her elbow out of my grip.

"Stop!" Lila cries. "Guys, stop it!"

Christopher steps in between us all then. "NOBODY PUSHED ANYONE INTO THE WATER!" he booms, the unexpectedness of it somehow stunning the whole boat into silence. Regan wipes her mouth with the back of her hand.

"We don't have time for this," Christopher continues, pointing hard at the swim grid. "There's a bloody great crocodile out there. He hasn't gone; he's still circling us. Do you *want* him to find his way onto the boat?"

"I'm ready." Desh straightens his shirt, seething. "Let's go. But for the record, she's completely batshit. Stay the hell away from me, Regan."

"Not a problem," she says.

32

REGAN MOVES TO THE railing with her back to us, the atmosphere on deck heavy with hurt. It feels like the seconds after a schoolyard fight: the crowd has stopped chanting, and the two kids swept up in it are now just breathless, on the verge of tears. *Jesus*, I think, *this is awful*. Regan is behaving like a child. Desh pushed a cat into the ocean just so he could rescue it? That's literally something a child or a mad person would say. And meanwhile, here's Lila witnessing conflict after conflict, none of them resolved.

Christopher herds Lila inside, and I turn to Desh, who's standing to my right with his shirt hanging open. He looks upset, a long way from a cold, calculating liar, and I'm about to suggest we get to work—break the mood, busy ourselves, get off this sandbar—when something on his chest catches my eye.

"What happened there?" I ask, pointing at three angry welts that have risen on his pec, each one pinpricked and beaded with crimson. Regan didn't scratch him. No, those claw marks aren't human.

He covers the spot I'm staring at. "Pearl scratched me, but . . . but it was earlier. When I first woke up. I must have startled her—I didn't know she'd snuck into my room overnight."

He shifts his weight from one foot to the other, scans the deck as if trying to locate the missing button. *No*, I think, my stomach sinking. *Don't be this guy. Don't be all the things Regan has told me.*

"I haven't seen Pearl lash out. Why would she scratch you?"

"No, I know, but I kind of rolled on her, and she . . . well, she went nuts. But this was before. She wasn't even in my cabin when I went back down to fetch my speargun."

"What speargun?" I ask, my tone flat, because all he came back with was the net and a towel. And how did he know he needed that? My head starts to pound, and I desperately want to sit down.

"My— It's downstairs. Under my bed. I heard you guys shouting, so I came back up."

"Liar, liar." Regan turns at the railing. "*Liar.*"

She shoulders her way past us and strides toward the cabin.

"Ivy." Desh looks so sad—so alone—and all the aloofness has gone out of him, as if he's genuinely reaching for me, and his standoffishness yesterday was just a glitch in his system. "Honestly. I wouldn't hurt a soul."

And I want to believe him, want more than anything to get back to the easygoing fun of him, the kindness he showed me when I was seasick, the zap of electricity I felt whenever our skin touched. Deep down, I still can't believe he could be threatening, and the cat-throw-rescue scenario is bananas even as a theory, but then I hear Regan's voice in my head: *Like* you *know what's real and what isn't.*

I just nod and head toward the cabin, too, my heart dull, my eyes stinging with exhaustion. I need time to think.

Regan is waiting by the galley sink. "You get why he did it, right?" The question lands like a pounce. She knew I'd follow her.

"No, Regan. I don't get anything."

She kicks her heel against a lower cupboard in a steady, irritable beat. "To impress you, obviously. To be the great savior. He wants to be the hero again." She waits for me to agree with her, but nothing about that idea seems rational. "Wow, you're so blind to it all."

I take a deep breath of damp air, prickles of anger starting to rise in me now. "Yeah, he's so into me that he'd shove a live animal into the ocean, where it could drown." She can't possibly miss my sarcasm. "Because I'd find that so impressive."

"No, but the *rescuing* would be. He's all about ego! Why can't you see that?"

Because the guy wears faded old clothes. Goes everywhere barefoot. He doesn't seem to care in the least bit about image. Why can't *she* consider that there might be a more innocent explanation?

"Plus, he found that net in point-four of a second," Regan presses, while I chew at a ragged piece of skin near my thumbnail. "And he knew exactly where Pearl was when he ran back on deck. Like, did he even *look*?"

I try to remember Desh standing at the portside railing, but it's true. He was never there. "Maybe he just thinks fast. He trained as a paramedic for a while. Did you know that? People who want to hurt others don't generally seek careers in—"

She steps forward from the counter, her face tight with frustration. "What is the matter with you? You're defending him when you've known him for, like, barely a week."

Because he's solid, I think. He's *Desh.* The nice guy, the green-eyed grinner, the laid-back boy who exudes charisma. He's not a person who's cruel to cats. He can't be. He's not.

"So? You're attacking him," I dig into past grievances, "when the night before last, you stayed up stargazing with him, giggling at all of his jokes. You brought your A-game, Regan, and he still didn't fall for you. He picked *me.* It must be blowing your mind."

Her eyebrows shoot up; she wasn't expecting that one. But I'm sick of the way she assumes leadership, acts so sure the whole time, foists opinions on me because I'm usually so malleable. Not anymore!

"Is that seriously what you think? That I'm *jealous*?" She spits out the word like it's rubbery old gristle.

"Aren't you?" We're chest to chest now, mirroring each other's crossed arms, neither of us budging an inch.

"No, Ivy, I'm trying to help you! Do you think you're the only one who's ever been tricked or hurt?"

I curl my lip at her, roll my eyes. *As if that's happened to you,* I'm saying. The world's her giant benefactor. Since we met, she hasn't had to recover from a single rejection or betrayal.

She sees my scorn, swears heavily under her breath, and sweeps away from me toward our cabin.

"I don't want your help, thanks!" I shout after her. "Or your guidance. Wherever I go, there I am!"

She replies with the clanging slam of our cabin door, and then the fumbling hook of the lock she manufactured. For a minute I stand still, watching the empty corridor, a little surprised I just did that. But something inside me snapped. I have to figure this out, once and for all—by myself and *for myself*—to prove that not all my instincts are garbage.

Once I've checked that Desh is still up on deck, I tiptoe down to his cabin.

If I've learned anything lately, it's that creeps always leave some kind of trail. They can't help it. Even the cleverest ones leave clues. As I think that, I see a flash of that girl's face in Thatcher's horrible collection—Veronika unconscious on her back, knees staged to expose the innermost pink of her flesh—but then she recedes again, steps back into my mind's shadows.

I close the door behind me. Desh's room smells like a mechanics' shop. The engine is in the corner to my left, leaving only a tiny space for a single bed, unmade, a tangle of wrinkled sheets. One metal cabinet beside it, bearing a novel, a flashlight, a pen. The window above his bunk is open as wide as it'll go, but that's okay. It doesn't prove anything, except that he's straining for a breeze.

I pick up the novel—*Heart of Darkness*, wouldn't have expected that—and notice he has a photograph tucked inside as a bookmark. I tease it out to see it's of Desh with a girl, both of them young teenagers. Desh's arms aren't as developed, he's thinner, but the grin is the same. They're sitting on a blue Vespa in bright sunlight, the cliff-top road behind them dusty, the girl in the forefront with long tanned legs. She's laughing at the camera, holding one hand out as if blocking it, and while I squint at her features, I'm struck by how similar they are to mine. Brown hair, cut into a simple bob at her jawline. Brown eyes. Straight teeth. She's fun. I can feel it through every pixel.

He looks happy, I think, trying hard to resist a twinge of jealousy. Happy and carefree and full of youth, and I wish for a minute I'd known him sooner, before he'd gotten guarded, and stopped wanting to talk about the people he cares about in his life. This girl doesn't look related to him, but she's important, obviously. A sweet glimpse of his past. I put the photo back, wondering what her name is, and start to thumb through the pages when the engine beside the bunk fires up, the whir of belts startling.

Upstairs there's action, and above me, I can hear the tread of someone moving fast through the covered cabin. *Shit*, I think, riffling quickly through the final pages. Something papery slides out and even though I don't have time—I should get out of here, whoever's coming is in the galley now—I unfold a faded newspaper article. This is it! The answer I'm looking for. I know in my gut that whatever's in here will tell me everything I need to know about Desh.

My heart is hammering as I skim. Most of the first paragraph is missing, torn halfway across as if someone didn't like what it said. But the headline is still there, dark and thick-lettered on the page.

Investigation Continues into Death Of Local Girl

I read it again. And a third time, as if it's written in a foreign language. Below the headline is an image of Vespa girl.

Hair longer now. Bone structure a year or two more sculpted. *Ali June Powers* reads the caption. *June 3, 1992–January 10, 2010.* I hold my breath, read the next sentence.

Police in Suva announced today that Desh William Turner, 17, has been arrested in connection with the death of—

The footsteps are coming down the stairs, and I scramble the book back to the cabinet, the article shoved into a random section. *Death of local girl?* I lurch to the door and listen as he knocks on our cabin.

"You're needed on deck," he mumbles. Regan doesn't answer.

This boy—this man—has a whole history of violence locked tight in a vise. *He was arrested for the death of a girl? Can that be real?* My head fizzes with white noise. Twenty minutes ago, I couldn't even imagine he'd hurt Pearl. I feel the last scrap of faith slide away from me, the final fragment of trust sputter and go out.

I hold my breath, praying to God he won't come in here. What would I do if he did? What would *he* do? I picture his hands round my throat, feel the hateful squeeze of them. Is that what he's like? A master of disguise. A hunter. A guy just like Thatcher.

Eventually his footsteps trudge back toward the galley. Only then do I crumple, slide down to the floor, my knees knocking, sobs lost in the drone of the engine.

33

BY THE TIME I go up top, we've been motoring for a while and Christopher's just cut the engine again. He's dropped anchor and is lowering the tender into the water with Desh's help. Regan stands watching them, stony-faced. What the hell is happening? Why are we stopping? Four hundred yards away I can make out a hazy scrub of land, mostly palm trees, a pale strip of deserted sand. No dock, but the dots of a few people, the fronts of squat buildings behind the trees. We're at a town? A tiny beach enclave? It's as if Christopher agreed to get to Cairns as quickly as possible, then decided to do nothing of the sort.

"Hey, what's going on?" I feel swamped, and this latest rolling wave of calamity will sink me.

Christopher turns. "There you are! We're low on gas." He pauses, his face apologetic, or perhaps he's sensing a metaphor. "We just need to fill a couple of containers to tide us over to Cairns. There's no jetty here, but we'll be quick. Twenty minutes, tops."

I don't nod, can't seem to move my face muscles. I don't
want to be on land, don't want to be on the boat. I'm done.
A rat giving up in a trap.

"It's an F1 pit stop," Desh says, attempting a quick flash of
a grin as he teases out ropes behind Christopher. *Don't talk to
me*, I want to tell him. *I've been in your cabin.*

I'd watched enough TV dramas, read enough true crime
to know that killers keep trophies to remind themselves of
their moment of power. That elusive second of omnipotence
when they're unstoppable, siphoning a life away like fuel into
their own tank. Usually the mementos are jewelry or panties;
sometimes even fingers or hair. But was Desh that kind of
monster? Jesus, did he have other things stowed in his room?
I'd run from there as soon as I could, sat in the bathroom
weeping, wondering what the hell he'd done to that girl.

2010 was a full decade ago. Had he been convicted, gone
to jail? It occurs to me that he might just be freshly out, that
this trip was his first taste of freedom. The working around
the world, the dive boats, the paramedic training, being a
chef: it was all probably lies. Why wouldn't it be? He'd
refused to share so much information that any detail he'd
given seems unreliable.

"Are you going to shore?" Regan is clearly pissed with me.
Her question is gruff and she's not maintaining eye contact.

"I-I don't know," I stutter. I am aware that I owe her an
apology, but dread telling her what I've found out. "Are you?"

"Christopher suggested I get a new phone," she says flatly,
warning me not to contradict him. "And there are only four
seats in the tender."

"Is Desh going?" I ask quickly.

"Fuck knows. Ask him yourself. You don't need me, remember?"

She moves away and I regret everything I said to her in the galley, all the ways I took it too far. I *do* want her help. I *do* need her guidance. But it's so humiliating to admit that every single guy I've picked has been worse than the last. I've gone from disloyal to predatory to "arrested in connection." What *is* the matter with me? Again and again, I can't imagine the destructiveness in people. I'm like a child, continuing to press my hand to the stove. I couldn't even understand my own mother, even when she tried to explain why she cheated, ruined everything about the home life we'd all known. *One day, you'll see* was all she could offer me. *You'll do things, too, that you don't anticipate. Have impulses you can't resist.*

She was wrong, though. We always have a choice. We steer toward things or away. Thatcher chooses to buy porn of young women, names them all as if they're pets. Desh was arrested for *killing a girl*—

"Are you okay?" Lila interrupts my dark thoughts. I just shake my head, say nothing, try to give her a smile. Every cell in my body feels numb.

"Okay, Flint Beach, guys." Christopher rubs his hands together, as if enthusiasm's still a thing. "It's tiny, a dot on the map, seven hours south of Cairns by boat. I doubt anything ever happens here."

"But there are roads in and out," Regan says, her brow knitted. *Lila has called her mom*, she means, but this stop was unexpected. Lila couldn't have told Helen about it. Beside me, she fidgets with her sleeves. Poor kid, how tangled she must be, wondering if her mom is close by. She'd run toward her, part elated, part unsure, and as sad as that is to imagine, we still can't tell Christopher about the phone call. He'd be furious, and Lila's so threadbare already.

"Dirt roads. Potholed, unpaved. This town won't get much for visitors. Nobody would think of it," Christopher says. Including my ex, he means, and I grimace. Could Desh have told Thatcher we're stopping here? He'd have known the fuel supply levels, and since he's a fucking ongoing gray area, who knows what connections he really has in New York, whose side he's really been on. Is getting off here the worst idea ever? Or if we spend twenty minutes on shore in a boondock outpost, would anyone spot us anyway? I wish I could ask Regan, but she's studiously ignoring me.

"I'll stay back." Desh looks around at everyone except Regan. "You three go. Ivy and I can hang out, fish, catch something for d—"

"No." My voice comes out thick and flat as a slap. He recoils, and Regan notices, surprised, but no way, no way am I staying alone on this yacht with him.

Christopher clears his throat. "Do you mind holding the fort, Desh? You're my best boat guy. Ivy most likely wants to be with Regan."

Desh shrugs and withdraws to the gunwale, leans against it. I can't look at him, but I'm sure he's staring at me. The whole left side of my face feels hot.

"So, team of four," Christopher says, turning to us, and I nod blandly. "Fetch your stuff. We'll leave in five minutes."

Regan and I head down to our cabin together, although neither of us speaks. We dig in our backpacks silently for our wallets. I want to sit down on Regan's bed, but she's busy pulling out a bucket hat, giving it a sniff. *Reags*, I want to say, *tomorrow we fly home.*

On land, it'll be better. No one will find us. And even if Desh has somehow sold us out, one person can't overpower four. We'll get some respite, calm down, get twenty minutes of peace.

And I'll dig for the facts. Find out what the hell Desh did to Ali June Powers.

34

THE TOWN LOOKS DRAB as we get closer in the tender. There's a tiny beach, and beyond the palm trees, the few shop fronts I can see are faded. It's like an abandoned set from fifties Hollywood, peeling and sunblasted. Everything's a parched pale blue.

Lila sits next to me in the middle of the boat, Christopher manning the engine, Regan up front. We're low in the water, which is filthy. Maybe the locals dump garbage nearby, or gasoline, because the whole surface is streaked like spilled oil. Even so, Lila trails her fingers, making little shimmering tracks as we putt-putt along, but I pull her arm in, tuck it under mine in my lap. That crocodile was only a few hours ago, and I don't know what's under the surface. Of anything right now. Or anyone.

I look back at the *Alone at Last*, see Desh gripping the starboard railing, and wonder what he'll do while we're gone. What he'll look through, what he'll touch. Will he really spend the time fishing? He lifts his hand in a wave, and quickly I face forward again. He's too at home with traveling, too sun-kissed, too beachy to be fresh out of jail. But whatever the Ali story is, he's kept it so *hidden*. For the tenth time in a row, I wish Flint Beach was Cairns, a bigger center with an easier means of escape, an airport, a finish line.

"What will you do on shore, Reags?" I ask.

"Call home," she says without turning around.

Right, I think. Not ready to talk to me yet, since her desolation's equal to mine. If there's a rock bottom, she's there too. I drove her toward it.

"I'm going to find Wi-Fi," I tell her, even if the conversation's one-sided, and my quest is now different from hers. I've turned on my cell, but so far have no signal. It's information I want, and in twenty minutes, I can get a lot.

"Is anything even open?" Lila asks quietly. "It looks deserted. I don't like this place."

I put my arm around her, and we huddle in the humid fug of midday, the air hot at the back of my throat like I'm breathing through a hairdryer. She's right: it is eerily quiet here, and the closer we get to the beach, the more rotten it smells. Tinny, like old fish heads, dried seaweed, brine. I cover my mouth with my sleeve, scan the beach parking lot for signs of shiny rental cars. Is anyone waiting for us? I squeeze my hands into fists. *Be rational*, I think. This is a nowhere town. A dot on the map. Nothing ever happens here.

The tender scrapes as we reach the beach, and Christopher shuts off the engine, raises it out of the water while we clamber out. The sand is gritty underfoot as I follow Regan and Lila toward a tattered set of steps, all of us holding our shoes.

I get that strange urge to sway again, as if land is too compact for my legs, too dense to stand on. We pause by the lowest step, where a dog has defecated in a coil next to a discarded beer can.

"Okay, not a town to buy postcards in," Christopher says, stepping over the mess and urging us upward. "Let's get in and get out."

We emerge onto the main drag, and I scan left and right. The street looks empty, just a scattering of rusted old pickups, a rained-on smudged sandwich board, a dog asleep in a doorway. If someone's watching us right now, they're well concealed. All the same, I take footsteps gingerly as if there are trip wires, something set to explode.

"Lila, you're coming with me. We're heading for gas." Christopher holds up his two empty containers. "Meet us back at the tender in twenty."

I watch them go, a sharp tweak of anxiety pulling at me. Should we all stay together? Regan doesn't seem as apprehensive. Already she's stepped away and is standing beside a pay phone with an orange Telstra hood, dandelions crowding the base.

She unhooks the receiver, wipes the mouthpiece with her sleeve. "So, I'm, like, calling my mom now."

"Good. Yeah, go ahead." There's an awkward pause, during which I realize she means *Get lost*. She wants me out of earshot so she can vent about me. *That's fair*, I think miserably. I did call her a jealous narcissist. Mostly I want to say sorry for that, to explain everything and catch her up, but I know Regan. She needs space from me first. "I'll walk down a little ways, see if there's internet."

"Don't go too far." The care in her voice sounds reluctant, her face drained, and I wonder if I really have blown it this time, pushed her so hard that she won't come back. "I mean, I'm sure it's fine, but . . ."

We nod at each other grimly, the way people do when they're both on their very last nerve.

I take off down the street, scanning, scanning, past a bakery that's not open, even though it's past twelve. A dive shop with a mannequin in the window wearing nothing but a mask. Further down, I spot a small corner store with its door open, the curved lines of a Wi-Fi sign on the glass. I glance back at Regan, who's pressing buttons forty feet away, and gesture that I'm going inside. She gives me an expressionless thumbs-up. The only other sign of life on the street is one scruffy guy on a bench out front of the store, sitting hunched forward, eating something that's dripping.

I peer inside. There's a long counter stretching away into shadow, with an old cash register on it and pepperoni sticks in a jar that's foggy and moist with heat. Flies buzz. I can't see an owner, or what's further down at the back, but there's definitely internet access. A hand-scrawled note on the window reads: *Buy Drink, get On Line.*

I step inside. I have to do this. Have to find out what Desh did to that girl.

As my eyes adjust to the dimmer light, I notice shelves along the wall littered with cigarette packets, lotto tickets, candy. An old metal fan is whirring, the breeze limp against my shoulders as it makes its turn.

"Hello?" I call out toward the back office, where a television is playing. I can hear the cackle of canned laughter.

An ancient office chair on bad springs rolls into view, a woman in it holding a cigarette, with a huge flowered muumuu hooked high on her veiny knees. "Wi-Fi, my duck? Or are you after a pie?"

"No, yes, Wi-Fi is good."

"Five dollars for ten minutes. Set the timer so everyone's honest." She points at a white kitchen timer with a dial, on a desk in front of a sole computer monitor. The screen is dusty, and the machine looks twenty years old at least. I can just use my phone. I pull out a plastic lawn chair, sit down, log in from the instructions on the wall, then swivel the dial so it ticks. I don't need creature comforts, I think. Just details. I'd pay fifty bucks for ten minutes if I had to. Deep down, I'm still hoping there's some context, the second half of the torn newspaper article, something that'll clash less with all the feelings I've had for Desh. While Google loads on my screen, nothing new dings to divert me toward Thatcher.

I type in *Ali Powers, 2010, Suva*. The search wheel spins. Eventually a page loads, several headlines blurring for me against the white screen. All of them are about a court case, and I taste sourness in my mouth as I swallow. Prickles of sweat start to form at the nape of my neck as I hover my forefinger over the first link.

ALI POWERS' DEATH ACCIDENTAL, TURNER BOY'S INVOLVEMENT A "MOMENTARY LAPSE OF CONTROL"

I'm about to tap the headline, my grip on the cell phone tight, when I'm aware of a silhouette in the computer screen's grimy reflection, feel the sudden presence of someone behind me.

"How ya going, Ivy?"

I freeze, then spin around in my seat.

Blake Coleman leans against the shop counter holding a Popsicle stick, his teeth stained blue as if he's rinsed them in ink. I shift, trying to stand, and the plastic legs of the lawn chair warp.

"Blake, what are . . . what are you doing here?" *How does he know my name?*

He smiles, wags his Popsicle stick at me. "I knew yous'd show up eventually."

BLAKE COLEMAN
RECORDED INTERVIEW
Date: January 10, 2020
Location: Cairns, Northern QLD
Conducted by Officers from the Queensland Police,
Far Northern Region

POLICE: Blake, can we talk more about your job?
BC: I told you. I'm retired.
POLICE: You say that, but it appears you have an
          offshore bank account.
BC: Do I? That's going to be hard to prove.
POLICE: And a company affiliated with you called
          Salty Dog Sails, through which you
          financed your boat.
BC: Fishing company. For fun. I do charters.
          Sunset tours.
POLICE: How well do you know Helen Farris? Did
          she ever sign up for a sunset tour?
BC: Don't think so. The name doesn't ring
          a bell.
POLICE: Helen's daughter, Lila Farris, has just
          admitted that her father smuggled her out
          of Hobart under cover of night. He was
          trying to get her away from trouble at
          home. Or to be more specific, Lila said—on
          record—that he was trying to get her away
          from her mother.
BC: Okay. [Pause.] Sorry, I don't know why I'm
          meant to be interested in any of that.

POLICE: Did Helen Farris hire you to find them?

BC: No comment.

POLICE: Did she wire you money for that purpose?

BC: No comment.

POLICE: This is a homicide case. We've had an arm
          wash up on the beach, a butchered corpse
          in the water—

BC: So, why aren't you interviewing Desh
          Turner? He *offed a girl* when he was seven-
          teen. When he was drunk and claimed he
          couldn't control himself, or whatever it was
          he said. I told you this, I put it right into
          your hands. You can't even follow the
          easiest leads.

POLICE: We're following several. One of them is you.

BC: [Audible sigh.] Go ahead, check my emails
          and phone records. There'll be nothing
          about Helen Farris in there. Or ask her! Put
          a polygraph on her or something. Have any
          of you wizards thought of that yet?

POLICE: Thanks for the tip, Blake. What if we put
          one on you?

BC: Go ahead. Fill your boots.

POLICE: Let's go back to the night of January 6th,
          and the party aboard the *Alone at Last* in
          Flint Beach.

BC: Are you listening at all? I told you before,
          it *wasn't* a party. It was heavy drinking.

POLICE: How would you know that without having
          been present?

BC: I saw the tall girl buying the booze. She
           looked like her life was on fire. If you ask
           me, she was drinking to put it out.
POLICE: Where did you see her? And when?
BC: I was in Flint Beach when they showed up.
POLICE: And you didn't see Helen Farris later the
           same night, boarding the *Alone at Last*?
           While people were distracted and . . .
           drinking heavily?
BC: Not to my recollection.
POLICE: You didn't assist her with this? Take her—
           or a man she might have traveled from
           Hobart with—over there on your paddle
           board once darkness fell?
BC: Jeez, you guys are inventive. You should get
           an agent, write for the movies.
POLICE: Blake Coleman, we believe you hunted the
           crew of the *Alone at Last* and helped pre-
           cipitate the violent events in question.
BC: [Silence.]
POLICE: We also believe that Christopher Farris—or
           a member of his crew—attacked Helen
           Farris's male companion when they discov-
           ered him on board, and a fatal altercation
           ensued.
BC: Are you arresting me? I don't remember
           being read my rights.
POLICE: Once Forensics confirms that Helen
           Farris's DNA is on Christopher's boat or
           yours—blood spatter, fingerprints, hair

follicles, anything—you'll be arrested for aiding and abetting a felony. Unless you just want to cut to the chase right now, and tell us the truth?

BC: [Laughter.] You fellas have some wild imaginations. Let me know when you get your hands on an actual fact.

POLICE: We'll speak soon, Blake. Interview terminated at 3:17 p.m.

35

"FLINT BEACH IS A BEAUTY. I always drop by." Blake watches as I stand, edging in front of my computer screen. "Such a shithole, completely collapsed, but not hiding it. Not apologizing." He picks at a molar with his Popsicle stick. "What are *you* doing here?"

My smile feels wobbly. "Not much." All this time I was fixated on Thatcher and Helen, I'd completely forgotten about Blake and his vacation schedule. *Flint Beach is the end of the line*, he'd said, but holidaymaker or not, something about his presence feels weirdly unnerving. I don't know him at all, and I don't want him to know me. "Christopher says nothing ever happens in Flint Beach."

"Christopher's not looking properly."

Our eyes lock, when suddenly the kitchen timer behind me goes off and I jump, fumbling to shut it off and shove my phone in my pocket. When I turn back, Blake's grinning at me with those lurid teeth.

"So, how's the trip been, since yous all ditched me and scarpered?"

"No, we . . . I don't know what happened there." Desperately I look for the shop owner so I can pay and leave, but she's disappeared from her chair. "I think Christopher's just a guy who likes to keep moving."

"Oh, I know he is."

I hesitate, confused by his confidence, while he tosses the Popsicle stick toward a garbage can, watches it bounce off the rim, then doesn't bend to pick it up.

"He has a lot on his plate," I say. Who the hell is this guy anyway? What does he know about the risks Christopher's taken, the lengths to which he's gone for his child? We *all* have a lot on our plate, not that Blake Coleman cares. Before, I'd thought he was kind of a sad sack, but now he seems like a bully with a chip on his shoulder. And he's ruined the only time I had to find out about Desh. As soon as I leave the store, I'll lose the Wi-Fi signal. *A momentary lapse of control. An accident.* Whatever Desh had done, it wasn't on purpose. *Stop, Ivy,* I hear Regan's voice in my head. *Stop working so hard to decipher it. Any instincts you have steer you wrong.*

I pull ten dollars from my wallet, tuck it under the computer mouse. "I have to go now. Have a good trip back to . . ." *Where was he from?* He doesn't fill in the blank. "Wherever. Enjoy your time hanging out in the shithole."

"You're leaving already? But you only just got here," he whines, so nonchalant and pleased with himself that it's all I can do not to punt the garbage can into his shin.

"We're not hanging around," I say.

Blake moves away from the counter, yawning into a stretch

that's about to block my path. But this jerk is the least of my worries right now. I sigh and step sideways, just as a new shadow in the doorway alters the light. Regan, clutching a brown paper bag to her chest.

"Ivy? Ivy, quick we—" But then Blake turns and Regan pulls up short, as if he's another dog turd that needs stepping over. "*You're* here?"

"See? It's all happening. I always meet the most interesting people in Flint Beach."

I receive his message with a sneer, and Regan matches it. She tightens her grip around the bag, which clearly contains a bottle of something. "Whatever. Let's go, Ivy. Christopher will be waiting."

"Bye, then." Blake leans lazily against the shop counter. "Best regards to Christopher."

Once we're out in the street, Regan grabs my hand, picks up the pace. I look over my shoulder. Blake hasn't followed us out.

"That was awkward. His trip ends here; he's turning around," I say. "Are you okay? Can we slow down for a second?" She doesn't answer, just keeps up a near jog.

"Regan, stop." I wrench my fingers free of hers as we near the steps to the beach. "I have to tell you something." She halts stiffly. "Look, I'm really sorry about earlier. You were just trying to protect me, and I shouldn't have—"

"It's fine," she says tightly, grimacing for a second, as if my apology's making it worse. "I'm past that. Let's just get back to the boat."

"But I should never have called you a bad friend," I press, wondering why she's so agitated. Christopher won't leave without us if we're a couple of minutes late. "Or accused you of being jealous. It was super uncalled for. You see things I don't, and you call people out on it. And you're right about people having secrets, you're right, and I respect that about you—I mean, honestly, maybe *I'm* the jealous one. You're, like, the bravest person I know, and everything you do just . . . lands."

"It really doesn't." She coughs the sentence out in a borderline sob. "And I'm really not."

I pause, drop the Desh revelation for a second, bewildered by how upset she is. "Did you get through to your mom? Is everything okay?" She gives me a look of such complete devastation that she doesn't even resemble herself. "What, Regan? What is it?"

"On the boat," she says, moving rigidly toward the steps. "Not here."

I follow her, wondering how badly her phone call home could have gone, then stop dead at the top step, looking down at the beach below. The tender sits empty and unattended where we left it, the sky behind it thunderous and black. Where the hell are Christopher and Lila? What time is it? Surely twenty minutes have gone by.

"Oh, no," I breathe. "I knew we shouldn't have split up!"

"Bloody gas station's closed," we hear Christopher shout to our left. "Bloody owner's stuck a sign to the door!"

We whirl around to see him and Lila crossing the sand, Christopher waving what must still be two empty gas cannisters in the air. As we meet at the bottom of the steps, I can see sweat at his hairline.

"*Gone Fishing*," Lila adds, looking at my face and then Regan's. "I thought that was only in cartoons. What's wrong?"

"Nothing." I try not to snap, but clearly she doesn't understand the gravity of the situation. "Is there only one gas station in town? What time is the guy coming back?"

"Locals say four if we're lucky." Christopher grips the back
of his neck, stares out at the our boat in the distance. "But
there must be a mechanic shop, a hardware store, something."

Regan's voice strains as she's drowned out by a rumble of
thunder. "Can we keep going and just stop somewhere else
before Cairns?"

Christopher shakes his head. "Not without spare gas. We
don't want to get stranded. I can make a run to the boat, get
Desh, bring him back here while we figure this out."

"No," I say hurriedly. Whatever happened to Ali, I'm
happy to keep my distance from him for a while longer.
"Let's not waste fuel. He's fine. We can just wait in the shade
together until four if we have to."

"Blake Coleman's here." Regan kicks at a loose piece of
driftwood, spinning it into the sea. "You'll probably run into
him, Christopher."

"Blake—Coleman? I thought we'd lost him." He glances
quickly at Lila. "You girls didn't tell him anything, did you?
Or invite him over again?"

"God, no," I say. "And don't worry, his trip's done. We
won't see him again. He's not on our list of problems." I bite
my lip. "Christopher, can I talk to you privately for a
second—"

But just then, Regan pulls on my arm, stress mottling her
face. "Ives, can we chat? Let's go somewhere, just you and me."

"Oh . . . really?" Whatever's upset her is starting to seep
out, and she doesn't even know about Desh yet. "Sure, we

can do that. We'll find a bar, there has to be one. Is that okay, Christopher—where will you guys be?"

"We'll come find you if we come up with an idea. Won't we, Lila?" He puts his arm around her shoulders, but she looks slightly forlorn, like she's drawn the short straw. "Otherwise, be back here at the tender at four. I don't want to waste more time looking for you."

I nod. Regan has already turned and is heading up the beach, on a mission. What is going on with her? I run after her, jog up the stone steps.

"Okay?" I say, joining her on the street, looking around for a bar to hide out in. "Just you and me. And, seriously, I'm sorry for being an idiot before."

She smiles, but her eyes don't. Together we cross the road, turning left down the sidewalk this time. But she's not walking beside me; her strides are fast and long, almost mechanical.

"Do you need to eat?" I ask, and she stops, although she doesn't seem to have heard my question.

"I'm more of an idiot than you."

For a second, I'm caught off guard. "Why? Have *you* gotten involved with a college professor, stolen his stuff, and made him chase you, then had a crush on a guy with a hidden pas—"

Suddenly she grips my forearm, her thumb pressing hard into my tendons. "Thatcher's not chasing you."

"What do you—? Ow, Reags, you're hurting me." I push the clamp of her fingers away.

"It's not you he's after," she says quietly. "It's me."

36

WE FIND THE ROYAL, a bar that's almost empty, the metal sign above the door creaky with rust. Sitting opposite each other in a booth against the backdrop of a loud Aussie Rules football game, the only other customer is an old guy at the bar, him and the barman both ignoring us, transfixed by the screen.

I feel sick. "Let's just rest quietly for a minute. Get our bearings." I smile, trying to look brave, even though I can't handle the thought that Thatcher's touched her, or been near her in any way. She's always hated him, been so disgusted, but the fact that she has her *own reasons* for that makes me want to both weep and throw up at the same time.

"Can you tell me what happened?" I ask gently, trying hard not to picture him here in the booth with us, whispering with his lips brushing her earlobe, fingertips where her neck meets her spine.

Her eyes swim with tears, her gaze broken and sad. The barman arrives at the side of the table, mumbles something and waits, clicking the end of his pen. I finally look up at him. He's about sixty. Sunburned. His T-shirt has a sloth on it asleep in a tree.

"We just need alcohol," I tell him, although I didn't even hear the question. "Stat."

He checks our faces hurriedly, the way servers do when they realize they've landed in the middle of a problem. "Righto. Two schooners of four ex?"

I nod and he walks away, returning with beers that he sets down gingerly in front of us, mouth clamped, as if trying to withdraw without getting involved. Once he's gone, we sit in silence for a minute. Neither of us touches our drinks.

"I'm such a coward," she says finally, hanging her head. "All this time, I let you think this was your mess. I've done everything wrong."

"Regan, you're not . . . I don't . . . Whatever's happened, just tell me. Did he hurt you? I can't bear it. I'll kill him, I swear to God." Another slurry of nausea passes through me, but I clamber to move around and sit next to her.

"No, stay there," she says. "If you hug me, I'll lose it, and I won't get this out." She presses her palms to her eyes, hiding her face from me, takes a deep quivery breath. "It started the summer after our first year, really. For me, it did. We were done school, but I didn't want to go home. New York was bigger and better than San Fran."

"You were with Thatcher the summer after freshman year?!" *Whatever happened, it went on for a while.* I stare at her, trying not to look so horrified, realizing how the tables have turned. I'd gone back to Michigan that freshman summer. Regan had stayed, gotten a job in a cool clothing store.

"No, but . . . That summer was awesome. I made money, people let me style them, and the owner of the boutique wanted my input on everything. When sophomore year started and you came back, college wasn't working for me anymore. I was jumpy, unfocused, impatient. I never even wanted NYU—it was my mom's thing—and I felt stuck, couldn't wait to get out into the world." She frowns, mad at herself. "I created a gap, a weak link."

"But then you landed that modeling contract. After Christmas. Your golden ticket out. You were barely in the city after that." She lowers her hands, and I see her crumpled face. "Oh, my God. That's not why you left. What the hell did he do?"

In a flash, I see Thatcher claiming her for his own in some way, his hands tracing the softness of her skin. Has she been to his loft? Does she know every detail that I do? The soft music on his Sonos, the dish towel over one shoulder, the bourbon, the couch, the seduction. But surely she was too streetwise to ever fall for his bullshit? Maybe he slipped unseen through the door of our residence, watched her asleep, his breath on her, poltergeist-close. He'd all but salivated when he saw her at that convention in May of junior year, more than a year after she'd dropped out. *Professor Kane, Regan's come to get me.* He couldn't stop staring, his focus now so malevolent in my memory.

"I first ran into him in November of our second year." She pauses, as if forcing the memory front and center. "At a student bar in the Village. The Drake. You know the one that's loud and the floor is sticky. You can't leave your drink unwatched. Professors don't hang out there."

But Thatcher would, I think. A room full of drunk twenty-year-olds? The ultimate hunting ground. And the second I think it, another thought sweeps me, shocking and hot. Holy shit, was he spiking young women there? Had my first instinct been right all along? The photos he had in his filing cabinet. *Were they students after all?* I rub at my upper arms, feel the need for a hot shower, a wire brush. If he didn't buy the images online, he took them himself. If that's true, then morning after morning when I woke up with him in his luxurious bed, climbed on top of him, his portfolio of girls was quietly growing in his study.

My throat is raw, but I don't interrupt her. *Please, Regan. Please don't be one of them.*

"At first, it was funny seeing him there," she says. "He was with a buddy, some broker guy he'd grown up with or known for a while. Thatcher is from a rich family; they've bought him everything, probably even his career. They didn't fit in at the Drake. They were all designer shirts and TAG Heuer watches, and I related to feeling like an outsider there. I thought I was better than that place too.

"'We took a wrong turn,' Thatcher yelled from his bar stool, 'but we're blending in.' 'Guess again,' I said, and he laughed. And it was exciting, especially once I figured out he was a professor. Sassing him, letting him know I wasn't intimidated by him. I had his attention, but it was only a joke." Regan takes another deep breath. "Except he was moneyed, and confident, and had friends in good jobs. He was never A-list, but he was doing better than I was and knew I wanted to climb. *Hey, I'll get a boost up the ladder,* I thought. And climb right on by."

I nod, my mouth dry, because I fell for Thatcher's sophistication too. With me, it was about books, theses, academic uniqueness. He packaged it differently for me. I strain to listen, stay focused. My mind keeps circling back: *he took the photos himself.* Veronika. Jordan. *Payton Nielsen.* That's why he needs them back.

"He'd hired a town car to get to the bars that night. With a driver waiting, and everything. So, I figured . . ." Here she wobbles visibly. "I figured, hey, he's kind of uncool, but he's not some penned-in sophomore with zero ambition. I'll take the upgrade, the new venues. I'll play."

I take a shaky sip of my drink, the crisis she's about to describe rolling toward me like a boulder. I am certain that Thatcher didn't take a wrong turn that night. Everything he does is calculated.

"By the time you went home for the Christmas holidays, I was hanging out with Thatcher a little, kind of in secret, but never as a date. I never went to his apartment. Not once. I was just a girl he could walk into a party with, who could run with his crowd, keep up with the banter, hold her own. I was always really clear about boundaries. And he was the perfect gent with me."

I nod, but under my thighs, my fists are clenched tight. When I was with Thatcher, he made me feel seen and heard. With Regan, it was all about glamor and the illusion of power. He was nobody without his family's money, and by New York standards, not very noticeable at all. I realize that now, but I can also see how shrewd he is. His victims might as well show up with placards, he reads so efficiently what each of us craves.

"Then a few days before Christmas, he invited me to a

party at a private club. His father was a member; I got the impression the people there would have more influence than Thatcher did. I could bring a friend, he said, and he'd put both our names on the guest list."

"Regan, no . . ." I hang my head, because we've arrived at the moment when the animal she'd thought was tame suddenly turned on her, all teeth and claws. Across the bar, as if horribly synchronized, there's a braying cheer from the TV.

She rotates her beer jerkily and it spills. "I invited this cool girl from my marketing class. She was fun, a foreign exchange student from Prague, so she didn't have family in the city. We had kind of paired up for the holidays."

"You never mentioned a friend from Prague."

"She'd gone home by the time you came back in the new year." Regan pauses, her chin wobbling. Great fat tears start to spill over and roll down her cheeks. "Her name is Veronika."

I stare across the table in horror, the whole of my body trembling. *Veronika*, the girl whose limbs and sagging mouth I can still see in terrible flashes, her legs pulled apart for the money shot.

"Are you one of them?" I blurt, crying now too. "Regan, are you in one of those polaroids?"

Had she been in the next envelope in the pile? The snapshots spark one by one in my head, but Regan's face is in all of them. Her head lolling and out of it, her makeup smeared, her body stripped by sweaty fingers. Rage flares in me, and I grip the edge of the table.

Regan sits slumped, every part of her wrecked. "I don't know. Isn't that the most pathetic thing? That's what I'm telling you, Ivy: I'm the weakest person you know."

37

"YOU'RE NOT WEAK—"

"Wait, you need to hear it all." She takes a swallow of beer. "Veronika and I went to the club. We walked right on up to the entrance, past two women who shot us envious glares. I think about their faces a lot now. We were no less thirsty than they were."

Which Thatcher knew, I think. Which is how he played you.

"Veronika was so excited." Regan pauses, her eyes brimming again. "She kept telling people, 'I'm Veronika Sedva. Remember my name.' The doormen were stern, but they let us through and we signed in at a flashy coatroom. Video cameras recorded us. We were both handed champagne."

"Did you drink it?"

"At a private gentleman's club in old New York? With a tenured professor as your guide?" She lowers her face. "I don't think they were spiked yet. But what do I know? I was an idiot every step of the way."

I reach across the table, take her hand, feel its clamminess. "I'd probably have had two glasses. I'm the kind of person who actually falls for Thatcher Kane, remember? And I'm the one suggesting we get on boats with total strangers we know nothing about." *One of whom has accidentally caused the death of someone they loved,* I think, sweat prickling. "The point is, we make decisions all the time that aren't well informed. Everyone does."

She exhales, relaxes her shoulders an inch because it's true. Life *is* full of quick decisions, tiny little moments that seem so throwaway, but are in reality a series of narrow escapes. Should I sip this or not, go right or go left, talk to the stranger who seems to be looking at me or keep my head down? We jump this way or that—all of us do, every day, in the blink of an eye—but as one choice rolls into the next, we don't notice the debris in our wake, the whole archive of our near misses.

"What was it like in the club?" I urge her on gently.

"Beautiful." She clears her throat. "I mean, at first. The hallway led into a main bar with sophisticated lighting, art deco furniture, everything plush. I'd never been anywhere like it. Thatcher seemed like he was waiting just for us, came right over in an expensive suit, loose tie. Even though no one really seemed to acknowledge him, he looked handsome, at ease."

Oh, I bet he did, I think, my fists tight. He's a chameleon; he can adapt to fit any room.

"He said we looked lovely, kissed our hands. I remember Veronika blushed." She shudders. "Thatcher'd promised to introduce me to his father's friend, who was a film agent in LA. Or so he said. The guy was in New York for the holidays."

"What was his name?" I murmur.

"Leon Alvarez, apparently. Thatcher brought him over; he was about seventy. Had a nose like a trodden-on toe. While he talked to us about Hollywood and Beverly Hills—his great life, his hired help, his expense account—Thatcher got us drinks. Leon gave me his card, told me to 'look him up' when I got to 'Tinseltown.' 'Nope,' Veronika said as soon as he'd gone. 'Old toad.'" She looks down at her lap. "Then Thatcher circled back, said there was another contact he had who might really change my trajectory. Someone bigger than Leon who he hadn't known would be at the club. Vero and I finished our drinks, and we took off after Thatcher down these weird twisting corridors.

"'Veronika Sedva! Remember my name!' I heard her shouting behind me, looser now, and I'd laughed, told her to behave, that we were meeting a bigwig, but even by then something wasn't quite right. The hallways were getting swirlier, the music around me muffled like it was thumping through soup. When Thatcher opened a door for us both, his features were warping into two noses, three pairs of lips in a stack."

I cover my mouth with my hand. *He had you*, I think. *Here come the teeth and the claws.*

"'Just through here,' he said, and I remember his voice echoing like a synthesizer. 'Vero,' I said, 'are you . . . ? I don't feel right.'" Regan pauses, and I wonder if I should move, sit next to her, whether it would help. She looks dogged, though, wants to press on. "She was ahead of me two steps, and I tried to get it together, but as I moved through the doorway, the floor seemed to slope like a ramp. I had no idea where the hell I was. Green walls. A blurred chaise lounge. And someone else in there—a man in the corner. His face rippling like liquid flesh." She shivers.

"Who was he?"

"There was something about him I recognized, but I was too messed up to figure it out. Mostly I just knew he was wrong, it was all wrong, and we needed to get out." Her hands are clenched on the table. "'Wait,' I said, 'wait,' and Vero must have felt it too because she turned around, but Thatcher took her elbow, guided her toward the chair. 'Whoops!' he kept sniggering as she stumbled. 'Look out now! Someone's had too much champagne!' And I knew that wasn't true, but when I tried to say so, my mouth just made sounds. Nothing worked."

"Regan." Our eyes lock across the table, hers wild, like a cub caught in a trap. "Do you need to stop? You don't have to—"

"No," she says, teeth gritted. "I want to. Get all of his poison out."

We take a deep breath in unison.

"Thatcher sat me down on the floor, my back to the wall. It was cold through my shirt. I felt a hand touch my hair, so I jerked away, tried to get up. 'Verka,' I slurred, no longer able to make syllables, but she was on the chaise lounge now, a kind of daybed, and they were pulling her top over her head, skinny arms high in the air. 'No,' she moaned again and again. I made it onto my knees, but then a TAG Heuer watch tracked past my vision, and I thought, *Thatcher's friend.* His broker friend from the Drake. *But he's not LA; he's just a money guy.* I strained to stand while they both laughed at me, and I stayed awake longer than Vero. They'd taken all her clothes, she was naked, unconscious on the daybed. I was barely able to blink, everything closing in, going dark in my head."

Stop, I think. *I can't take it, I can't hear this.* But I say nothing, just stand and move to her side of the table, put my arms around her, fold her into a hug. She's breathing so fast against my ribs; she feels fragile like never before. And again I think to myself, *I'm going to kill Thatcher.* If I see him, I really think that I will.

"'Ready?' the broker asked me." Regan's crying now, and I shift her closer an inch. "The last thing I felt was his finger in my mouth, hooking inside my cheek like I was a fish. It was salty, and I tried to widen my jaw, spit it out, but my tongue was so floppy and thick. 'She's good,' Thatcher said from somewhere over top of me. 'Lock the door.'" Regan huddles into me. "Then I passed out."

We're silent for a long time, clinging to each other. Every photo I could barely look at of that poor girl, Veronika, Regan was *there*. In the same room, the same kind of helpless, only a few feet out of frame. Whistles sound from the game across the bar, but I don't say anything more. I'm just here for her, and she knows it. I'm also so angry I could tear the table from the floor.

"I woke up in a yellow cab," she says quietly. "Dawn was breaking. There was a metal grill between me and the driver, and I fucking lost it, Ives, because I thought it wasn't over, that he was taking me somewhere worse." She washes a hand over her face. "Turns out he'd been asked to take me back to the address on my student card. Thatcher or the other guy told him I was some dumb kid, they'd found me hammered, they were doing the right thing. I still made him stop, let me out. Walked home in pieces while it snowed quietly around me."

"What happened to Veronika?" I ask softly.

"We found each other later that day, hugged and sobbed. But neither of us knew about the photos until you . . . until you told me you found them in his loft. She still doesn't know."

"You didn't . . . Did you think about going to the cops?" I can't look at her. It's a question that sounds so judgmental, even though I know it's never straightforward at all.

"Veronika made me swear not to tell. Or if I did, not to mention her name. 'It didn't happen,' she said. 'The door is closed.' She was leaving, going home, back to her dad who was in politics. And I owed her whatever she needed: it was my fault, I led her straight to Thatcher. She flew back to Prague, but every message I sent bounced back." She shakes her head, so many layers of despair in her that she seems shell-shocked.

"That night, I called Thatcher, so furious I could barely see. I was going to leave him a message. *Motherfucker, you're going down for this.* I didn't for one second think he'd pick up. 'Hey, party girl,' he said, and I could hear the smirk in his voice, the casual clink of his spoon in a cup."

I feel like standing up and yelling in the booth. How the hell does he do it? Get away with it again and again?

"I said I was going to the police, taking a drug test, proving what he'd done, but he was so calm. 'What drugs? Are there drugs in your system?' I googled it afterwards. If it was GHB, it would have been gone already. 'And sorry, Regan, what are you saying you've done? Groomed a foreign exchange student, delivered her to a club, and spiked her?' I'd stopped then, terrified. Apart from the fact that I'd promised never to mention Vero, I was also the one on camera, showing her where to sign in. Was I an accessory? I couldn't believe how stupid I'd been."

"You didn't do *anything*," I say, but she sniffs, hating herself, twisting my meaning.

"Yeah, I blocked him and shut down like a coward." She

exhales. "I never heard from Thatcher again. And I lied about it to you ever since."

Suddenly, the barman steps into view. "Girls, you need food, or . . . ?"

"What time is it?" I ask quickly. "Shit, we were meant to be on the beach at four. Could we just get the check?" We need to get out of here, go home, get her home. I'm so overwhelmed by what Regan has gone through, and can't imagine dealing with—

"Ivy, wait. There's something else."

I look up. Her eyes are steady on me, but they're scared.

"A student has come forward and accused Thatcher of sexual assault. That's what I found out today. All hell's broken loose at NYU. My mom says they've suspended him; it's all over the news."

"What?! That's *great*!" A huge rush of satisfaction surges in me, the first I've felt in a while. Thatcher will be exposed after all, lose everything, his whole career on the line. But why isn't Regan celebrating? If anything, she looks even more terrified.

"It's Veronika who's going after him," she says. "The report was filed from Europe. Her name hasn't been released, but it has to be her. She's pressed charges two years later."

"Why is that bad?"

"Because she doesn't have any evidence. No one else has come forward, and even if they search Thatcher's apartment, he'll have gotten rid of the photos you saw by now. He's not stupid; he'll have wiped the place clean."

"But you can corroborate Veronika's story! You'd know every detail; you'd say exactly the same thing as her."

"Don't you get it? That's the problem. I'm the only one who was there, who can *back her up*." The cold realization of what we're really up against dawns on me. The reason Thatcher would come all the way to Australia. It's not about me, or even the photos he can't be certain I've burned. No, it's all about Regan.

He needs to make sure she never talks.

38

AS WE RIDE BACK to the *Alone at Last*, the sky is already dark-ening, although the sun won't set for a few hours. Christopher and Lila found some fuel and were waiting for us on the beach. I wasn't sure whether I would tell Regan about Desh once we were on our way; I'd have to decide if she could handle another shock, even if it seemed like one that was a distant, terrible mistake in his past. I felt that maybe I should tell Christopher, though, for Lila's sake—if Desh had been reckless ten years ago, he might be again. After tomorrow, he would be the only remaining crew on the boat. Christopher could evict him in Cairns if he wanted to.

As Christopher navigates us through the swell, a warm strand of seaweed slops over the edge of the tender, sticking to my thigh like dead hair. I flap at it, fling it back into the water. The closer we get to the boat, the more fatigued I feel.

"One thing," he pipes up from behind us. "And this is a team decision, so let's discuss: I reckon we should cut the motor at sundown. It's not safe to journey on through the night."

"Really?" Regan and I turn in unison.

"I know, I know we're keen to move fast. We all feel the same way about that. I mean, I'm eager to get to Cairns for *your* sake." He pauses, and while we don't buy Christopher's altruism for a second, I also catch Lila's eye. *She knows*, I think. She knows deep down her dad is rescuing her. Everyone in this tender is secretly dealing with so much.

"Flint Beach's waters are riddled with riptides and atolls," Christopher says. "Sandbars just like the one we ran aground on last night. Without GPS, it's very hard to navigate, so I'd prefer that we wait for the tide. We can do what we did this morning—move when there's maximum depth."

"But . . ." Regan stares beyond him back to the distant beach. *Thatcher*, she's thinking. Thatcher with everything to lose. "Will we be out of reach of the town? And will . . . will tomorrow be Cairns?" She sounds like a small child asking if there are monsters under the bed.

"We'll moor somewhere safe and secluded," he says, as we near the swim grid. "We're all shattered, so if we tuck ourselves away for the night, we can forgo boat watch altogether. Then if we set off at, say, six a.m., we should still be in Cairns by midday."

"Okay. I mean, I guess." Regan nods doubtfully.

"We trust your judgment," I add. "The last thing we want is to get stuck again."

We turn back to face the front. The horizon, the offing, is a faraway line. *Stay on target*, we're both thinking. It's still a straight shot. But then, slowly, Regan lifts her arm and points. I follow her gaze, and there, moored in a shimmer of heat about two hundred yards away from the *Alone at Last*, is a black shape, hunched as if poised to spring. It's Blake Coleman's cruiser. The *Salty Dog*.

"Forget him," I say. "He's done, and heading back south. We won't see him again."

———

Regan and I stay close once we're back on the boat, resolving not to leave each other's side until we set foot in America. By five, we're ready to go, and when Desh comes up top to help Christopher pull anchor, we slip around the stern and go down to our cabin. Questions pile tight in my head, all of them versions of the same thing: *What happened back in Fiji, exactly?* But I won't let myself approach him, won't ask. It doesn't matter what tiny ember I seem to still have for him. I've been wrong so many times.

When he comes down to the galley to prep the javelin fish he caught for dinner, we head back up on deck. He's crouched, looking in a cupboard when I pass by him, and I try hard not to imagine that at some point, he must have crouched over Ali Powers too. I stumble, hurrying to the stairs. Once we're up by the spinnaker, Lila joins us with Pearl, but neither Regan nor I feel chatty.

"What is wrong with you two?" Lila tugs at the hem of her T-shirt. Behind her, a few wisps of cloud are doing their best, but mostly the sky is moody, a storm threatening but not quite breaking.

"Don't worry," Regan says. "We're okay."

"You're lying." She looks at me with her sad hazel eyes, the tilt of her little snubbed nose defiant. "I'm not a baby. If it's secrets, I swear I won't tell."

"We're not . . . It's nothing, Lila," I say. "Why don't you go fetch Guess Who? Bring it back here, and we'll all play together."

She gets up, pads into the covered cabin while Pearl stays with us, twitching her tail. Will Lila be okay once we've gone? I'm worried for her, and not just about the coming days. What kind of life is she going to have once they stop running? Still, when five minutes go by and she doesn't return with the board game, I have to admit I feel slightly relieved.

Regan and I nibble what we can of our dinner, sitting cross-legged together up by the swim grid after Christopher's shut off the motor and gone to bed. It's past eight p.m., and we're moored in a tiny cove, by all accounts on our own, although as ever, it's dark now, and hard to see too far into the distance. All I know is we're about three hours out of Flint Beach. Everything is quiet.

Regan fetches the bottle of wine she bought earlier, uncorks it, and pours big glugs into two tin mugs.

"I know I should be giving this to Christopher like I'd planned," she says, taking a sip. "It was meant as a Goodbye and Sorry I Called You a Crook gift."

I stretch my arm out, and she passes me my mug. "We need it more than him. Although that was nice of you. Nice gesture."

She shrugs, her hands fidgety in her lap. "I just need to take the edge off. I'm so tired, but I don't know if I'll fall asleep tonight."

"Maybe we should sleep in shifts. We can lock our door, and I'll stay awake for a bit. That way, you'll be out like a light. I'll look after you." I want to do that for her, keep guard after everything she's been through. I can do it; I won't drop off.

"Maybe." She considers the idea. "I have been falling asleep faster out here. You know, in between being totally horrified."

I smile in spite of myself and set my wine down on the deck. "It's all the fresh air. We'll miss that when we get home."

She raises her eyebrows at me as if to say *Will we, though?*

I pause, bite my lip. "Reags, something's bugging me. About Thatcher. Sorry to talk about him again, but there's this piece I need to iron out."

She leans in so our shoulders press together. "He's evil. You can't apply rational thought."

"No, but . . . just, why would he date me at all? And for so long? Was it to keep tabs on you?"

She sits up, her face sympathetic. "It might also be because you're aweso—"

"Seriously, I'm not upset that his attention was fake. He's a monster. I'm not fighting for a place in his heart." I shift, pull my shirt over top of my knees. So many times he could have drugged me while I was at his apartment, added me to his horrific collection, but I never woke up feeling drowsy or odd. *Because he didn't need me for that*, I think, shuddering. My value was purely as an access point to Regan. She'd blocked him, and he couldn't let her win. Or maybe she was simply his favorite. Either way, he wanted any information he could get. *Your habits, bunny. Your weekends, your schedule, your friends.* When I sublet Regan's place, he must have all but drooled.

"I shouldn't have rushed us onto this boat," I say. "We should have both just gone home at the start."

She takes a shaky gulp of wine. "I fed into it. I was freaking out too. And I've been shitting myself ever since you said he had porn. It's like having your innards dragged out and not knowing which parts of you he took. I . . . can't even explain."

I nod, trying to imagine being robbed to the core like that, and also wondering what I might have missed, what evidence I might have burned. The image of his hand? His furniture? Some recognizable part of his loft? Maybe not all the young women he groomed were led to a lockable room in a private club.

"Do you think he took the photos as . . . what? As trophies? Or to blackmail the students afterwards. If they didn't do what he wanted."

"He didn't blackmail me."

We're both quiet for a long minute, and I can feel the shame simmering in Regan. I can't believe everything she's been through. "I just hope that once we're home and you give your statement to the faculty and the cops, it'll be enough," I say. "That Thatcher won't be able to persuade them that you and Veronika are in cahoots, or something, both equally obsessed with him." I kick my heel against the hard deck. "If only I hadn't burned the photos. They were tangible proof."

There's a long, strange silence, enough that I turn to see Regan's face completely taut, her skin bone-pale in the darkness.

"Pass me back that wine," she says quietly, and I hand her the bottle. She refills her mug, then slowly stands, begins to undo the fly of her jean shorts.

"What are you . . . Regan, what the hell are you doing?"

She pulls down the denim a few inches, puts one hand flat against her skin, tugs the pink cotton of her panties aside.

"I need to show you this. Here. This is what Vero and I both knew he'd done."

Warily, I kneel upward, my breath catching as I realize there's a mark below her bikini tan line. Circular, ivory white, seared into the tender part of her flesh. It's a cruel ridged curve of scar tissue, about as wide as a quarter, but deep like it's been pressed there with force.

"What the fuck . . . Regan, what is that?" But I know. I already know from the swirled letter *K* that stands out on her skin, remembering the ornate stamp I found wrapped in tissue paper in that manila envelope. The one I'd thought was just his pretentious way to seal letters. I stumble to my feet and grip Regan's arms, fold her into me. She's shaking like a leaf.

"Thatcher did this? He fucking *branded* you?" As we separate, a roar of fury escapes me, and I bellow into the dark of the night. He wasn't sealing envelopes with wax. He was marking his victims like livestock.

"I'm so ashamed." Regan's shoulders are hunched, her voice tiny as she does up her shorts. "But I'll show everyone back home. I'll do it. Because, Ivy, *I* am the tangible proof. If Veronika and I both have the same brand, our story might hold. Then maybe others will come forward. The marking must be visible in those photos. It's the detail he knows will end it for him."

"Holy shit. Oh, my God. Regan! Stay here! I have something . . . I need to . . . stay here!" I rush toward the covered cabin, because I have the proof, too. I have the actual stamp to match her horrible trauma—Thatcher's DNA surely all over it—and it's here, in my day pack, in our cabin. I'd planned to throw it out because I thought it was nothing, a tacky gimmick, completely forgotten about. But as I run down the galley steps, and along the corridor, adrenaline pumps in my veins because we've got him! With Regan's testimony, Veronika's, and this branding seal, Thatcher's done for! It's far more damning evidence than those photographs ever were, and he knows it. He texted me eighteen times to get it back because I *am* a part of this. I do have agency. I'll be goddamn essential in the way his world burns to the ground.

I fling open my cabin door, stumble toward my pack in the far corner, beyond my bed. The room is dark, lit only by weak shards of silver through the skylight, and I trip on a flip-flop, stumbling. It's only then that someone behind me laughs. A soft sound. Fond. Caring.

"At last. I've been waiting for you."

39

I CRY OUT, tripping over the edge of my bed and crashing to the floor, then scrabble backward on palms and heels. Desh is sitting on the edge of Regan's mattress, his hands resting on his dark knees, the top half of him obscured by shadow.

He leans forward, smiling, eyes glinting like dark emeralds. It's the patience of a prowler, waiting for me in my cabin, knowing he would eventually get me alone. I hold my breath, every nerve in my body alert, while he tucks a curly strand of hair behind his ear.

"Please don't be scared of me." His smile fades, and he puts his head in his hands. "I know you've found out about . . . all of it. But please. I'm not scary at all."

"I know. I know that. It's okay." I keep my voice low as I struggle to my feet, my shoulders hunched, but inside my heart is jackrabbiting. Desh watches as I edge toward the door, one arm out front of me—*easy now, easy*—as if I've fallen into a pit with a tiger.

"Ivy, please." He slithers to the floor, his back against Regan's bed, his movements like someone in agony. "Ali wasn't . . . I didn't hurt her. The article you read, the one you stuffed back into my book, that isn't . . . It doesn't explain what really happened."

"How did she die?" I ask carefully, fighting the urge to sit down next to him, to offer any kind of comfort. *Don't do it. Make sure, make sure.*

"It was a one-second mistake that changed everything. For everyone." Desh wipes his face, which appears to be awash with sorrow, then takes a huge breath. "And I can't get it back ever, or change it. Ali was my girlfriend, my first love. We were kids on summer break, coming home from a party."

"You got in a jealous fight," I say, my nod grim. "You lost control. Pushed her harder than you meant to, and she fell." I can see it: the flash of temper, everything spinning away from them, and two teens' lives ruined.

"No!" He looks up at me, green eyes wide. "No, it was my fault—I was driving our scooter, but it was never a fight. I pled guilty to manslaughter, against my lawyer's advice. I'm not a killer, Ivy. I was a stupid kid who drank a couple of beers at a party, then took a corner too fast on a gravel road. And Ali died because of that choice."

I watch him while he reaches into his pocket and pulls out a tiny flashlight and a folded piece of paper, holding both out for me. Gingerly, I take them. Under the skylight, I click the beam on. It's a different newspaper article, this one with the headline: *POWERS FAMILY SUES OVER UNMARKED CONSTRUCTION.* I skim it quickly, then look back at

Desh's tear-streaked face. He's watching me, his eyebrows arced as if I'm the only verdict that matters.

"I'm not lying," he says. "I've kept a whole bunch of reports. Read it again, please."

Phrases like "fractionally over the limit" and "road signage absent" jump out at me, my brain churning with new information. The way this article portrays it, Desh was only partially to blame.

"If it was an accident, and the roads were that poorly maintained, why didn't you argue it in court? You could have pled not guil—"

"Because I was driving. It was me. I caused her death." He wipes his eyes again, hugs his own ribs. "And because it was Ali, and she was amazing. Her parents needed someone to blame. Someone to hate. And I needed to be accountable, or I knew I'd never get over it my whole life. I haven't drunk alcohol since that day, and I won't, ever. I'm completely sober; I just don't draw attention to it. It's easier than telling my sad story."

I think back over the nights we've spent in each other's company. It's true. He's never had a beer or a glass of wine. What if my first instincts about him were right? Actually *right*? He's a good guy. Not like Thatcher at all.

"I tried to become a paramedic to . . . fix things." Desh shakes his head. "But in the second week, we were in this lecture, and there were all these slides of accident scenes and I just starting bawling. Like, really loud. I had to get helped out of the classroom. It was not a good fit."

Compassion floods me, but I'm still wary. "Why would you hide the photo of Ali? If you love her, I mean."

He smears at his nose with his knuckle. "Because it's painful, Ivy. And I miss her. Haven't you ever done something you wish you could take back?"

Jesus, I think. *Hundreds of times.*

"I made it a rule not to be anyone else's boyfriend," he says. "For a full decade, I just kind of . . . ducked and dived."

I smile, because I can imagine it. Desh's charisma. The guy at the center of the fun. But there's always been something quieter and more soulful about him. I felt it in the hammock. A depth that felt comfortable, that I couldn't trace the source of.

"The last few days, you've spun me out a bit," he goes on. "I've been . . . inward because Ali died at this time of year. It's always . . . I find it difficult. But this year, you were here. And the truth is I like you and it's new, and . . . it scares the shit out of me. I don't want to feel anything or lose anyone. I got spooked and shut down."

A warm relief spreads out in my chest. Desh's coldness, his avoidance—it wasn't him being mad or horrible. He's freaked out. Because he *likes* me. I press my mouth closed, try not to smile.

"And then when you thought I'd hurt Pearl, I . . . That was so much worse. You shut down on *me*, and I couldn't handle it."

Above us on deck, there's a thud of something, a whomp, and we both glance up. But then it's quiet. Probably Pearl, on cue, jumping down from the boom.

"You rescued that cat so fast," I say. "It looked superhuman. Although, for the record, I never really thought you'd tossed her into the sea."

"I'm good in a crisis, I guess. Just not one I've caused." He sniffs. "I wouldn't hurt anyone or anything on purpose, Ives.

Hand on heart. I fought for ages to save Ali, but she was . . . There was no one to help me, and I—"

I see his chest heave again, and imagine what that would have been like for him. Watching her slip away, probably sitting next to her limp body with his head in his hands. He'd have been out in the middle of nowhere, his first love dying in his arms because of something he'd done in a millisecond of miscalculation.

"I believe you," I say. "I do."

He exhales. "I know you're getting off the boat tomorrow, but it felt so important to explain everything before you go. Can we . . . I'll be in California in May, and I—"

"You will?"

"My brother, Rafi, wants me to chef on this old barge he's bought in Santa Monica. He's turning it into an Airbnb, super high end."

"I thought he was a dick."

"He really is. Massively. But he's smart, and I don't know. His ideas are good." Desh shrugs, arms loose by his sides. "I'd just be stoked to see you again. Off this boat, I mean. In a . . . different context."

I nod, wondering how much of my smile he can see. "I think I'd be stoked too."

I slip down to the floor and wrap my arms around him in a hug. And it feels good, right, even though his arms stay close to his body, so it's kind of like hugging a tree. When we separate, his face is relaxed again, the old Desh, the one who isn't being distant or suffering in torment.

"I'm glad I sat in here for an hour like a loser," he says. "You came sprinting in so fast, you nearly headbutted the wall."

"I know!" I turn and crawl over to my day pack, dig through it, pull out Thatcher's seal. It's made of brass to withstand such high temperatures. Disgust passes through me as I see the fragments of what I once thought were wax. Yet it's mingled with a sense of power. Victory. In my head I hear Regan's voice: *Motherfucker, you're going down for this.*

"What is that?" Desh stares as I put the solid little chunk of metal in my shorts pocket, zip it in there, then move past him, my fingertips brushing his arm.

"I'll explain later. I have to go do something now though. It's, like, crazy important."

"Go," he says. "I'll be in my cabin."

I hurry out into the corridor, jog through the galley and up the steps. Regan, I think, you are going to *lose your mind* when you see what I have. We've won! And my instincts *are* good! I stride through the cabin, hurry back toward the swim grid.

"Reags!" I shout, turning around. "Regan?"

Her bottle of red wine is on its side, a circle of crimson seeping into the deck like blood at a crime scene. I stoop and right the bottle, looking around, but the whole space is empty. *Weird*, I think. Is she sitting at the bow, by the spinnaker? Puzzled, I move to the narrow walkway beside the roof of the sunroom, thread my way along the railing in the dark.

"Regan!" I yell, more urgently now, a shrill noise starting to sound in my head. But the front deck is empty, as is the helm, the whole aft, the boom. Above me, the sky hangs broody and sullen. The mast wire clacks.

Icy fingertips tickle up my neck to my scalp. Regan is not on deck. She is nowhere to be seen.

40

I TURN IN ANOTHER CIRCLE, trying to think clearly and not freak out. What is the most likely scenario here? That Regan is in the bathroom. That she came down below while I was talking to Desh, and I didn't hear her.

But as I step back toward the sunroom, the soles of my feet suddenly feel wet. There's liquid all around this part of the deck, the wooden boards flecked dark as if water has been flung high from a pail. I hunker down, hands in the dampness, then notice something bright lying half-hidden behind the boom. A long sleek thing, dropped there, shiny and metallic.

Isn't that Desh's speargun? I squint in the shadows, then move to where it lies, but as I grab it, my fingerprints etch along its yellow side like rust. What the hell? I turn my palms over one at a time, check the bottoms of my feet. Everything looks brown, like I've walked through a puddle of paint. Did I step in the wine? Or . . . is it fish blood where Desh might have gutted one earlier? But that was hours ago. It would have dried by now.

I stand up. The weapon feels light in my hands and I realize that the sharp spearpoint is gone. The gun has been fired. Fear starts to hammer in me then, and I rush inside, throw the speargun to the cushioned bench, and slither down the galley steps to the long corridor. My shoulder slams into the bathroom door, but it swings open easily. No one inside. Our cabin is empty too. *Fuck!* I think, staggering. *What am I . . . Fuck!* I turn back to our doorway in desperation, just as Desh emerges from his room.

"What are you doing?" He peers strangely at my chin. I smear at the skin there and his eyes widen. "What is that? What's all over you?"

"I can't find Regan," I pant. "She's nowhere."

"What do you mean 'nowhere'? What the hell is all over your hands?"

"Blood, I think it's blood." I push past him and sprint down the corridor, grab the huge flashlight from the galley, push open the door to Christopher's room. He and Lila are in there—sleeping soundly as my beam sweeps a jagged scan across them—but Regan is not. There's no time to wake Christopher up now. He dithers in a crisis. I take off up the stairs, Desh right behind me.

He grabs a second flashlight from a hook near the depth gauge as we pass through the empty sunroom. "What are you saying? Why is my . . . Is that my speargun?"

"I think there's been an accident." Maybe Regan picked up the weapon to put it away, but she was so bleary with stress and fatigue, she triggered it and it went off in her hands, maybe hit her in the leg. The thought is terrifying. But who else's blood can it be? Pearl's? Any possibility feels unmanageable.

"Check the other side!" I shout to Desh, running down the length of the boat with the flashlight trained on the water. I dread seeing Regan's shape at the surface, face down, T-shirt billowing. Would it be better to find her or worse? But all the way along the starboard side there's nothing. Just the silky lap of the swell.

Desh does the same on the port side, meeting me at the bow, and as his flashlight swings erratically, the beam catches a shape out at sea. The glint of something that doesn't look like land or rock. Something black and too shiny. We both stop, point our lights that way. And there, moored fifty yards from our boat, is the *Salty Dog*.

"What the . . . Why is he here?" I breathe, staggering forward a step to grab the railing. Blake Coleman's been moving in the wrong direction. He's not heading south at all, I realize. He's followed us north from Flint Beach, creeping closer as soon as night fell.

"We need to get the tender," Desh says, his voice steady, although his hand trembles as he takes my wrist. "Right now. If Regan fell overboard, she won't be far. We'll do a methodical search, follow a pattern, a grid." He pauses. "And then we'll check out Blake's boat. We can board it together."

I nod and stumble along behind him toward the swim grid, where the tender is tied. As we reach the boom, though, Desh suddenly stops short, so I nearly run into his back. He bends then turns, holding a flip-flop. Just one. It's Regan's— she was just wearing it—but now the rubber strap has been wrenched free of its plug. I put the back of my hand to my mouth. She is not okay.

"Come on," Desh says, his face pallid. "We need to be quick."

Together we tug the tender closer and clamber in. Desh unties it and pulls the cord for the motor, while I move to the front of the boat with both flashlights sweeping like head-lamps, searching the surface anxiously. Behind me, the motor coughs and splutters. Desh reefs on the cord, again, again, but there's not enough gas in the tank.

"Shit!" he says. "We didn't refill this yet. We need the spare gas. Wait, wait here." He scrambles out, barefoot and lithe, and climbs the swim grid, disappearing across the deck. Suddenly I'm alone with just two flashlights in the total dark-ness and the sound of my own shallow breathing. Water laps around me and I'm aware that a crocodile, a shark—any-thing—could leap out of the water, pluck me from the edge of the boat, I'm that low to the surface. I move to the middle of the bench, still scanning the water. I just need to find Regan. Where the hell is she, what's happened to her? It has to have something to do with Blake—why is he here, what is he *doing*? Did he board our boat without permission again, and did Regan try to stop him? Is *that* why she picked up the speargun? Desperately I peer after Desh. We need to get to the *Salty Dog* right now, before anything else happens to Regan. I can't just sit here doing nothing.

I turn off the flashlights, drop them, pull off my hoody. Fifty yards is about one lap of a pool. At most, it'll take me one minute to swim. I hook the tender's rope back onto the stern, then open the little black box Christopher keeps in the tender for emergencies—his flare gun, a couple of flares, a whistle, duct tape. There's also a diver's knife, and I grab that, clench the neoprene sheath tight in my palm. Then, without letting my brain have any more say, I put one foot onto the spongy rim of the boat and dive into the water.

My only thought, like a primal beat in my head, is *help her*. Move. Keep moving. The sea is soupy and warm, and I kick out, trying hard not to picture the world below me, the whole inventory of species that are hunting and feeding. I swim breaststroke in the direction of the dark boat. One minute in the water. One minute in the water. Nothing's coming. I switch into speed mode, face in the water, a flailing front crawl, the knife tight in my fist making me awkward.

Something brushes against my shin, feathery as a caress, and I gasp, stop, wheel around in a circle, my head and shoulders exposed. But it's seaweed, just seaweed, and I fling it aside, flap away from it, trying not to cry. I'm halfway. I can do it. I can do it. Twenty more strokes and I'll be climbing out of the water.

The *Salty Dog* bobs silent and dark, although a little light glows in the forecabin. Someone on the boat is awake. I glance back at the *Alone at Last*. No sign yet of Desh in the tender. I take a deep breath and kick onward, trying not to make too much sound. Half a minute later, I've reached the side of Blake's cruiser. It sits high in the water from where I am—the hull slick and sleek, motors lining the stern, the side ladder retracted and secured—and for a second, my head reels with the likelihood that I won't be able to climb aboard, that I won't find any footholds or have enough upper body strength to pull myself up. I'll have to tread water with my legs dangling until Desh catches up in the tender.

But then I spot a bumper that's been left out on the starboard side, its ropes tied to the railing. I swim until I'm directly under it, clamp the knife in its spongy sheath between my teeth, then with an almighty kick, surge upward from the water, grabbing the bumper with both hands. I hang there, trying hard not to drape my wet body against one of the porthole windows. My knuckles and wrists scrape and bruise but I don't let go; instead, I wriggle and scuff until I can reach the rope. The fibers cut into my palms, but I can do this, I'm doing it. Adrenaline courses through me, because I know Regan is here. I will rescue her; I just need to be quiet.

I wrap one wet hand around the cool of the metal railing. Pull my body up, feet slithering, but with enough purchase now that in seconds I'm onto the roofed upper deck. For a few seconds, I crouch there, waiting, knife down, getting my breath. There's an orange paddleboard stowed under a bench seat, but other than that, nothing left outside. Down a few steps is the lower half of the cruiser where the *Salty Dog*'s living area must be. From up here, I can see part of a polished glass door, through which everything inside looks quiet. Carefully, I move down the short stairwell, anti-slip treads rasping under my toes. The door glides open on expensive rollers, barely making a sound. I take the blade out of its sheath, and step inside.

41

ALL LIGHTS IN THE downstairs of Blake's boat are off, but the roof over me is all skylight—four clean wide panels of glass specter the boxy space in ash-gray. It's cloudy outside, barely any stars, and I glance around, heartbeat thudding while I drip onto the polished laminate flooring. Along the whole wall to my right is a white leather couch; on the opposite side, a pristine stainless-steel fridge and galley. Liquor shelf stocked. TV screen, off. Shiny table. It's tight but top dollar; a playboy bachelor pad, shrunk. Four steps, total, in any direction and two closed doors. One in front of me that must be the fore-cabin. The other behind the stairs, a room under the outside deck. There's a pair of men's Nike slides kicked off by the low table. Blake is in here. But is Regan?

I find I'm shivering, sit down on the couch for a second, nauseous. I feel out of body. The dive knife trembles in my right hand, the titanium of its clean serrated blade terrifying. What am I doing? Storming the cabins, seeing if Regan's tied up in there? But can I defend her and myself? Like, how? Stab him? I lean forward, set the knife down on the table, my fingertips fluttering over a litter of receipts and papers. The top layer shifts, and I see town names on some of them. Airlie Beach, Magnetic Island, Flint Beach. My breath catches. That's exactly the route we covered, from the very first random town where we spent New Year's and then boarded the *Alone at Last*. I dig deeper into the pile.

Buried in scraps and scrawled notes, I find two things that send shivers down my spine. One is the ad we saw in the Airlie Beach hostel, with the picture of our yacht on it. The other is a log book. *Salty Dog Sails* on the front cover, sections tabbed by . . . boat names? *Time Flies. Liberty. Sea Esther.* Each tab has a client name, contact information, whole pages of notes and payment calculations. I thumb through the log book, and there it is. The newest tab. *Alone at Last.* Opening the page, I read the notes, my scalp tingling. *January 2, parties head north toward Bowen, target sighted. January 3, target paused, approached vessel, Lila asleep below deck.* Holy shit. Lila.

Blake's a tracker. A pro. He was never on vacation, heading home after Flint Beach. He's a paid investigator, hunting Christopher and his daughter down. Helen must be the one who's hired him; she might even be on this boat. I stand up with a stifled gasp. Is *she* the one Regan grappled with earlier?

Then a sound, and I stare at the front cabin to see the door handle turning, and before I can do anything other than grab for my knife and half crouch, a figure emerges. It's Blake, bare-chested in silver basketball shorts. Paunch. Skinny arms. Huge watch. Holding an empty glass. He stops dead when he sees me, then looks quickly toward the other cabin. *There*, I think. Someone else is in there. He isn't alone on the boat.

"Ivy McGill." He sets his glass down on the table. "You're full of surprises."

"Where is Regan?" I say.

He leans back, closes his own cabin door. "Why would she be here?"

I hold out the knife, although it's clear to us both that it's shaking. "If you've hurt her, or done anything, I swear to God . . ." I trail off as he just stares at me, his eyebrows high. "You're following us. I know what you are. Is she in this back cabin? Have you—?"

He holds up both hands. "Slow down a minute. I don't have your friend. You're barking up the wrong tree. Although it's impressive. Did you *swim* here? That's fucking ballsy. Well done."

I ignore his approval, my calves pressing into the spongy white sofa as he moves to the galley, takes a bottle of whiskey from the drinks shelf, gently, gently unscrews the cap. His chest is covered with a whole tattooed scene of a navy dive boat, frogmen with guns, bullets traveling through water, a rippling Australian flag. Christ, he's seen much bigger fights than this. I mustn't shift my focus off him, not for a second, but I also need to keep an eye on the back cabin door. Helen could be standing behind it, six feet to my left, picking her moment to charge. Blake swigs his whiskey and grins, shaking his head.

"Look at you." He tilts the bottle toward me, as if it's a toast. "I had you down as such a pushover, but here you are swimming through sharks and crocs for your mate, on a rescue mission, bloody kamikaze. Look at that Rambo knife!" He sighs admiringly. "Good on ya. That's awesome."

"You're here to get Lila back." I try hard to make my voice steady.

"Do you reckon?"

"You're being paid by Helen Farris to grab her and bring her back to Hobart. Her dad has been trying to save her from her mom."

"Righto. Sounds full-on. And so . . . how would that involve your friend, exactly?" He sips again, smiling. "It *is* Regan Kemp you've boarded my boat to extract?"

"She got in the way," I say, hating that he knows everyone's full names. "She's brave, and she tried to stop you. Or stop Helen."

I hazard a glance at the steps to the upper deck outside, imagining the ocean flat like a cement wasteland, stretching between this boat and ours. Where the hell is Desh?

"Brave? It's not the adjective I'd choose," says a voice from the other side of the stairs. "Try overconfident. Impetuous. Weak."

I feel my knees buckle. I know that voice. Know it far too well. It's the same one that whispered seductively in my ear, praised my work, told me it would destroy me.

42

WHEEZING WITH PANIC, I lunge for the steps but Blake is already there. He shrugs with regret, as if to say *Sorry, kid, love your spirit, but the game's the game.*

"Stay back!" I hiss, pointing the knife at each man in turn. Thatcher's eyes burn with hate. He's in pastel shorts and an undershirt, his hair rumpled, but behind him, I can see both bunkbeds in his cabin are empty. Only a bag on the floor. Still he's tensed, ready to pounce, but seems unsure if he's allowed to with Blake in the room. Or maybe he's hoping Blake will take the lead, be the one who gets his hands dirty. Just as I think that, Blake sets his whiskey onto the counter, leans across, and twists the knife out of my hand.

"Regan! Regan, help!" I yell, but the boat remains quiet. What have they done to her? What have they done?

Blake grabs my arm, shoves me back to sitting while Thatcher's fingers clench and unclench. Can I get past either of them from here? The forecabin is closer to me now than the stairs. "Stop that. Shut up and calm down."

"Mind out the way," Thatcher says to him, trying to push past, but Blake won't budge.

I stare at his stony face. "You work for *him*? You've helped him track down Regan?" In a blaze of clarity, I see that Blake's stalked us all the way up the coast, maybe from before we even arrived in Airlie, and relayed the information to Thatcher, no doubt picking him up from the ferry at Magnetic Island. How far would Blake go for money? In horrible slow motion, I imagine Regan, alone on the top deck, kicking her red wine over in shock at the sight of him looming out of the dusk. She wouldn't have stood a chance.

"Did you . . . did you shoot her with the speargun?" I stammer. "Is she here, in your cabin, bleeding—?"

Blake steps across to a drawer in the galley, opens it, tosses my knife in. "Look, we're just here to chat. Isn't that right?"

"Absolutely." Thatcher leans back against the sink then, a parody of someone open to talking things over. If I step within range of him, I know he'll strike. It's Blake I need to reason with.

"Blake, listen, if you knew who this man really was, you wouldn't help him. What he does to women, to girls . . . He-he's *evil*." It's a last-chance move, and even as I say it, I know it's hopeless. Blake is a bad guy. He doesn't care.

Still, as he sits down beside me, he frowns for a second.

"Ivy," Thatcher says. "You stole something that's mine. I would like it back now."

I can feel the stamp, his brand, in my pocket. I will myself not to look down. "It's gone. I didn't know what it was. Honestly. I burned your photos and threw the stamp overboard."

Thatcher considers me silently for a moment. I can't hold his gaze. It's like being locked in my worst nightmare, unable to jolt awake. Then he nods once, as if in confirmation. "No, you didn't."

"Okay, you're right. I mailed it to Dean Blau at NYU, you fucking sicko. There! That's the truth. And Regan and Veronika will use it against you—they'll tell everyone how you spiked and attacked them two years ago. They'll show where you *branded* them! They'll both testify, and you'll go to jail!" I look over at Blake's doorway, begging for a spark of hope. *Please, Regan*, I think. *Please be in there, not injured, not bleeding to death*. Beside me, I sense a shift in Blake's posture—he's totally focused on Thatcher now.

"Oh, you're all so infatuated with me." Thatcher moves a step closer, and my whole body stiffens, shrinks away from him into the cushions. "You know, it's very difficult teaching girls your age. The slightest compliment, a single word of praise, and you dedicate your lives to making up stories about me, placing yourselves at the very center. I've told the dean all about this. She understands."

"Did you mention you're fucking burning the letter *K* onto every student you assault?"

He's by the stair rail now, moving in. "Come on, now. I can't control the girly fan clubs my students create. The cultish things they do to claim membership."

"Wait a minute there, professor," Blake says, getting up. "*Branding*?"

"She's lying. She's a lying, stupid, little bitch who steals

valuable items to pawn, because she's poor and has nothing."
Thatcher goes to grab me, but as I raise my arms, Blake
pushes him back a step so he's trapped at the galley counter.

"Hey, this was a straight deal," Blake says, while my brain
scrambles, daring to hope he'll help me. "Find the girls, get
your family heirloom back, fair enough. But you never sai—"

Thatcher grabs the bottle of whiskey and rams the thick
bottom rim hard into the bridge of Blake's nose. His head
snaps back, and he stumbles against me, woozy, smearing
blood on the couch as he slumps. As I wriggle free of him, I
see Thatcher open a drawer, and I spring for the forecabin,
panic coursing through every vein.

"Help! Regan! Desh!" I scream. But no one is in here, no
one is coming, no one can help. I climb onto the queen bed,
feet snagging in the rumpled black sheets. "Regan," I sob, my
back to the wall, hunching into myself, because there's nowhere
she can be other than in the water, hurt, bleeding, attracting
predators from every part of the deep. She's out there right
now, probably trying to staunch a wound, straining to keep
her chin above the wash of the swell as her strength leaks away.
Or has she already sunk beneath the waves?

I look up to see Thatcher leaning with one shoulder on
the doorjamb, so self-assured, wearing the expression of mild
amusement that I know so well. *See, this is what I find so
refreshing about you, Ivy.* Except this time, there are no loft
invitations, no cooking lessons, no stories he's fabricating
about how clever I am. No book lending, no bourbon, no
sickening couch.

All there is now is the dive knife in his right hand. And
no way out.

43

WE STARE AT EACH OTHER, my vision so acute and primal that it's as if he's spotlit in a tunnel, everything around him black. There's a porthole above the bed and I push at the glass, hopelessness sounding in my head like a high-pitched hum. The window is shut tight but I claw anyway, thump it with the heel of my hand. "No!" I shout. This is not how it ends for me. This is not how he wins. I turn and brace myself, get ready to kick.

"Oh, Ivy. Stupid little Ivy. You were always so worthless," Thatcher says. "So invisible, and average, and . . . *plain*. It amazed me that Regan ever befriended you. Someone of her caliber. Her shine. But it was circumstance, I can see that now. And pity. You're pitiful. A dead dog in a"—he steps forward suddenly and grabs my ankle—"*ditch*."

He pulls me down hard. My head slams against the headboard and my eyes swim. I shuffle back against the wall, looking up at him, aware that the outline of the brass seal in my damp pocket is visible against the pale of my thigh.

"You don't have to do this, Thatcher." My voice lowers, and he lets go of my ankle. "You don't have to hurt me or Regan! We'll be quiet if you just tell me where she is, what you've done—"

He smiles, languid and horrible, and that's when I know. This is it. There's no bargaining, no plea that he'll hear. Like rapid-fire, my brain searches for anything I can hit with, or throw. But everything's soft in here, just comforters and sheets. *Desh*, I think. *Where is Desh?* But if he was here, what would Thatcher do to him?

"I'm taking back my seal." Thatcher stands over me, shifting the knife so it looks ready to stab. "You're so easy to read, Ivy, it's laughable. But I'm done asking nicely. I'm just going to slice it out of you." He raises his arm, the knife glinting and high. I grab a satiny pillow just in time to slow the downward force of his thrust. The knife rips the fabric and feathers swirl everywhere, like snow. The blade snags, I jolt, and Thatcher pitches forward, his body falling on top of mine, writhing in a repulsive, intimate press as we pant and struggle for purchase, both of us spitting out goose down.

He manages to wrench his fist free and draw his arm high again, knuckles white around the hilt of the knife. I scream, full-lunged and terrified, just as Blake rushes in behind him, blood on his face and a wide-ridged lump across his brow. He's holding something—flappy, transparent—and while my brain tries to process that, he kneels hard onto Thatcher's back, traps both his arms, flings the knife to one side, then slips a clear bag over Thatcher's face.

In one swift action, Blake pulls back and twists so the plastic is tight. Thatcher's nose is smushed five inches from

mine, one dark eyebrow trapped sideways, his eyes starting
to bulge and his face redden. He retches and gags, spittle
coating the plastic in front of me, foaming in a crease near
his throat. I cry out again, turn my head from the sight of it
all, my fingertips scrabbling at the wall behind me. Blake
holds on, unrelenting, and Thatcher's body flaps and thrashes
on the bed like a gasping fish.

"Blake!" I yell, trying not to hear Thatcher's horrific wet
bubbling. "Blake, stop!" My eyes meet his, and he tilts his
head. *Really?* he's saying. *This guy, you want to save?* And then
I think of Regan, all the awful places she could be right now,
all the ways Thatcher's hurt her, everything she's been through.
It must have been him who boarded our boat—Blake was
conned, didn't even know what he was enabling—which
means Thatcher's speared, branded, assaulted, and spiked her.
There must be a ton of other victims, too: Payton sobbing on
the stairwell, Harlow jerking away from him on the Village
rooftop, other young girls he's demeaned so thoroughly
they'll never say a word. And what about the next ones, the
ones he's working on, just beginning to charm? The man is
a predator. He won't stop hunting.

I force myself to look at Thatcher, at the burst spidery
veins in his eyes, the purple bulge of his tongue as it smears
against the bag. *You deserve this*, I think. *And I am witness to
the justice. If they hanged you in a public square, I'd watch.*

"Do it," I say, and Blake tightens his grip. Ten long seconds later, Thatcher stops thrashing. The crackling breath
rattles quiet. Blake prods him, then wipes one palm against
the other while I sit with my knees quaking.

"Is he dead?" My voice sounds elsewhere, as if I'm

speaking from another room. "Was he . . . Did he hurt Regan? Where is she?"

"I don't know. Get up."

I do as I'm told, stand with my arms limp by my sides. Blake is moving calmly, efficient in everything he does. He ties a knot in the plastic bag where it meets Thatcher's Adam's apple, the corpse now face down at our feet like a scarecrow with hay for a head. "Strip that bed. Do it carefully, give me everything. Don't worry about the feathers, I'll get them when I clean up."

I start to work, pass him the bedsheets, my fingers clumsy. "Please, please, we have to find Regan."

"There is no 'we.' You're getting off my boat and you're saying nothing to anyone, ever. Do you understand me?" His eyes are cold and definite. "I helped you, Ivy. Remember that."

"I-I will."

I swallow drily as Blake does a confident sweep of the room, wiping his brow with his forearm, checking his hands. They're covered in his own blood, but nothing of Thatcher's. But won't Thatcher's fingerprints be all over the whiskey bottle, the dive knife, the boat?

"I've got it from here," he says. We lock eyes, and I shake my head, completely overwhelmed. He must know what's happened to Regan, but I won't ask again. He saved my life, and we're accomplices now. Suddenly, there's the sound of an engine getting closer. *No!* I think. *No, Desh, don't come on board!* The situation here is so precarious. I don't know what might make Blake snap, change his mind.

"Who's this now?" Blake listens with his head cocked.

"No, no . . . I'll head him off. And I won't say anything about what . . . happened. I swear to God."

"Yeah, best not. Go on then. Scarper." He gestures for me to leave, and I step past him shakily, stumbling on noodly legs toward the main cabin. There are no signs of a struggle in here. Just the whiskey bottle on its side on the floor. But as I reach the glass door, Blake calls out, and I turn to see him standing in the bedroom doorway.

"Ivy," he says. "He didn't leave my boat. Not once. Do you hear me?"

I recognize this as a pact—*what happened on the* Salty Dog *stays on the* Salty Dog—and I nod quickly. Pact accepted. Christ, the man just murdered Thatcher Kane with a plastic bag. Even if Blake did it to save me, he is not a guy to ever tattle on. He'd find me and everyone I love, I have zero doubt.

I turn quickly and hurry outside, where the clouds still engulf the stars. Desh cuts the throttle ten feet from the back of the *Salty Dog*, clambers to the front of the tender, wobbling, gaping up at me. "What the hell! I couldn't find the bloody fuel, and then I thought you'd been— Are you okay?"

I climb over the rail and jump straight in, skinning my knee on the rubber siding, gripping the bench. "Go," I say. "Go!"

"Wait, what? Is Regan in there?" His skin shines waxy as I shake my head no. Quickly, he sits, begins to maneuver us away.

"Hurry, please Desh, we have to find her!"

"I checked everywhere," he says. "Thought you'd fallen in too. I didn't know what to—"

"I'm sorry, I just dove in and swam. It was stupid—"

"It's okay. We'll find her. We will."

I set my jaw, a fine spray cooling my hot face. Regan is brave and strong, and I'm no dead dog. This is not over.

DESH WILLIAM TURNER
RECORDED INTERVIEW

Date: January 10, 2020
Location: Cairns, Northern QLD
Conducted by Officers from the Queensland Police,
Far Northern Region

POLICE: Shall we get started, Mr. Turner? I'm sure you know why we've called you in. You're a key witness in two major crimes.

DT: I don't think that's true.

POLICE: Okay, let's start with the facts. You took a job as cook on the *Alone at Last*, leaving Airlie Beach on January 1st. Did Christopher Farris check your references before he hired you?

DT: Christopher Edwards. He said his name was Edwards. [Long pause.] I've no idea if he checked me out. I doubt it. It was a casual hire and . . . fast.

POLICE: Do you think he would have employed you, had he been more cautious in his approach? You know, vetted even a little bit?

DT: [Pause.] Yes. I think he would have. He'd have learned that I'm good at my job. I get on well with people. I work hard.

POLICE: Okay. Well, just to be clear, Mr. Turner, we're not here to drag out the well-documented skeletons in your closet. We don't have time.

DT: They're not skeletons. I own what I did.

If you want to talk about Ali, let's talk about her.

POLICE: [Pause.] We'd rather talk about the head-less body of a white male we found floating near Flint Beach on January 8th. As yet, we've been unable to identify him.

DT: Okay, but I don't know who it is. And I don't know what happened to him.

POLICE: It's so strange, though, don't you think? Two boats moored within the vicinity of a butchered corpse, and not a trace of his DNA on either vessel.

DT: I don't know what to tell you.

POLICE: Head and hands removed. With precision. This wasn't the tear of teeth or jaws. This was a professional job. Requiring the kind of knife skills that a trained chef might have.

DT: Chefs don't normally cut up people.

POLICE: That's true, but there's very little about this case that feels normal. No ID or passport on the victim. No Missing Persons report filed.

DT: Dead end, then.

POLICE: It would seem so. [Pause.] Did you make contact with Blake Coleman on board the *Salty Dog* late on the night of January 6th?

DT: No, I did not.

POLICE: Do you know if any other member of your crew had any contact with Mr. Coleman?

DT: I don't. You'd have to ask them.

POLICE: So strange. No traces of anyone else's DNA
           on that boat, either. Doesn't that strike you
           as odd? After all, it's a cruise boat, isn't it?
           Sunset tours. Know anything about that?

DT: No, sir.

POLICE: Why isn't there a single tourist's fingerprint
           on board?

DT: How would I know? I was never on that
           boat. [Pause.] Look, I'm not . . . I don't think
           I'm of any use to you. I don't know what any
           of this means, but I've had conversations in
           rooms like this before, and I've said stuff
           that's been twisted and made to sound . . .
           [Pause.] I'm just done. I don't want any
           more trouble.

POLICE: Fair enough, Mr. Turner. No, that's fair.
           Except you know more than you're telling
           us.

DT: What? No, I don't. I'm not a witness to any-
           thing.

POLICE: But there was more that went on. Things
           you definitely *did* see. That you *were*
           involved in.

DT: What happened to the *Alone at Last*, you
           mean? But that was an accident.

POLICE: Was it? How about you talk us through the
           events of January 7th? Start as the clock
           ticked past midnight on the 6th. Take it
           from there, the early hours. How was

Christopher Farris doing? And where was his wife, Helen?

DT: She w—

INTERCOM: CS Abbott, you're needed out here. We have a major development. Another body has been found.

DT: Wait, wait! Where's Ivy? Do you have her safe? I haven't seen her since the boat c—

POLICE: Interview ended. [Sound of door opening.] Inspector Knightly, mark it down. Interview ended at 7:12 p.m.

44

WHEN WE'RE BACK ON THE *Alone at Last*, Desh stops outside the door to the covered cabin, stills me with a hand on my arm. "Ivy, are you sure you're okay? Did Blake do anything?"

"No." I swallow, wondering if he can see all the multifaceted horror I'm trying to bury in me. "No, he helped. And he didn't hurt Regan, or grab her. I'm sure of it."

"But who else could have done this? She's definitely not on our boat."

I can't tell him, can't mention Thatcher. I think of Blake's warning, the pact we've made. *You're saying nothing to anyone, ever.* "I think maybe the speargun went off and threw her backward. Come on, we need to radio that there's been an accident."

Together we step into the sunroom, where Christopher's spare fuel cannisters are now side by side by the bench. Desh grabs the radio receiver from its nook, clicks the side in and out. "Mayday, mayday," he says.

What will Blake do with Thatcher's body? Will it be found when they go looking for Regan? I push the implications of that away. Can't focus on that.

"This is the *Alone at Last* . . ." Desh adjusts buttons, turns dials, tries again. "Mayday, mayday. Ivy, it's . . . This thing's junk." He rattles the radio, checks the wires at the back. "Has it been dead the whole time?"

"It can't have." I feel a wave of dread. "Let's get Christopher. We'll just head for shore."

"Yeah," Desh sounds perplexed. "Does he *know* he's been sailing without radio contact? That's nuts! We-we can call on a cell phone once we're in range."

Of course, I think, *my cell phone!* I still have that voicemail from Thatcher, saying he's here, and all eighteen of his threatening texts. But is it good to have proof of him or not? I see his suffocated face again, the swollen eggplant squelch of his tongue against the plastic bag. Willing the image away, I barrel down the galley steps after Desh, and we hammer on Christopher's cabin door.

He opens up fully dressed, as if he's been lying down in his clothes. Not a hair out of place, either, although his eyes look tired.

"What's up?" he says. Behind him in her bed, Lila shifts under the covers and turns over. I step forward, grab his sleeve, pull him into the corridor.

"Regan's gone overboard," I say. "She's not on the boat. The speargun has gone off, there's blood, and one torn flip-flop."

"What? What do you mean?" Christopher wraps his arms around himself, hunching with each hand in an armpit, as if we're telling him the bilge pump is broken, not that our friend might be in critical condition. "Did you see her go in?"

"No!" I say, anger rising, because is that really the most relevant question? He's so useless in a crisis! We're wasting time.

"She could be hurt, we need to get back to Flint Beach—call for help." Desh leads Christopher into the galley, where he sits down on the bench like he's elderly, looking around with that same air of bewilderment, as if he's never seen our faces before. "Skipper, I can start the engine and get us there. Stay down here if you want. But we need to act fast. This is a real emerg—"

Just then, Lila pads through the doorway, frowns sleepily at us. "What are you all whispering about? Dad, what's going on?"

"Back to bed, please." Christopher's voice is crisp.

She ignores him, looks around. "Where's Regan?"

"There's been an accident." I wave off Christopher's objections, because Lila's eleven, for God's sake, not four, and she needs to be told things, included so she can help. "Regan is in trouble. We have to turn around and alert the coast guard."

"What?" Lila blanches. "What kind of accident?"

"Let's pull anchor." Christopher stands suddenly, springing to life, clearly hoping to spare his daughter any detail. "Come on, we'll get moving. Lila and Ivy, you girls keep looking out over the water, and we'll get the motor started for Cairns."

Desh blocks Christopher's path to the stairs. "Cairns? We're not— That's bloody miles away!"

"And there's no point just looking in the water," I snap. "You said there were riptides—don't those drag? We need to get back to Flint Beach! As quickly as possible!"

Christopher busies himself tucking his shirt into his shorts. "Cairns has a much bigger Search and Rescue department. Twenty times the size. Helicopters, motor boats, the whole shebang. You saw Flint Beach, guys! It took me all day to get two cans of gas. Is that really the best we can do?"

Desh shakes his head. "It would help if the radio worked, Christopher. How long has it been broken?"

"What?" Christopher says again. "It's not . . . We haven't needed it."

Desh rubs his face. "Wow."

"If we sail back toward Flint, we'll be in range of cell service once we reach shore," I suggest. "We can call Cairns and everyone."

"I thought . . ." Christopher pauses, watching me carefully. "I thought you'd prefer we didn't use our phones."

"No, it's . . . I don't care anymore," I say. "This takes priority."

Christopher weighs it. "I still think the city is our best shot. Call ahead as we go north. You'll find range." He claps his hands together, decision made. Desh and I gape at him, and Lila chews her nails.

"Dad, can we even sail in the night? You said the boat scrapes because there's no water. And what if we scrape a hole and the crocodile comes back?"

Christopher stares at his daughter, his eyes slightly wheely and wild. "Every problem has a solution. Isn't that what I always say? Come on, we need to get dressed and get ready."

He takes her back to their cabin, his energy bizarre. One minute he's overwhelmed, the next he's taking charge with terrible ideas. And he already is dressed! Desh's face is creased like his stomach is sore, but I know it's confusion he feels. This can't be the best plan.

"Your cabin," he mouths, and we slip in, close my door. Pearl looks up from where she's curled on my pillow, blinks, goes back to sleep.

"Right, he's *lost it*," Desh whispers, "and we're not waiting to report this in a town six hours away. What if there's no cell service for ages heading north? I can't believe he hasn't fixed his radio." Desh runs a hand over top of his head, while I wonder if Christopher disconnected it on purpose, to stop Lila sending out homesick call signals on random channels, like messages in a bottle to her mom. "Look, I say we take the tender, you and me, and we head for Flint Beach without them. Bring your cell."

"Without Lila?" I ask, my heart dropping. Her little face, her stalky legs in her nightdress, the way she's chewing her nails.

Desh throws out his arms. "She has to stay with her dad. Christopher's dead set on Cairns. I think it's the wrong move, but Lila's his kid."

"Okay. Yes. Whatever's fastest." As torn as I'll be to abandon Lila, I think again of Regan sputtering in the swell. "Christopher will freak out. Let's go now while they're still in their cabin."

But Desh isn't listening—he's turned away, toward the open skylight. When I follow his gaze, I see fingertips, a full row of them gripping the edge of the window. Someone is up there eavesdropping. But who? Christopher and Lila are in their room, we're the only other two on the— *Blake*. He lied to me. We don't have a pact, and he's come to tie up some loose ends.

The fingers above us tense and retract silently, like a spider when a shadow falls across it. Desh sprints from the room, down the dark corridor, through the galley and up to the top deck.

"Wait!" I shout, four steps behind him. "Be careful!" He doesn't know who he's dealing with, doesn't know what Blake Coleman can do without a second thought. Racing outside, I skid to a stop beside Desh, who's spinning in a slow three-sixty. The deck is empty.

"Strange," Desh whispers.

Fifty yards away, the *Salty Dog* glints on its mooring, its windows tinted and impenetrable. So, he definitely hasn't left yet. What is he up to?

"Let's go back to his boat," Desh suggests. "Together. He'll have a radio we can use."

My eyes widen in the darkness. "I don't think . . . I asked him that already when I was over there. He said his is on the blink."

It's a feeble lie and Desh frowns at me, looks back at the cruiser. *Really?* he's saying. *Every available radio is broken?* I'm about to add more—Blake's private, very guarded, wouldn't want us showing up again unannounced—when we glimpse a dark figure on a paddleboard, heading around the other side of the *Salty Dog*, out of sight.

"Why is he fricking paddleboarding in the middle of the night?" Desh murmurs, then a few seconds later, the cruiser's engine starts, a startling roar in the night. I know that Blake was washing the blood off himself, or—God help me—towing or dumping a body. But why come over here? Why listen at our hatch? Whatever he was up to, he's getting the hell out of here now.

"Come on," Desh says, tugging me toward the tender. "Let's head for shore. Now or never."

I stumble to the stern, my imagination spewing ghoulish images of body parts, meat cleavers, acid. But what do I really know? I can't predict Blake's plan for Thatcher; I'm basing everything on the worst of TV. I jump into the tender and fumble to untie the rope, throw it back onto the swim grid while Desh lowers the engine, double-checks something, bending to look. He swears, completely aghast.

"What?" I say from my seat. "What is it?"

He holds up the fuel supply line that connects to the motor. With both hands, because there are two drooping ends of it. The hose has been cut cleanly right through the middle.

CHRISTOPHER EDWARD FARRIS
RECORDED INTERVIEW
Date: January 11, 2020
Location: Cairns, Northern QLD
Conducted by Officers from the Queensland Police,
Far Northern Region. Also present: Oliver Ciprios, legal
counsel for person of interest.

POLICE: Christopher, new developments have come
           to light. Is there anything you'd like to tell
           us before we proceed?
CF: Should I answer that?
OC: No. As we discussed, my client has nothing
           further to disclose at this time.
POLICE: Fine. Let's go back a few weeks. You're
           living in Hobart. You haven't come up
           with your plan yet to buy a boat. You've
           embezzled money from the Rosebud and
           your wife, Helen Farris, has reported it to
           the police.
CF: She withdrew her statement.
POLICE: Okay. But your marriage has collapsed and
           you've moved out of the family home.
OC: Inspector Knightly, how is this a new devel-
           opment? According to my client, you've
           already been over all this.
POLICE: It's context, Mr. Ciprios.
OC: Can we focus? Mr. Farris is keen to absolve
           himself of any involvement with the discov-
           ery of the bodies—

POLICE: We'll get to that. Christopher, we've spoken with your daughter, Lila.

CF: No, you can't do that without me! She's a minor, you can't—

POLICE: Lila had a support person present. She chose for that person to be . . . someone other than you. [Pause.] She's explained that under the terms of the separation, you had visits with her most weekends. You'd pick her up, take her for a pizza, that kind of thing.

CF: [Long pause.] That's correct.

POLICE: She also stated, albeit reluctantly, that you [sound of papers rustling] "left Hobart in the night to get her away from Mum." Would that also be accurate?

OC: Don't answer that.

POLICE: We've talked before, haven't we, Christopher, about Helen's temper, her tendency to bully you, the ways in which she might have been furious with you?

CF: Not about our daughter. She knows I look after Lila. That's my job. I'm a father, a *good* father. A good leader, a man under pressure, doing his best.

POLICE: Even so, Helen has been quite the threatening presence in our minds. Was she threatening in yours?

OC: That isn't— Inspector, what kind of question is that?

POLICE: Okay, true or false: Helen asked you to take
            Lila for two weeks over the Christmas
            break, so she could attend a yoga retreat.

CF: True. I mean, I think that was her plan.

POLICE: So, why didn't she go?

CF: She did. She did go. [Pause.] I don't know.
            Maybe she changed her mind, then.

POLICE: What might have put her off?

CF: Maybe when I went to pick up Lila, I ruined
            Helen's chi. Perhaps she didn't feel like
            yoga afterwards.

POLICE: You upset your ex-wife? Is that what you
            mean?

CF: Just that we weren't on the best terms. We
            didn't agree on a lot of . . . fundamentals.
            Sometimes even looking at me made her
            upset.

POLICE: [Pause.] Do you think she might have been
            upset that you told Lila to pack enough
            clothes for more than two weeks? That
            you'd suggested Lila bring everything she
            could fit in her suitcase, but not mention a
            word of it to her mother?

OC: I'd advise you not to answer that.

CF: [Silence.]

POLICE: You were sick of being kicked around by
            Helen, weren't you, Christopher? Sick of
            her disloyalty, her derision, the perimeter
            fence she'd built around your daughter. You
            were taking Lila and leaving, never to return.

CF: How do you—

OC: My client has no comment at this time.

POLICE: Except Lila couldn't keep the secret. She's eleven and needs her mum. She told Helen the truth, and then when you arrived to pick your daughter up, all hell broke loose.

CF: No. It didn't.

POLICE: That's why Helen didn't go to the yoga retreat, isn't it?

CF: Lila and I have been on a very special trip together. It's been therapeutic. [Pause.] I don't know what Helen did if she didn't go to yoga. We're not in touch.

POLICE: It's okay; we found her. We finally tracked her down.

CF: [Silence.]

POLICE: There's a swimming pool at the family house in Hobart, isn't there, Christopher? [Pause.] I'm sorry, you'll have to speak up.

CF: Yes. I said yes.

POLICE: It's where you killed Helen Farris. On the night of December 21st, 2019, between the hours of four p.m. and six p.m., you drowned your ex-wife in the swimming pool while your daughter was inside watching television, the volume turned up loud enough that she wouldn't hear your latest argument.

CF: [Long pause, faint sound of moaning.]

POLICE: It's time to tell the truth now, Christopher. It's time. Your daughter has no idea that her

mother is dead. She left her a *voicemail*.
Can you see how unbelievably sad that is?
You rushed Lila out of the house, doubled
back alone to bundle Helen's cold body into
your car, then dumped her in the ocean by
Devil's Point. You purchased the *Alone at
Last* the next day, paid cash, dyed your
daughter's hair, and swore her to secrecy.
You've been on the run with her, and she
doesn't even know why.

CF: Please, I need to see Lila. I need to speak
             to her. Oh, God, what have I done?

OC: Stop talking. Don't say anything more.

POLICE: You've been hurrying north, knowing you
             had two weeks in the clear when Helen
             was meant to be at her retreat, so no one
             would expect to hear from her.

CF: I didn't, I thought it for the best—

POLICE: Christopher Edward Farris, you are under
             arrest for the murder of Helen Sophia
             Farris. Do you understand what has
             occurred? Do you understand that you—

CF: I should have . . . Oh, God, Helen, I'm so
             sorry. [Loud sobbing.]

POLICE: Mr. Ciprios, please remain in here with
             your client. CS Abbott and I will be back
             shortly. We have more to discuss with him.
             More charges to bring regarding the attack
             on Regan Kemp.

45

"BLAKE CUT THIS?" Desh holds the broken fuel supply line. "Why?"

"I guess he's . . . he's just a bad guy," I manage, while inside my head, everything is blaring. Why was he here, and why would he disable the tender? I left him wiping the *Salty Dog* clean. So his plan with Thatcher is to . . . dump him on us? *Oh, my God.* To dump him on *me*.

He's towed the body over with his paddleboard, and now the corpse is floating somewhere nearby. He knows Regan is missing, that I'll soon call Search and Rescue, and when they come out here, they'll find Thatcher's body, and the only link will be to me. Has he gotten rid of Thatcher's phone? Any communication between the two of them won't be traceable, no doubt sent to and from anonymous accounts. Blake's good at this; he'll have covered all his tracks. If he's kept the phone at all, it's because he's double-crossing me.

"Why do you think that?" Desh helps me out of the tender. "That Blake's a bad guy? I thought you said he helped you?"

"I'm not . . . I don't . . ." *I'm trapped*, I think. Can't tell Desh anything, can't *not* alert Search and Rescue. Regan has to be helped, no matter what. "We need to check the engine."

Desh's green eyes are steady on mine. "You think he disabled our whole boat?"

I nod tightly. He waits a beat for me to speak, then nods in response. Together we hurry inside, where we meet Christopher and Lila at the top of the stairs.

"Ready?" Christopher asks. "Apologies for the delay. Lila and I had to have a team talk."

Lila's eyes are downcast, and I get the impression she'd rather swap teams. "Where are you two going?"

"We've found a new problem," Desh says. "The fuel line on the tender is bust."

"Bust?" Christopher repeats, as if it's his first time hearing the word. "What do you mean?"

"Listen." My mouth feels like sand. "Somebody has cut it. Someone who doesn't want us on the move, or who wants to . . . pin something on us. Christopher, we have to get to Flint Beach. Cairns is too far."

He doesn't answer, just looks at Lila, his face hangdog and forlorn. "You were running away from us? From Lila and me?"

"No, she was not—" Lila begins, and I pull her into a hug, put my arms around her. The last thing I want is for her to feel rejected or unloved.

"No, we weren't. I'll explain later, but we're in trouble now," I say over top of her head. "All of us, Christopher. Not just Regan."

He says nothing, his shoulders slumped, watching Lila burrow into my ribs. *Can you see how frightened she is?* I want to ask him. *You need to manage this, or step aside.*

"I'm checking the main engine, and then one way or another we're heading back to Flint," Desh says, with an assertiveness worthy of a coup. "We'll motor if we can, if the engine's not damaged. Otherwise, we'll sail and I'll fix the broken fuel line in the tender."

Christopher sits down at the table. "Do what you think is best. It's all I was ever doing anyway." His voice is soft, but there's a strange defeat in his eyes, a blankness I haven't seen before. It's as if, by questioning his decision-making, we're undermining everything about him.

Lila pulls out of our hug, obviously sensing it too. "Dad? Every problem has a solution."

Her voice chirps with earnestness, but he just stares at her with his jaw muscle tweaking. Apparently that's not always true. "You stay here. Sit with me. They don't need you hanging around."

—

Blake Coleman might have made it to the tender, but he didn't get below deck. According to Desh, the engine is fine, and for a couple of hours we chug back to Flint Beach under an inky thumb smudge of sky. The further we get from where Regan must have fallen in, the more I feel we're abandoning her. *We'll come back*, I keep telling her in my head. *We're getting help. Please fight.* I try not to think about Thatcher floating out there too. Or the hideous possibility that Regan might run into him, that his carcass arms might nudge her, his squashed face next to hers, damp inside the bag.

Lila and I huddle under a blanket by the swim grid, tired beyond belief as we watch Desh crouch in the tender, fixing the fuel line. Christopher has his back against the door of the covered cabin. Every time I look around, he's watching us intently, an injured animal, ostracized, but still trying to hang with the pack. Perhaps he feels this whole thing is his fault.

"Is your dad feeling upset about Regan?" I whisper to Lila.

"Well, he's the leader," she says. "He's meant to be in charge. That's why he's cross you've overruled him. Don't worry, he'll get over it. He does this a lot."

"Right," I say uncertainly. At least Christopher's mostly growl. No bark, no bite.

Once we're about four hundred yards from shore, Desh shouts to Christopher to shut off the motor. Christopher says nothing, but does as he's told. Then we all head to the tender.

"We're good," Desh says as we climb in, "but be gentle on that hose. Ivy, any signal yet?"

"No, we need to get to shore." I sit next to him on the front bench, my cell in one hand. "Christopher, do you want to drive?"

He takes the tiller, mildly placated, and sits in the back, Lila just in front of him with the blanket still over her shoulders. The *Alone at Last* looks suddenly forlorn, lilting there, completely empty. We all take a second to register it.

"What about Pearl?" Lila suddenly begins to cry. "She's mine! We can't leave her."

"She's— We won't be long!" I grab hold of her as she starts

to stand. "I promise, we'll come straight back here. We'll leave her some food and water."

"I'll go." Desh loops the tender's rope lightly over the swim grid and clambers back onto the boat, using my shoulder as a handhold. "I'll just be a second, guys. Quick as a flash."

He jogs across the aft deck toward the covered cabin, leaving me alone with Lila and Christopher. I turn to find he's staring right at me. He won't take his wolf eyes off me.

46

I TURN AWAY AND watch Desh hurry into the sunroom to feed Pearl. I see him hesitate, then bend down. When he stands, he's holding his speargun. He looks back at us in the boat. Doesn't head further inside.

"What is he— What are you doing?" Christopher suddenly shouts, his voice sharp and raw as we sit side-on to the stern.

"Stowing it—hold on!" Desh shouts back, disappearing below deck. But the doubt in Christopher must have scared Lila, because she stands and pushes the tender away from the swim grid, and we're now drifting further than Desh could possibly leap.

"Don't!" I cry. "Lila, stop it—he's just putting things back where they're safe!"

I turn in my seat to find she's still swathed in the tent of the blanket, only her little hands poking out. But I frown: she's holding the flare gun. The one Christopher keeps in his metal box for emergencies. She's aiming it at the floor of the tender, one eye squinted closed as if it's a game.

"Wh-what are you doing?" I stammer. "Put that down!"

"Lila." Christopher hunches beside the engine, bony, quiet, and dark, like a crow. "Pumpkin. Please pass me that back."

"How come you all love Pearl so much?" Lila moves the gun from one hand to the other. "She's my cat. And she fucking hates me."

"What are you talking about?" I'm astounded by the f-bomb, her tone, and the way her little hands grip so tightly around the flare gun. Any second now, she'll trigger it accidentally, shoot a hole straight through her knee. Should I dive for the gun, wrench it away? She's so tired she can't think properly, her face expressionless, just like when she's sleepwalking, that same horror movie void. She's not herself at all.

"Christopher!" *Do something! Parent!* Why is he sitting so still?

"I read once that cats can distinguish between good and bad people," Lila says. "They're not meant to *care*, though. Or *judge*." She scrunches up her face. Christopher sags further into himself, looks like he's a waxwork melting.

"Pearl loves you very much," I say. "Of course she does. Right, Christopher? We all do."

Her father reaches out with a shaky arm toward Lila, but she shoulders him away.

"No, Pearl's an asshole. And so is Desh, by the way, who you also all love. You know, he's hardly acknowledged me this whole time. Maybe he can spot bad people too." She sniffs, then shrugs. *Oh, well. Their loss.*

"Lila, you're freaked out," I say. "We all are, but nobody's against you, and you're not a bad person."

"Pass me the flare gun, sweetie." Christopher's voice is a rasp. "Let's stop this now."

"Look, can you help me reach the swim grid?" I lean forward, my chest on the rubbery rim of the boat, hands in the water. I realize I'm talking to her like she's a toddler, but what else can I do? Maybe I can distract her, make her join in. "We just need to paddle a little bit. Come on, or Desh won't ever catch up."

"Did you hear *anything* I just said?" She kicks hard at my ankle.

"What the hell is your problem?!" I saw an ex-lover *die* tonight! Does she have any concept of what that's like? But I rein my anger back in, because it won't help. We're all falling apart. This is just her eleven-year-old version of it. "Let's think about Regan, Lila. We all need to calm down and help out."

Her hazel eyes study me for a few seconds, head tilting. "Oh, I don't think we need to do that."

Dread begins to thicken in my throat. "What . . . why do you say that?"

But she doesn't answer. Without breaking eye contact, she raises the flare gun to shoulder level and fires it straight at the covered cabin. It explodes in a shocking bright ball of red flame, shards of wood and fiberglass splintering twenty feet high into the night sky while Christopher and I hunker, arms covering our heads. *The fuel cannisters.*

Within moments the entire covered cabin is engulfed, smoke funneling upward while my ears ring.

"Desh!" I scream, and I scramble to my feet, lurch toward Christopher, toward the motor, so we can get back to the boat and help. Lila is still crouched under her blanket, smiling at the fire. She points—*look at that, look what I did!*—like a kid amazed by July 4th fireworks. It's like she's possessed.

"What the fuck, Lila!"

"You're just like the others," she says, cocking the gun, reloading it with a second flare, her fingers fumbling and eager. "Pretending to be on my side, then talking shit about me. Your dumbass best friend let it all slip. *Are you muddled, all messed up about missing Mum? Let me be your buddy, I can take care of you.* I told her, 'Hey Regan, I'm a fuck of a lot less muddled than you are.' And then *I* took care of *her.*"

She hurt Regan? My mind is rattling, but I hear Blake's voice clearly: *Ivy, he didn't leave my boat. Not once. Do you hear me?* Holy shit, it wasn't a pact Blake was offering me: it was a warning! He was saying that he'd had eyes on Thatcher the whole time; he knew it wasn't him who'd gone after Regan. Blake was trying to tell me: *You have another enemy.*

"Mum talked about me all the time, too—"

"Let's not talk about Mummy," Christopher breaks in, leaning toward his daughter. "Let's keep that just for us."

Lila ignores him. "She told everyone *everything.* You know what shuts people up? Wine and a shit heap of sleep meds. It was funny watching her disappear while she sipped. She was like a robot running out of battery. Her legs and arms turned to goop. When I pushed her into the deep end, I don't think she even knew it was water."

Oh, God, Lila's insane. She's hurt her mom, Regan, Desh— all of it's *her*! I pull myself up to sitting, force my expression to look genuine. "I *am* on your side. I'm not pretending." First chance I get, I'll grapple her to the floor of the tender, wrestle that flare gun out of her hand. My fingers itch for retribution.

But even as I'm thinking it, she stands, straightens her arm, and points the reloaded flare gun straight at my head. There isn't a tremor in her, not a trace of human empathy. "Yeah, Mum said that too. She was *so on my side*. Like when she told the whole school I was 'troubled.' Or drove me to the fat ugly therapy lady who kept taking notes, the fucking bitch."

"Lila, I'm your friend!" I shout, petrified, the flames of the *Alone at Last* whipping into the desolate sky. I see Christopher lunge, hear a crack, watch the flare explode out of the mouth of the gun. Lila shrieks, and a burst of pain explodes in my hip. I fall backward, slithering over the edge of the tender into the water, unable to hold on to anything. One gasp, then I'm swallowing water, flailing in the dark of the sea.

CHRISTOPHER EDWARD FARRIS
RECORDED INTERVIEW
Date: January 11, 2020
Location: Cairns, Northern QLD
Conducted by Officers from the Queensland Police,
Far Northern Region. Also present: Oliver Ciprios, legal
counsel for person of interest.

POLICE: We've said many times, Christopher, that
           it's the truth we need. [Pause.] Are you
           ready to give us that now?
CF: I'll tell you everything. And I don't need
           counsel. There was only ever so much
           I could do.
POLICE: We want to ask about your daughter, Lila
           Grace Farris. Following further investiga-
           tion, we have reason to believe that the
           statements Lila has provided may not be
           reliable. We know you're protective,
           Christopher. That fatherhood means a
           great deal to you. But there has to be a line.
CF: Please, let me say this, before anything
           else: Helen was never a bad mother or a
           bullying wife. She wasn't derisive, or dis-
           loyal, or bad-tempered in any way. She was
           lovely. She had every right to report me for
           embezzling money: I wasn't honest with
           her at the start. And I didn't listen to her
           when I should have. I let her down.
POLICE: [Pause.] We can see you're upset, but

we need you to go back to that night in
Hobart when you turned up to collect
your daughter.

CF: No, before that. Months before. Helen was
convinced that there was something . . . the
matter with Lila. That she had a, a pathway
in her brain we needed to address. She said
we couldn't continue to ignore a problem
and hope it went away. It's just . . . Well,
I felt that Lila was going through a patch.
You know, a preteen wobble, something
typically hormonal. I was in denial. [Pause.]

POLICE: Go on, Christopher.

CF: Do you know what it's like to watch your
own child's unhappiness? There's no pain
greater. Or I thought there wasn't. Helen
and I argued a lot. She couldn't sleep.
[Long pause.] Then I tried to fix Lila, hired a
local specialist whose rates I told Helen we
could afford. But we couldn't; that's why I
borrowed money from the Rosebud when it
was already near to closing its doors. And I
hid this from my wife, so that when she discovered the funds gone, it looked like theft,
when it was only ever love. Protection.

POLICE: So, December 21st, you show up to your
home to take Lila for two weeks. Helen is
set for her yoga retreat.

CF: Yes, two weeks was always the arrange-
ment. What Lila told you about secretly

packing for longer, that was . . . None of it's true. [Pause.] I arrived at the house at around five p.m. Nobody answered the door. I could hear the TV blasting. [Pause.] I went around to the yard.

POLICE: The swimming pool is back there. What did you see when you got through the gate?

CF: Lila. Sitting alone on the diving board, hugging her knees and rocking. When I said her name, she turned, and she looked so . . . so haunted. Like she'd seen something so harrowing, her eyes would never close again. I went toward her, and then I saw . . . Helen was in the water. Face down. Her cardigan billowing around her like a shroud. I jumped in, shouting her name, turned her over. [Long pause.]

POLICE: Christopher? You're doing very well.

CF: I . . . I dragged Helen from the pool, tried to resuscitate her. The kiss, the kiss of life. But she was so cold, her cheeks and her lips . . . [Sounds of crying.] And all this time, Lila sat on the diving board, watching me, so rigid and still. "What happened?" I yelled at her, hugging Helen upward, but my wife's arms dragged on the wet pool deck, her neck lolling. "She's been drinking," Lila whispered, and to be honest, Helen had been doing that more lately, plus taking sleeping pills. We were . . . We hadn't been coping well. She used to sit out by the pool every night, on her own, even after I'd moved out, I think. It was her quiet time.

POLICE: So, you tried to resuscitate, but found you were unable to.

CF: Yes, it was too late, I was . . . I shouted at Lila to call an ambulance. "Dial 0-0-0, get help!" And she ran for the phone, but when she came back, her eyes were so big. "We can't, Daddy," she said. "They still think I hurt Vicky. They'll blame me." [Long pause.] You see, Lila had been in so much trouble at school lately. There'd been an incident with another student. A girl in her class she'd been close with. Vicky Danvers. I don't know why, and I didn't believe it at the time, but Vicky's parents claimed Lila had drugged her, ground something up, slipped it into her water bottle. She'd apparently done it at school. The girl had spent the night in the hospital, been discharged, and then the whole thing had come out. Lila was expelled. [Pause.] If we called the police or the paramedics, she was right, they'd suspect her. And I thought that was why she'd been sitting so terribly quietly. It felt like a perfectly orchestrated tragedy: Lila is accused of something nonsensical at school; then my wife dies catastrophically, in *sight of* my child, the very nature of the accident cruelly reminiscent of Vicky Danvers. At the time, you see, my only thought was that Helen had mixed alcohol and meds, and stumbled into the pool.

POLICE: So, to be clear, you chose not to call Emergency Services.

CF: Lila is eleven. Withdrawn and unhappy. And I thought, *Helen wouldn't want this*. Her death was clearly accidental, a terrible miscalculation she'd made, but she'd be devastated to have it land on Lila. [Sound of a sob.] I believed I was doing the best thing for us all.

POLICE: What did you do next, Christopher?

CF: I . . . sent Lila inside. Wrapped Helen up gently in towels and a tarp. And then, while Lila stayed home, I drove my wife out to Devil's Point. It was our place. I proposed to her there.

POLICE: You disposed of Helen's body in the sea. Can you speak up, please, for the record?

CF: No, I-I didn't just chuck her away like a bag of old bricks. I had a . . . There was ceremony. I told her I loved her and said goodbye. Devil's Point is notoriously wild, a place we'd both adored, but it has infamous undertows. I thought her body would never be found.

POLICE: So, you placed Helen's body carefully in the ocean, then took off with Lila to protect her. Is that what you're saying? Christopher?

CF: Yes. I said yes.

POLICE: Okay. Is there any other reason you decided
         to run?

CF: [Long pause.] Perhaps, if I'm honest, I was
         also worried about myself. I had motive,
         after all. And spouses always get the blame.

POLICE: Thank you. Can you tell us when you first
         realized the true nature of your daughter's
         character? [Pause.] Nobody is questioning
         your parenting, Christopher. Or your devo-
         tion. But there must have been a moment.
         When you *saw*.

CF: In the tender. With the flare gun. Or, before,
         with the fuel line tampering. But I was lying
         to myself then.

POLICE: You had no inkling of your daughter's
         involvement in Helen's death until that
         moment?

CF: Lila murder her own mother? Would it have
         occurred to you, as a dad? Lila was all but
         catatonic when I found her. [Sounds of
         crying.] Now I think she must have watched
         Helen's last breath bubble upward. She
         viewed it from the diving board, like . . . like
         a tourist at Sea World.

POLICE: [Pause.] When did you realize that Lila had
         attacked Regan Kemp?

CF: I thought it was fish blood on the deck.
         Desh had caught and gutted one only hours
         earlier. We'd eaten it for dinner that night.
         I wouldn't let myself believe . . . anything

else. Even when Lila climbed out of the
skylight in our room, ran off in the middle
of my team talk, the one I was trying to
have with her while Ivy and Desh were pre-
paring to leave the boat. I wanted her calm;
I could sense her energy . . . peaking.
Anyway, she ran away and I wrote it off as
a tantrum. She was back within minutes.

POLICE: Having damaged the tender. To prevent any
help reaching Regan.

CF: [Pause.] It's a terrible realization, that
your child is . . . this. It's quicksand. You
have no idea.

POLICE: But you did try to help in the end.

CF: By pushing my daughter into the crocodile-
infested sea? And then, when I hauled her
back in, by knocking her out with the flare
gun? Yes, because I'm a terrible father and
a useless husband. I miss Helen. Oh, God,
I want her back. [Sounds of crying.]

POLICE: Christopher, the charges brought against
you will alter now. But, to be clear, you're
still in breach of the law.

CF: What will happen to Lila? Please, I'm begging you, I need to see her.

POLICE: I'm afraid she's not . . . interested in that.
For the time being. [Pause.] Christopher?
Okay, Inspector Knightly, stop the inter-
view. The subject is too upset to continue.
We have all we need from him at this point.

47

I FLOUNDER IN THE WATER, gasping, my right hip burning with pain. What is— Where the fuck is Lila? Crazy, insane, violent Lila, who the hell did she just become? My brain replays the last seconds, like a movie on rapid rewind. Flare gun, fuel canister, fire. Twenty feet away, the *Alone at Last* is burning and I try to splash, make it back to Christopher, who's screaming in the tender, "Calm down! Calm down!" Is he yelling at me? He's pivoting desperately, ragged and wild, reaching out from this edge and that.

"Help me," I sputter. "Christopher, get Desh, help Desh." He'll be alone and trapped in the bowels of the boat, scalded or panicking, thick smoke choking him in the corridor, the wood creaking around him as it warps. Pearl, too, tucked under one arm, pressed to his ribs, as he tries to find any kind of escape. "We have to, we have to keep Lila in the—"

"Look out!" Christopher shouts. "Look out!" *Fuck, fuck!*

I try to turn, but my spine is searing. Is there a shark? I'm leaking into the ocean, the swell around my thighs blood-warm.

Suddenly I feel a thud at my back, something ramming me, grabbing me, and I shriek, swallowing water in a splashing reel of panic. Is it a creature from below me? Is it teeth, is it jaws? But my flesh isn't ripping, and this grip on my shoulders feels like hands. Oh, my God, is it Blake, come to finish me off? Or Regan, heavy-limbed, her death rattle after hours in a riptide? I pull urgent fingers away from my neck, twist around in agony, and catch a breath. There's a pale face in the water. Huge eyes. Hair pasted back.

"I can't swim!" Lila looks terrified, her top half juddering with the effort to keep her chin above the waves. Our eyes lock together, and I grab the skinny flesh of her upper arm. She's a scared child, helpless and afraid. Whatever she's done, whoever she's hurt, I cannot let her drown.

"Over here!" Christopher yells from the tender, bent over the side, flapping at the water with his hands. "Grab on!"

But we've drifted, we're too far away, and I'll need to drag Lila to him. She's so small, so weak a swimmer, so afraid. "Lie flat," I pant. "I've got you."

I reach for her, but she dips in the water, ducks under my arm, turns me deftly so I'm now facing the tender again. "Have you?" she replies, and I gasp as she hooks her sharp elbow around my throat, then grinds her knee once, twice into the wound at my hip, the pain so intense that blackness starts to spread at each side of my vision.

"God help me, God help me." Christopher jerks, jerks at the motor in the tender, but the engine won't catch, the fuel line has come undone again. "Lila, Lila! Stop!"

I choke as she kicks and heaves, as if I'm a driftwood log
she's climbing onto. She's strong in the water, scarily strong,
and as saltwater floods my eyes, ears, lungs, I feel her pressing
down on me with everything she has. Her face glimmers
above me through the water. She's smiling.

REGAN ZOE KEMP
RECORDED INTERVIEW
Date: January 11, 2020
Location: Cairns Hospital, Northern QLD
Conducted by Officers from the Queensland Police,
Far Northern Region

POLICE: I know this is difficult. You've been through
           so much. I'll try to keep these questions
           simple for you, make them yes and no as
           far as I can. Do you think you can manage?
           [Pause.] We can stop or call for the nurse
           at any time.
RK: [faintly] Okay.
POLICE: Good, well done. You're incredibly brave,
           Regan. Do you know that? You've battled
           so hard. [Pause.] Oh, I'm sorry, no, I've
           upset you. CS Abbott, grab a tissue.
           [Pause.] We'll keep this short. Are you
           alright to keep going?
RK: Yes.
POLICE: Thank you. Righto, firstly, do you take any
           medicine regularly? For insomnia or anxiety?
RK: No.
POLICE: The reason I ask is because the doctors
           found trace amounts of benzodiazepine in
           your blood work. It's a drug that's used off-
           label as a sleep aid. Combined with alcohol,
           it can be very dangerous.
RK: I don't take it.

POLICE: Okay. Then I'm sorry to tell you this, but
           it's likely you've been administered it in
           small amounts quite regularly over the
           past week. Without your knowledge.
           [Pause.] I know, I know that's upsetting,
           on top of everything else. [Pause.] The
           thing is, Regan, that benzodiazepine is the
           same drug prescribed to Helen Farris,
           Christopher's ex-wife, back in Hobart.
           She had a lot of it in her system when her
           body was found. So, you see, it's a very
           important link, forensically.

RK: Her *body*?

POLICE: Yes, unfortunately Helen's remains were
           found yesterday evening. It appears she
           was deceased before the *Alone at Last* was
           purchased by Christopher. Which leads me
           to my second question. Did you find out
           what Lila had done to her mother? Did she
           slip up in some way and then panic?

RK: No. What? I—

POLICE: Are you okay? You've gone— Nurse! Can we
           get— We need some help in here!

RK: [Gasping breath.] She murdered her mom?
           Jesus, she came out of nowhere. I was up
           on deck, drinking wine. Ivy had gone below
           to get something. [Pause. Sound of nurse
           entering.] No, no, it's okay, I don't need help.

POLICE: It's . . . We're okay. Regan, this is very
           important. Take your time.

RK: Suddenly Lila came toward me with the speargun pointed at my chest.

POLICE: Did she say anything? Had there been trouble between you before?

RK: No. Or I don't think so. She said I was changing Ivy. Taking her away, gouging her for secrets. "He didn't alter me, I'm not muddled, I don't need help." [Pause.] She was babbling, said something about a cowrie shell, the message. "I told her don't bring you." [Pause.] I remember being, like, *What are you talking about?* And standing by the swim grid, backing away. She kept saying, "It's just like Mum, she was on *my* side first." None of it made sense.

POLICE: And what happened next?

RK: I tried to get through to her, told her, "Lila, you can trust me." She laughed in my face. Said she'd drugged all the people who said that.

POLICE: That's . . . okay, that's the benzodiazepine.

RK: She was acting totally crazy. Asked if I'd missed my cell phone. If I'd enjoyed her acting. "Don't hurt me! No, Mum, don't do that again!" We'd found her sleepwalking once, we thought, but now I'm sure she was awake the whole time.

POLICE: Did she talk about the death of her mother?

RK: She was all half meanings, like a bad dream. I think she called me "people-smart" like her mom. Then she said, "You're Helen all over again. Let's see how well *you* swim." [Pause.]

POLICE: Take your time, Regan. You're doing great.

RK: She . . . she fired the gun. The spear hit my left shoulder, knocked me back over the swim grid. I remember the ache of it, the way my flesh felt loose in the water, like it was flapping.

POLICE: But your arm was severed at the elbow joint, not the shoulder. [Long pause.] I'm sorry. That— I could have put that more sensitively.

RK: The pain was . . . I was half passed out, I think. Or I hit my head, or . . . I don't know. I remember trying to shout up to the boat, but I was in shock. [Pause.] The water was dragging me further and further away from the swim grid. She was there. Lila. She stood there for a full minute, watching me. Then she turned, and I was alone, and no one could hear me.

POLICE: How long were you in the water before you found the atoll?

RK: I didn't find it. Last thing I remember, the stars were blurring, and I couldn't keep my head up. *I'm gonna die*, I thought. *This is it.* I'm pouring blood. And there'd been a crocodile . . . [Sounds of crying.]

POLICE: You're okay, Regan. You're safe and okay.

RK: [Silence.] I didn't find the atoll. A cruiser
          clipped me. It was flying, didn't see me in the
          dark. My arm got tangled in its prop. I was
          so drowsy by then, I didn't feel much. I only
          remember the thump. I think the guy driving
          that boat stopped and helped me, though.
          It's hazy, but I remember him dragging me
          onto a sandbar, tying something tight
          around my upper arm.

POLICE: But you were alone when you were found.
          You're saying someone applied a life-saving
          tourniquet, but then left you bleeding and
          unconscious on an atoll? Can you describe
          him at all?

RK: No, I was barely awake, and he was quick.
          I passed out, then woke up here.

POLICE: Okay, thank you, Regan, you've helped a lot.
          Just one last question, if you can manage
          it. Is there a white man in his thirties—
          likely about six foot tall and dark-haired—
          who might have been in the vicinity of the
          boat earlier in the evening on January 6th?

RK: [Long pause.] Like, Christopher, you mean?
          I think he's more fifty than thirty. Or Blake
          Coleman?

POLICE: No. Another male. As yet unidentified.

RK: A . . . dead male?

POLICE: Correct. We're not sure if he's connected to
          Helen Farris, or the case in general.

RK: [Long pause.] No, I don't know anything
         about him.
POLICE: Okay, well, you can rest now. We'll check in
         with you again tomorrow. Your statement
         has been invaluable.

48

WHEN I OPEN MY EYES, I'm in a bed, a tube attached to the back of my hand. Starchy blanket. Scratchy Velcro at the neck of my hospital gown. Pain when I try to sit up.

A woman stands from a chair in the corner. Police uniform. She's young, with short sun-bleached hair. "Go easy, Ivy. It's okay—you're going to be fine."

She steps toward me. She has kind eyes. Behind her, the walls of the room are a shiny beige, while to her left, the light around the shuttered window is so harsh that it must be blazingly hot outside. "My name is Inspector Maeve Knightly. You're in Cairns Hospital. You're safe now."

"Regan? Desh?" My voice is a scratch. Inspector Knightly looks for a glass of water, brings it closer, waits while I try to trap the straw with my lips.

"They're both okay. Regan's here. Upstairs. She has injuries, but we found her in time."

Tears well in my eyes, slip downward, and tickle my neck. *She's alive, and so's he. They're alive and the nightmare is over.*

Knightly smiles, sets down the cup, hands me a Kleenex. "She had the same reaction two days ago when we told her you were okay."

"I thought she was . . ." I dab at my face, can't finish the sentence. "We couldn't find her, and we never made it to shore, and my cell was—"

She nods. "Search and Rescue dispatched a boat from Flint Beach. They found Regan very quickly, following an anonymous call from an untraceable phone. A male caller. Do you know who that might have been?"

Blake Coleman. The name switches on in my head like a light bulb. So, he helped Regan, called it in? "No," I say. "I've no idea."

Inspector Knightly absorbs that the way people do when they don't quite believe you. "Whoever the mystery caller was, he saved her life. And yours."

I try not to show the complete unlikelihood of that on my face. Blake helped us, risking himself? It feels so improbable, and yet I can't let myself react.

"Is everyone else okay?" I ask. "Did you find everyone?" I mean Thatcher, have they found Thatcher, but I need to be cautious.

"It's . . . There's a lot going on. We have questions."

Oh, God, I think, shifting, only to wince with very intense pain.

"Ouch, that must be sore," she says. "You've had a skin graft. No lasting bone damage, but you'll need to go slow for a bit." She pauses, leaning against the side of my bed. "What do you remember, Ivy? What's the last thing?"

"Being in the dark ocean. Struggling . . ." I grimace, feeling all over again the rush of water into my throat, up my nose, my ears tickling with the change of depth as Lila pushed. She'd been so demonic, sheer determination and glee in her effort. "Where is Lila? Did she . . . Is she . . . ?"

"In custody. We have the situation contained."

"So Search and Rescue found us? Everything is a blur. They pulled me out?" How, though? It felt like I had only seconds left before my lungs split.

"No, we believe Christopher got you into the dinghy. He saved you before pulling his daughter out of the swell." She waits, watching my face as fresh tears roll down it. Christopher. How awful he must be feeling. Lila was everything to him; he sacrificed his whole world for her. She took all of it, malevolently, and won't ever give it back.

"How did Desh get out? The fire, the fire was—" I shudder at the memory of those flames, funeral-pyre high.

Knightly passes me another tissue, a twinkle in her eye that says *You like him*. Something about her feels so relatable, like we're friends talking about boys at the mall. "Desh is okay. In fact, I have something for you. He wanted me to pass this along."

She hands me a note, then helps when I struggle to open it. Desh has folded it so many times, it's square, thick, a little grimy. Like he's carried it for a while gripped in his fist. I take a breath, check Knightly's expression, which is steady now, all the playfulness gone. Then I start to read.

DESH WILLIAM TURNER
RECORDED INTERVIEW

Date: January 11, 2020
Location: Cairns Hospital, Northern QLD
Conducted by Officers from the Queensland Police,
Far Northern Region

POLICE: You've been medically cleared, Mr. Turner.
            There's no reason for you to still be wander-
            ing the hospital hallways.

DT: I know, but . . . Why won't you let me see Ivy?

POLICE: She's not ready for visitors.

DT: Is she . . . She's going to be okay, though?

POLICE: With time. Sure. She needs to heal. [Long
            pause.] What are your plans now, Desh?
            Now that you're free to leave?

DT: I'm . . . I have a flight booked home to the
            States, but I was maybe going to change the
            date. Delay it a few weeks.

POLICE: You're fond of Ivy McGill. It's clear. You seem
            to really care about her.

DT: I do.

POLICE: But you haven't had the best luck with
            romantic relationships. Have you? All that
            previous trouble in your youth. And now this.
            Is it just coincidence, or does life always spin
            like a whirlwind around you?

DT: [Silence.]

POLICE: I'm just asking because if you care about
            Ivy, you might want to consider what's

best for *her*. She has a long road ahead of her, a lot of trauma to process. Do you really think she's in any state to embark on a love affair? Or that *you* are?

DT: What I think is that it's none of your business. Respectfully.

POLICE: [Short laugh.] Okay. I know you're probably sick of people like me. Old blokes asking you questions, in rooms like this, recording every single thing you say. But I'm trying to help you, Desh. Genuinely, you seem like a good kid. You've had more than your fair share of grief for someone your age.

DT: [Silence.]

POLICE: I've been married for twenty-seven years. That's the whole time you've been alive, and believe me, I've seen a few things. What I can tell you with maximum certainty is that lasting, solid relationships don't start in the middle of a murder investigation. You can't make smart choices when the world's topsy-turvy, on fire. Trauma is not a reliable foundation on which to build.

DT: You're saying I'll hurt her. I'm too helter-skelter. A bad omen. That everything I touch goes wrong.

POLICE: Or just that there might be a better time for this. Give her some space. Get your bearings.

DT: Go home.

POLICE: Yes. I reckon that's best. For her, anyway.
           I'd say it's about calming down now. And
           doing the right thing. Wouldn't you?

49

DEAR IVES, the note begins, Desh's handwriting all capitals, pressed so hard on the paper that in some places, the pen has punched all the way through. I'M SORRY I HAD TO GO, BUT I KNOW YOU'RE SAFE AND BEING LOOKED AFTER.

"Wait." I look up at Knightly. "He's *gone*?"

"I believe he had to fly home," she says. "Does he explain it?"

I pause, because it's unlikely she hasn't already read the note. It's not like it's in a sealed envelope. "Is he hurt? Badly burned?" Oh, God, maybe they've flown him back to the States so insurance will cover it. I think of his beautiful skin torched, scabbed, scarred. My dad always said burns are the most painful of any injury, that they cook in your flesh long after the fire has gone. My breath catches, and Knightly puts her hand on my blanket.

"I think just keep reading," she says. I swallow, try to focus on the next line.

I KNOW WE SAID WE'D MEET AGAIN BUT ALL THIS HAS BEEN REALLY HARD. I'M NOT GOOD AT POLICE STUFF. OR THIS. ~~GIRLS SEEM TO~~ *MAINLY I JUST WANT YOU TO BE OK AND I'M NOT SURE IF I'M HELPING. I HOPE YOU FEEL BETTER. DESH*

No, I think. *No!* He didn't even say goodbye! But then I picture him, beat up, shell-shocked, and triggered, interviewed by cops all over again. His mind must have gone straight back to Ali. Or maybe he found out what's actually happened around me—put all the pieces together that Knightly's not quite able to—and wants nothing more to do with me now. *I'm not sure if I'm helping.* More like *Ivy, I'm not sure if you're good.* What would he have written in the sentence he started and then scratched out? *Girls seem to*—what? *Get me in trouble?* Fair enough. If I was him, and had learned my lesson, I'd steer away from the chaos too.

I refold the sheet of paper, battling the lump in my throat. There's a beat of silence.

"It appears Christopher Farris—that's his real name—was also the one to save Desh," Knightly says. "Mr. Farris returned to the burning boat and managed to get Desh into the tender."

"His—really?" I'm exhausted by everything I didn't know on this trip, but more than that, I keep wondering how long it'll be before I forget Desh's clear green eyes, his smile, before I can no longer picture him jogging over barefoot in his pale-blue hoody. I hand the note back to Knightly, don't want to keep it. *I lost him*, I think. He flew home. Even if I understand it, I can't believe he just left.

She pockets the folded paper.

"Mr. Farris has stated on record that he deeply regrets ever inviting you, Regan, and Desh onto the *Alone at Last*. He called it a 'grave misjudgment' on his part."

"He got a lot of things wrong." I smudge my nose, unable to be angry at Christopher. He's the saddest guy I know. "But that's brave to help Desh in the fire. And can you tell him from me that I get it? When it comes to grave misjudgments, I'm kind of a pro."

She smiles, then leans back against my bed. "I'll pass that on. We're wrapping up our investigation. But there is one last riddle I was hoping you could help me with."

Here it comes, I think. Moment of truth. This is the question that shuts the door or opens another one. I know it, and so does she.

"Okay," I say. "I mean, I'll try." Stay measured. Get it together. Don't let your face muscles twitch.

She stands, moves to the window, her fingertip shifting one plastic slat of the blinds so that hard sunlight bursts onto the wall behind her. "What is your connection to Blake Coleman?"

I pause before answering, and before I do, the door of my room opens and a man of about fifty walks in holding two paper cups of coffee. He stops, surprised at the fact I'm awake.

"G'day," he says. "You're looking better." He's ruddy-faced, quite round in the belly. Gray-haired and broad-headed, like a human bullmastiff. "I'm Chief Superintendent Bill Abbott. How are you going?"

I nod, say nothing. Take stock while he hands Knightly her coffee.

"Ivy was just telling me about her dealings with Blake Coleman," she says, blowing gently on the surface of her drink. Something about her partner entering the room has changed things, burst the bubble she'd created, broken the connection. She must realize, but she's hiding her disappointment well.

"Blake boarded our boat once," I say, feeling more confident now. "And I ran into him again in Flint Beach."

Both police officers nod.

"That's it?" Abbott asks.

"He's not very . . . personable. I don't think he wants to be." I look from one police officer to the other, keep my eyebrows high, as if I've made a useful observation.

"Did you ever find him to be frightening?" Knightly leans against the wall.

"No, I found him to be gruff. But those kinds of people can be decent. You know? If you dig." Blake saved my life twice in one night. He didn't double-cross me. He's nothing like what I'd thought. But is anyone?

"Interesting," Abbott says, sitting down in the empty chair. "It would seem fairly obvious that Mr. Coleman called Search and Rescue on Regan's behalf, gave direct coordinates of the atoll she was on. He also warned officers about Flint Beach, said a boat called the *Alone at Last* was likely in trouble there. Right, Inspector Knightly?" She tilts her head. Yes, she thinks it was him, but she's not committing. "We've checked his GPS, and we're not aware of any other boats in close proximity."

"How would Blake know what was happening? And why would he call in anonymously?" Knightly asks, looking at me.

"I don't know. Because he's doesn't want thanks or medals? He probably mentioned Flint Beach because it was where he'd last seen our boat. And he knew the *Alone at Last*; he'd been on board."

It sounds viable. There's another loaded moment that stretches between the three of us.

"Did you ever go over to the *Salty Dog*?" Knightly sips, grimaces, then walks to my bedside table to set down the cup. I'm figuring out her style now. She asks big questions by pretending they're little, hiding how hard she's concentrating.

"Why would I? Like I said, Blake didn't seem like he wanted to make friends. Is he in trouble?"

Abbott exhales through his nose. "I'm afraid we can't discuss that with you."

"Oh. Okay. Well, I'm sorry not to be more helpful." *Is there a pact after all?* I wonder.

"Righto, well, thank you. I think we'll leave it there for now. Get a nurse in here to check up on you. Also, we've replaced your mobile that was lost—here, a new iPhone, set it up at your leisure."

"Gosh. Thanks a lot," I say, fully aware that they'll be monitoring it. Seeing what I Google. Watching the cloud. Abbott stands, but Knightly makes no move for the door. I get the sense that they do this a lot—one pushing, one pulling—and they're more in tune than they're letting on.

"There's a corpse in the morgue, Ivy." Knightly studies me, and I feel the roots of my hair heat up. "Dark-haired white male in his thirties. Roughly six foot, hundred and eighty pounds." She waits, but so do I. "No reaction to that?"

"I'm not . . . I was just waiting for more information," I say.

"Yes, as were we." Abbott stands with his hands in his pockets.

"You're saying Blake is connected to that?" I ask, feeling strangely protective. "But if he's a good guy who calls in Search and Rescue, would he also be the kind of guy who'd commit murder?"

"It's interesting, isn't it?" Abbott says.

"Doesn't sound very likely." I rotate my feet carefully under the starchy blanket. "But what do I know? I'm usually wrong about everything."

"Are you? Perhaps you get more things right than you think." Knightly smiles, joining her partner by the door. She turns before she opens it. "Once you're better and you've been discharged, you're free to fly home with Regan."

"Really?" I don't mean to sound so surprised. Both of them hesitate.

"I'd say your trip is over," Abbott says. "Perhaps one day you'll come back to Australia under happier circumstances. Choose *not* to take a crew job with complete strangers. Meet boys *without* complicated pasts."

I lower my eyes. Say nothing.

"Take care, Ivy. If we have further questions, we know where to find you." Knightly leads the two of them through the door, and I wait until it clicks closed behind them. Only then do I exhale in a steady breath, until there's no air left inside me.

We made it, Regan. We survived.

50

WE SIT TOGETHER IN two bright-orange chairs, the plastic molded in the shape of human thighs. The departure lounge is busy, a hum of adventures about to begin, but we're not rushing to buy a book for the plane or loading up on duty free. We're much stiller than that.

Our sneakers rest on the shiny linoleum, Regan's backpack propped against mine. To our left is a huge board full of the day's flights. The Uber driver came with us as far as security, even though he didn't have to. He saw, though. He saw Regan struggling, how she's bandaged and bound in ways that make everything difficult. She sat rigid in the wheelchair I found for her, hating everyone who offered to help. And just now when the airline employee at our gate approached us, suggesting she board us early, I could see the scream building in Regan that she doesn't know how to let out.

"Thank you, but I'm not a child," she said. "I'm fine. We'll be fine."

We'll be fine, we'll be fine, we'll be fine. How often we've said that to each other on this trip, even on day one in the cab, as we drove to meet Christopher for the very first time. We were never fine; we were barreling into the middle of a hurricane, and this is how we emerge. Burned, broken. Missing pieces. Both of us with less of ourselves.

Regan leans forward in her seat, tries to unzip a side pocket on her pack, but she's already holding her passport in her one hand, and the whole backpack tips. She lets it fall. Sits without moving while I right the pack, undo the side pocket for her.

"What do you need?" I say, crouching. She doesn't answer. The question is too big to contemplate.

We've mended in the hospital for two weeks. Reunited the minute we were allowed—I hurried to her room, wheeling a swaying bag of saline on a hook. Mostly we just cried, and I climbed right up onto her bed with her, lying on my good hip, on the side of her body that hadn't changed. *I'm so sorry, I'm so sorry,* I kept saying, my arm around her neck while she shook her head, mouth pressed tight, as if she just couldn't deal with her physical reality.

We spoke of Thatcher only in code. In whispers, never saying his name fully or out loud. Hospital staff, detectives, security cameras, even other patients—in that building, we never felt safely alone. The cops had bought Regan a new cell, too, but like me, she was leery of using it. There was the very real sense of an ongoing investigation, and she repeated only what the police had already told her, hedging at it, as if the words were grenades without pins.

"Ivy, a six-foot-tall man died. In his thirties. They don't know if he's part of the case."

"I heard that," I said, my hand squeezing hers. *Careful.*

In the departure lounge, the loudspeaker overhead announces general boarding for our flight to New York. We'll stop there first, although neither of us know what will happen next. But Australia's letting us fly home, so they can't have identified Thatcher yet.

A crowd has gathered in front of our seats, lining up to get onto the plane. Two teenage girls with headphones around their necks clock Regan's injury, the wrapped stub where a forearm should be. They whisper, cast weirded-out stares, once, twice. *Fuck off!* I want to shout at them, because I don't know what to do with my scream either. Thatcher is dead, but he's still haunting everything. He did this to Regan. We would never have been more than a cameo in Lila's story if it wasn't for him. We would never have boarded that boat.

"Regan." I turn to see tears in her eyes. "I watched him die."

"Wh—?" The revelation shocks her out of her self-loathing for a minute. She knows who I'm talking about, and immediately checks to make sure we're not surrounded by interested parties, anyone with eyes or ears on us. But we're alone. Our cell phones are switched off in our packs. It's the first time we've been completely unattended.

"It was as horrific a death as you could possibly imagine." My voice is a tiny notch above faint. "Slow and with full awareness. I thought you deserved to know he's definitely the body they found, and he's one hundred percent gone." Because she can't go home like this, missing whole parts of herself, including what really happened, the facts.

Her lips bunch. She exhales, then mouths, "Did you kill him?"

Our eyes bore into each other; even if I had, she'd keep it in the vault of our friendship, I have zero doubt.

"No," I reply.

"You *saw it*, though?"

"He tried to stab me. Someone intervened and . . . took him out." I feel dizzy for a second, remembering the snowflake drift of those pillow feathers. The awful sideways press of his eyebrow in the bag. I'll tell Regan all that I can of this, so she can put it to rest, but some details I'll never divulge. Mostly to honor Blake's pact, but also to spare her the disease of it. To make it about closure, not spread.

"It was Desh?" She stares forward, watching the line of fellow passengers file down the tunnel onto the jet.

"No. He saw nothing."

"On our boat?"

"No."

"Okay. Okay." She's blinking fast, tallying scenarios. There's really only one guy it could be, and I watch as her brow lifts for a second. *Atoll man saved us both.*

I put my palm face up on her thigh, and she pats hers down to meet it. A sweaty grip, an agreement. She knows it's Blake, but she also understands. Suggest that name to anyone, and this whole nightmare resets.

"I won't ask you," she says, reading the weight of what I'll always have to hold. "But if you need to talk . . . near it . . . I'm here."

I lace my fingers through hers, a promise, a fresh resolution. We've kept too much from each other in the past couple of years, and look how it nearly destroyed us. We can do better than that. We can be closer. "I know. Come on. Let's go home."

Epilogue

EARLY JULY SUNLIGHT STREAMS in through the barge window. Outside, the bay twinkles, the sky Santa Monica–pale. I turn over and see Desh's head on the white pillow beside me, the smooth skin of his tanned back, the line of muscle in his shoulder as it presses against the sheet. He's sleeping. I can hear the soft rise and fall of his breath. It's early, not even seven a.m.

I'd been so unsure about visiting Desh here. Despite the note he left me, the concrete farewell tone of it, and the sense that neither he nor the two Aussie cops thought we should be fueling the spark, I couldn't stop thinking about him. I couldn't sleep in the hospital, the low hum of machines at night reminding me too much of an engine. Of Desh's cabin. Of him. By the fourth night, I knew I couldn't leave it like that, couldn't let it end in a one-way note, and I found him on Instagram. Three posts, fifteen hundred followers. I DM'd him.

I'm okay but not great, yet. You WERE helping.

He replied within the hour.

For months, we texted and talked constantly. He told me he'd thought a lot about whether it would be right for him to ask me to visit. Especially on a boat. And I wasn't sure I could do it, it just felt . . . too close, too soon. I needed to spend some time with my dad. Poor Dad. I'd moved straight back in with him in Michigan, where we watched *Jeopardy!* a lot, neither of us ever knowing the answers. As COVID hit and we were locked down together, I think Dad was almost relieved to hold on to me. I could feel the desperation in him that I be alright, that the damage I'd endured wouldn't last, that up close like this we could carry on as we were before, in some version of a happier past, where he was just a loving dad with a quiet little girl. There were moments when I thought about Thatcher's mom—her handwriting on that calendar in Montauk—and whether she was distraught over him. Do all parents know deep down who their children are? Christopher hadn't, and I pictured him rushing to help Lila, to minimize her loss and pain. That was before he realized she was the source of it. That she created the agony, because for her, it was justified.

"Come sailing," Dad suggested once it was spring. "It's just our dinghy. Tiny. You and me."

But I shook my head, wouldn't go anywhere near it, and then in May, Desh invited me to California. I wavered, but Dad encouraged me to go. Even so, Desh had to work hard.

"It's different here, Ives," he'd promised me. "Our hemisphere, our stars. New hammock." I could hear him smiling, and it was just like that first night on the *Alone at Last*, the same persuasive optimism. *He'll lighten up. We'll win him over.* "Plus this boat's not rocky. No storms in the offing. You won't even need ginger soup." I'd laughed then, and I have to say, I think he's right. No squalls, no tenders, no sandbars. This time, very importantly, the barge is stationary.

The two iron boats are ones his brother bought—the first for staff, the other for guests—and they're connected by a planked walkway and a beautifully lit deck. The old girls barely sway. Each is stolid and staunch, built to last, like war wives arm in arm through the fray. And they're named perfectly, too: *Primrose* and *Emerald*. I love that, all the timeless sisterhood in it.

Sitting up in bed, I stare out at the wide milky sea and think how Regan would love it here. It's luxurious, stylish, immaculate—her world, since she's continuing to hit it big in New York and LA. At first, she took a break from modeling. She laid low at home in San Francisco, got used to her prosthetic arm, the loss she felt physically a metaphor for everything she thought she'd have to let go. But then her resiliency kicked in. She gave her head a shake. She'd felt like a victim in the Cairns departure lounge; she's now fierce and differently abled. When things opened up a little this spring, she walked back into auditions like they'd be *lucky* to book her. And they did, more than ever.

In lockdown, she'd joined TikTok, hit it hard with all her marketing skills, her unique, inimitable style. The number of followers she has now makes my head spin, but although she's getting seriously famous, she's still not caught up in the hype. Her mission statement is clear: she's a figurehead for all the ways in which humans are beautiful and strong. And since she got back in touch with Veronika Sedva, they've been using Regan's platform to build a foundation for young women being targeted in nightclubs and bars. They're fundraising, taking Zoom meetings with major club owners on the West and East coasts, gathering money for new tech to combat the spiking of drinks, in time for when all bars are open again. There's a lot of media interest. Regan will be the face of a new revolution, a literal comeback.

"It's funny, Ives," she said last week when I called her. "My life now means *more* than it did. How's that for closure?"

We still don't say Thatcher's name out loud. We not only begrudge him the breath but also need to be vigilant. The NYPD is still looking for him, and the trail hasn't gone cold yet. Nothing about it has. Not for me, anyway. When I found out Blake removed Thatcher's head and hands, I thought I was going to puke. Sometimes, I wonder what happened to Thatcher's face. Like, where is it? Still in a bag? It's such a creepy thought, and when I close my eyes, I see his last expression, vapor-sealed, pressed tight against clear plastic. It's so horribly preserved—perhaps literally, but also in my mind. At some point, I'll probably need help with that. Impartial, professional counsel, more than Regan can offer. So I can get closure too.

I stand quietly and pull on Desh's hoody, liking the salty-air smell of the fabric. Just being around him makes so much of my tension dissipate. When I kiss him, I feel those fluttery bird wings inside me, but they're warm now, no longer harbingers of panic. There are moments when I know he's watching me, wondering how okay I can be, the questions inside him waiting patiently. *What happened on that cruiser with Blake? Who is that dead guy they found?* But Desh knows trauma, and he understands the heaviness of some answers. He won't push me. I love him for holding that space, for the generosity.

Out in the main room of the barge, Rafi's making coffee

with a high-end espresso machine. Steam hisses as he stands with his back to me, dark hair just like Desh's but tidier, more groomed. He's Desh, if you gave him an LA makeover. Swapped out his slides for dress shoes, his fresh-air skin for cologne. The Turner boys are both headturners, there's no denying it. But I'd pick the surfer brother every time.

"Coffee?" Rafi passes me a cup. "Check this out." He holds up a copy of the *LA Times* travel section, a photo of himself and Desh sitting on the Airbnb deck, a cocktail in Rafi's hand, a chef's hat in Desh's.

"Hey, you both look awesome," I say. "You'll be getting celeb bookings in no time."

He smiles slowly. "Yeah, in fact we're booked solid for a while, assuming we can stay open. You know, if COVID doesn't come back bigger. And if it does, then I have other projects. Desh'll take *Primrose*, I'll live in *Emerald*. We'll pivot."

"Cool. Good for you." He's definitely the business brother. Less likeable, more analytical, but he'll keep Desh solvent. They make a good team.

He picks up his car keys from the counter. BMW, of course. "I have to get going, but you should stick around. Long term, I mean. Desh is crazy into you."

I cough and feel my face go beet-red. Are brothers meant to blow each other's cover like that? It seems against the bro code.

"For real," he says. "We haven't seen him like this for . . . years. A full decade, at least."

"That's good. I mean, that he seems happy again now." It's obvious I know all about Ali and the tragic accident. That one second, the momentary lapse of control. There's a pause, during which I get the sense that the whole Turner family has been waiting for Desh to find peace. Or be more settled. Somehow, they associate me with that, and I'm already a firm favorite.

"But you have a scholarship at NYU, right?" Rafi asks, and I nod. I was reinstated, following the departmental deep-dive into all the gross power plays of Thatcher Kane.

"I'm almost done though. I began spring semester classes online."

"Finish it up here." He shrugs, puts his cell in his pocket. "Why not?"

I'm surprised by a tingle of possibility. Stay in Santa Monica. Further from my dad and mom, but nearer Regan, who's in LA more often than she's not. Much closer to Desh.

Once Rafi has gone, I leaf through the paper, stopping with a jerk midway through to see an article on Thatcher. *New York Professor Still Missing.* Beneath is a photo of him leaning against a bookshelf, his smarmy teacherly pose. My body rushes with adrenaline and I press my forefingers to my thumbs, like Dad taught me, for moments where I feel overwhelmed. I already spoke with the New York police—they interviewed all of Thatcher's past students. *When did you last see Professor Kane? Was he ever . . . unprofessional in his dealings with you?*

I'd been ready, though. Listened more than I spoke. I figured out fast that they had no cell records for him at all. The only trail he left traceable was the above-board communication around school. He must have destroyed anything incriminating before he left New York, then bought a new burner phone when he landed in Oz. That's why his number had changed. He didn't want to be tracked to Sydney, not when he'd flown over with such hostile intentions. He probably hired Blake under an alias and must have traveled on a fake passport. All those creepy friends of his would have helped him out. The police had no idea whatsoever that he'd left the country.

"He made false accusations about me plagiarizing my work," I told them. "Perhaps it was his first step toward targeting me."

The detective accepted that. There were enough girls coming forward now with allegations, all of them with identical branding scars. I'd lost the seal—it had been in the hip pocket that Lila hit with the flare gun. Initially I'd been furious about that, but now I think it might have been the universe looking out for me. Because how did *I* get the ring? And where *exactly* did I lose it? The last thing I wanted to do was hand them a link to Thatcher and me, or talk more about Australia, where Interpol still had an unidentified body.

"That email was the only recent contact you'd had with him?"

"That's right," I said, my voice rock-steady. My original cell was gone, and the cops had no reason to subpoena the records. Every phone in connection to our trip had been lost. Or, in Thatcher's case, destroyed by Blake. Given everything else he did for us and himself, I knew he was too smart to have kept it.

"You haven't seen him in person at all?"

"No." *He's in four different pieces in tropical Queensland. Hewn where Blake wouldn't transmit DNA.* "But I know he attacks students. My best friend, Regan Kemp, has told me everything. He hunts with another guy. A broker. You need to find him."

"We're following up on that. Ms. McGill, how do you feel about Professor Kane's disappear—"

"I'm thrilled." I held their gaze, safe in my uncontestable alibi. Thanks to his own duplicity, Thatcher had never set foot in Australia.

I leave the *LA Times* on the countertop, take two cups of coffee back to bed. Desh sits up when he sees me come in, looking at me as if I'm his favorite thing in the world. I set down the cups, crawl over to him, kiss him while I breathe in his sleepy fresh-linen scent.

"Hello," he says. "You look great in my hoody."

I snuggle in, kiss him more deeply, my hands at his cheek-bones and throat, but suddenly there's a thud behind us, and the bed shudders. In a series of startling snapshots, I see a crocodile's tail, the butt of a flare gun, the thump of a dropped head in a bag. I gasp, then exhale in a long wide sigh.

Pearl has joined us. Desh adopted her, flew her back with him when he left Queensland. Of course he did: she chose him, sat with him through most of his meal prep on the *Alone at Last*, however much he complained. She might have scratched him in his cabin that night, but she also claimed him. It was Lila, the true Lila that only Pearl saw, who bundled her out of the porthole into the sea. How could she have done that—that, and everything else? Sometimes I think about what it must be like inside Lila's head. All the fury and violence and vengeance. Of all the horrible places to be trapped, she strikes me as the most condemned.

Pearl picks her way up the comforter now, turns in a hairy circle, her tail swiping each of our chins in turn. Then she settles between us, a humorless great aunt of a chaperone, here to make sure Desh and I don't touch.

"It's okay." Desh grins, pulling me closer. "We'll work around her."

Acknowledgments

Firstly, I need to thank my whip-smart agent, Joe Veltre, Queen Hayley Nusbaum, and everyone at Gersh for all their hard work in getting my books out into the world. Nothing would happen without you.

To my editor, Lara Hinchberger—thank you for untangling every tangle, and for having such a calm, clever, sophisticated eye on me throughout. Let's always envy-google expensive cruisers together.

The entire team at Penguin Canada has been exceptional: Crissy Calhoun (the greatest copy editor, I'm a lifelong fan), Dan French on marketing, and a special shout-out to Emma Dolan for devising a cover that literally made me gasp when I saw it.

The Offing is essentially a travel thriller, and my travel companion in writing it was Robyn Harding, who held me to task and told me what a dummy I am in exactly the right measure. There's so much I appreciate about our friendship, but I don't think I'd get anything written without you making me laugh every step of the way.

Big thanks and love to Chevy Stevens, too, whose early read of and commentary on the first fifty pages was both insightful and hilarious.

To Eileen Cook for reading and being a genius, to Sioux Browning who schemed with me on plot swerves, to Ali Popoff (the real Ali Powers) and Leo Grypma who helped me with clearing space and committing to what I love, and to Susan Barth—seriously pro Coroner, who I've had on speed dial with murder and death questions since 2018—I appreciate all of you, and thank you for your help.

Books also need the wonderful community of bloggers and readers, and I want to thank those of you who reach out to me with lovely comments, post anything encouraging to do with my books, and check in on me when all I manage to post on Instagram is a photo of a croissant. Or my dog. I dream of the day when we'll all meet in person, and sense it's coming soon.

To my mini family of writers on the inside—Sam Bailey, Hannah Mary McKinnon, Nicole Lundrigan, Laurie Petrou, Dan Kalla, Marissa Stapley, Kate Hilton—in an industry that requires us to work quietly alone, thanks for always being a text away.

And lastly, but never least, to my family in the UK—Mum, Dad, Joey, and Sal—whom I never see enough of each year: thank you for always being proud of me, and always having my back. And to my sweet little family here—Clint, Cash, and Rue—all my love, and thanks for listening to snippets, offering your thoughts, and helping me to keep things level in a business that's full of ups and downs.

ROZ NAY's debut novel, *Our Little Secret*, was a national best-seller, won the Douglas Kennedy Prize for best foreign thriller in France, and was nominated for the Kobo Emerging Writer Prize for Mystery and the Arthur Ellis Best First Novel Award. Her second bestselling novel, *Hurry Home*, was shortlisted for the Crime Writers of Canada Best Crime Novel award and *The Hunted*, her third, was nominated for Best Crime Novel in 2022. Roz has lived and worked in Africa, Australia, the US, and the UK. She now lives in British Columbia, Canada, with her husband and two children.